UNKNOWN FEARS

UNKNOWN FEARS

John Gardner

This title first published in Great Britain 2004 by
SEVERN HOUSE PUBLISHERS LTD of
9–15 High Street, Sutton, Surrey SM1 1DF.
First published only in Great Britain in 1992 by Orion Books Ltd
under the title *Blood of the Fathers* and pseudonym *Edmund McCoy*.
This first USA edition published 2004 by
SEVERN HOUSE PUBLISHERS INC of
595 Madison Avenue, New York, N.Y. 10022.

British Library Cataloguing in Publication Data

Gardner, John, 1926-
    Unknown fears
    1.   Suspense fiction
    I.   Title II. McCoy, Edmund. Blood of the fathers
    823.9'14 [F]

    ISBN 0-7278-6134-4

To Miranda, Andy, Laura and Emma

Printed and bound in Great Britain by
MPG Books Ltd., Bodmin, Cornwall.

Blood of the fathers, courses down the years,
Baptizing children for long gone misdeeds
and unknown fears

Brother Frances of Shrivingfold (1424–1501)

Acknowledgement

I must thank Simon Wood for putting the germ of an idea into my head, and for checking the manuscript to ensure there are no errors regarding the Autumn of 1888.

Foreword

MY FATHER NEVER knew his father who was killed in a building accident before my Dad was born. So, obviously, I never knew my paternal grandfather. However, the family came from Hackney – 56 Churchill Road – and there was a tradition that my grandfather gave evidence at the inquest of Elizabeth Stride – Long Liz – who was a Jack the Ripper victim. I have never gone in search of the facts of this tale, probably because I would like to think it true and don't want to be let down, but I have no doubt that it is the reason I became a Ripperologist.

Using an absurd candidate as Jolly Jack I folded the Ripper Legend into my book *The Return of* Moriarty in which I fashioned the evil professor into what reviewers called 'A Gaslight Godfather.' Whitechapel was one of the Professor's haunts and he had a prime suspect (as I say, highly unlikely) done away with because the police presence in the area was bothering him. In real death that particular suspect committed suicide by filling his pockets with stones and leaping into the Thames, just as Moriarty has him drowned.

A few months after *The Return* was published I met the author of the best and most exhaustive Ripper book, Donald Rumbelow, and still count him among my friends. I also count among my friends the author of the most ludicrous Ripper-revealed book, Patricia Cornwell – or I did number her among my friends until now. Who knows what lurks after she reads this?

My friend Simon Wood is also a keen Ripperologist and it was in a telephone conversation in 1991 that we discussed the perennial theory that Mary Jane Kelly (or Marie Jeannette Kelly) was not, in reality the Ripper's last victim: by which I mean that the mutilated corpse found in Kelly's room in Miller's Court in November 1888 was not that of Kelly. I still believe the terrible and disfigured state of the body was an attempt to make the authorities believe that Kelly was dead – a great start for a conspiracy theory. Certainly there is a lot of evidence to show that Kelly was still alive on the morning after the murder was committed, so why would someone wish to misdirect a person or persons into believing that Kelly was dead?

In 1991 I was living in Virginia and we tossed ideas back and forth in transatlantic telephone calls over a period of a few weeks. The seed had been sown and I couldn't get the possibilities out of my head.

It was a time of much creativity and I was tied into several projects, finishing off the latest Bond – *The Man from Barbarossa* the best of the Bonds, I think – and starting to block out a long planned novel titled *Maestro*. In the midst of all this work the ideas surrounding the Kelly murder plagued me, invaded my dreams and cried out to be written about.

My then agent – now gone to the great literary agency in the sky – was spending the early spring, as was his custom, in Key West. I called him and put the problem to him. "What on earth is the object?" he asked me, changing the subject.

There were two possibilities: (1) I could write the story which was like a cuckoo in my head, then leave it and offer it to my publisher at a later date. At that moment neither my British nor American publisher would be over the moon about an unscheduled manuscript. Or (2) I could write the story and publish under a pseudonym.

By this time, with the assistance of my friend Simon Wood, I had come up with the fictional link between the Kelly murder and the present – the IRA, and the reader now must see the novel within the setting of the early nineties. The Gibraltar shootings of three unarmed members of the IRA by the SAS is still controversial; but in'91 we were nearer to the incident, so my version of a similar action in Hong Kong seemed a reasonably contentious start. Note also that I do not say who the targets are – simply 'the prince and princess.' No personalities.

I tried to carry on working on the contracted books but it was no good: the idea still burned a fire in my head. So, I hopped on a 'plane and flew down to Key West. Over dinner my agent listened to me describe, not the entire plot but the starting point and finally said that he supposed I should write it as quickly as possible then get back to the "real work." To be truthful he was not really interested and only became animated when I sent him a completed MS of what was to become *Blood of the Fathers* some five weeks later. I do not normally work that quickly but occasionally it happens.

"Do you realise what a great film or TV this would make?"
He asked after reading it. He sold the book to Orion for a
respectable sum and negotiated a film option. Of course
nothing ever came of it, which is the usual way with film
options.

I now realise with hindsight that my agent was heading
towards his long sunset when he offered it to only one
American publisher. I've even forgotten who it was, but I
clearly remember the letter in which the commissioning editor
turned it down. 'Here in the States,' he wrote, 'we're not
really turned on by terrorism.' Possibly it's a good job that I
can't remember who it was; he also said that I didn't seem to
know a great deal about the realities of publishing.

Obviously he hadn't worked out that one was required to sex
up – as we'd say today – the world of publishing to make it
play to the reader.

Anyway, that's how it was left. Eventually the book was
published – only in the UK – under an assumed name of
Edmund McCoy. Don't even ask, but shortly after its
publication I went to a convention for thriller and mystery
writers in Toronto. On walking into the room set aside for
specialist booksellers the first thing I saw was a pile of *Blood
of the Fathers* by Edmund McCoy. On top of the pile was a
small notice that said John Gardner. So much for the cover.

ONE

– 1 –

Anyone standing on Hong Kong's famous Peak at dawn that morning could have been forgiven for imagining they were watching a piece of superb theatrical staging: the opening scene of a new Andrew Lloyd Webber musical, perhaps. First there was a breeze, then day leaped into the sky, a pearl wash, lightening and slowly changing to light blue, cloudless; then into the clear deep cobalt as if the whole thing had been set, on cue, by a superb technician. God is certainly the greatest director of all, and the topography of Hong Kong is one of his more perfect stage sets: crags and bluffs, the distant misty hills and mountains, the great wide bay that is the harbour, and the crowded man-made horror of its crushed buildings, rising for air and elbowing together, too close for comfort. So, as the light came up, the view sharpened, became almost idyllic. The twin Star Ferries began to plough across the water, and the wake of the day's first Macao hydrofoil plumed out, leaving a white scar over the still water.

As the sun rose, so Hong Kong became dressed overall for the royal visit. God, in his infinite wisdom, had laid on a perfect day, and the oppressive heat which, for the past week, had hung over the Territories, vanished. By mid-morning the temperature rose to the low, bearable, seventies – and death stalked in sunshine.

The streets, in both Hong Kong and Kowloon, seemed noisier, the cooking smells more pungent, the raised voices and the babble louder. Photographs of the royal couple stood in every electronics store along Jordan Road, and in the smart boutiques of The Landmark shopping centre. In the harbour junks sported bunting;

flags splashed colour along the waterfronts, and the trams seemed to be carrying even more bizarre posters than usual. Death came unannounced.

Across the Fragrant Harbour everything glittered, from the steel and crystal temples of the money men, to the seething apartment buildings. The hills and mountains stood sharp against a clear sky, and there were those who stood and looked, saying surely Hong Kong must be one of the most glamorous places on earth. Death came without glamour.

The crowds were out in force, Hong Kong Chinese, Europeans and tourists of all nationalities. The Chinese, always excitable, were more volatile than usual, for this was, maybe, the last chance many of them would get to see royalty. The royal family would not come once the colony was returned to the People's Republic of China in 1997. The Europeans, though equally exhilarated, were more blasé about the long awaited day. Most of them would be returning to the UK within a few years. Unlike so many of the Hong Kong Chinese, they had British passports and would not have to face the difficulties of escaping from China. Yet some visitors would not even escape this day.

This was a time for smiles, cheers, and waving the Union Jack, even though street hawkers were selling hats with the red star of the People's Republic emblazoned and prominent. After 1997, a good three-quarters of the men and women in the streets would wear those hats. Death was bareheaded.

The royal yacht rode at anchor, with two destroyers as watchdogs snapping at junks and motor launches who ventured too close. By eleven-thirty the honour guard had assembled on Queen's Pier; traffic was diverted from Connaught Road, and the police were now moving the crowds, funnelling them away from the saluting dais from which the prince would review a detachment of Gurkhas immediately after setting foot on land. Death was also moving on foot.

The small dais had been erected on the Connaught Road side of City Hall, so the royal couple would only have to walk a short distance from the pier, and the police had been carefully briefed to shepherd the mill of people to either the far side of the road, or towards the Star Ferry Pier. They, then, would be neatly corralled before the royal couple arrived. Death was ready to enter, stage left – sinister.

The three targets were lost for a few moments as they came close to the dais, jostled by the crowd, eight deep, pushed along the river of people heading towards the Connaught Centre and the ferry.

The Special Air Service captain, using the code Buster One, spoke low into the tiny microphone disguised as a stick pin on the left lapel of his bomber jacket. 'Buster One, I've lost sight.'

'Buster Three, I can see one head. I think they're coming towards me,' a voice said, clear, into his earpiece. Buster Three, a sergeant, was loitering at the outer fringes of the crowd as it broke and was shepherded towards the Star Ferry.

Buster One craned forward, pushing against giggling girls, and men holding small children on their shoulders. He was tense, strung out: the good humour of the crowds was just an added difficulty, a fact which had to be overcome if the job was to be done neatly and without too much fuss. An endless tape ran in his head. Jesus, this is not going to work. Too many people. We won't get them clear of the crowd. You have to push them into the open, he had been told. Manipulate the crowd. He saw his wife and the two kids, playing in the garden of the neat little house back in England, near Hereford, and heard his father, singing an old Noël Coward song, 'Mad Dogs and Englishmen'. His father, an unlikely Coward fan, used to warble the number in the bath – 'In Hong Kong they bang a gong/And fire off a noonday gun' . . . Well, there would be noonday guns in Hong Kong today. Christ, the crowd was thickening not thinning as they had planned.

There were six SAS soldiers in the team. Three pairs: two on the ground near the Connaught Centre; two close to the Star Ferry Pier, and the pair led by the captain who had shadowed the three men since they had come off that same Star Ferry from Kowloon three hours earlier.

The captain pushed forward, jostling to get closer to the targets. He glanced at his number two, nodding, then turning his head towards the three plain-clothes Hong Kong police officers who were close behind him. His hand strayed to the small of his back, as if to reassure himself that the pistol was still there.

Again he spoke into the mike. 'Buster Three and Four, get ahead of them. Five and Six, cut them off on the flanks.'

The soldiers were dressed in jeans, soft shoes and bomber jackets, not unlike the three targets who also wore jeans. Two of the targets sported denim jackets over checked shirts, while the third wore a short-sleeved shirt, and carried a leather satchel, slung over one shoulder.

Buster One was half out of the crowd now with his partner to his left. He saw the carrier bag was missing at the moment Buster Five reported it – 'Two's lost his carrier bag. Must be a button, Boss. Has to be.' The target, fingered as Sean O'Brien, had lugged a heavy plastic carrier bag all morning.

'The girl said it'd be a last minute thing.' Buster One thought the new voice was Buster Six, a lieutenant. 'Gotta be a button, boss. No way it's anything else.'

'Okay, just do as you've been told. Make it good. The cops'll see to everything once it's over.' Buster One quickened his pace, frowning as two Chinese children ran between him and the three targets. 'Keep Prancer and Dancer inboard,' he said slightly louder, a reaction, for the last remark was aimed at Buster Leader, the senior officer in charge of the operation they called *Eradicate*. He was holed up in an office high above them in the Connaught Centre. With him were equally superior police and diplomatic ranks. Prancer and Dancer were the prince and princess who would not be allowed off the yacht until it was all over. 'Speak now or forever hold your peace,' he said again, thinking of Buster Leader. He knew the man would say nothing, but the words were for the benefit of the tape, removing any blame from the captain, placing it squarely on the officer in charge.

They were in the clear now. The three men talking animatedly, oblivious of death stalking them – inevitable now.

Then, the man known as O'Brien glanced behind him. His eyes locked with those of Buster One. Recognition flashed like a spark between them and his hand moved towards his jeans.

Busters Three and Four spun around as Buster One shouted clearly, 'Stop! Police officers! Don't move!'

O'Brien's hand continued to travel backwards. Kevin Casey reached for the satchel, and Donnough Flynn made a move for the inside of his denim jacket.

4

One of the SAS soldiers – later it was claimed to be Buster Five – shouted, 'It's a bloody button! Stop!'

The first shot overlapped the 'Stop!' Twelve shots in all. Six pairs. Each SAS soldier fired two rounds. A dozen 'Splat' – soft kill option – slugs from six H&K 9mm pistols. 'Splat' rounds prevented any shoot-through, so no innocent bystander would be hit by a bullet passing through one of the targets. No overkill.

O'Brien died before his body hit the ground. Flynn was whirled around by the force of the first bullet in his shoulder, the second took off the back of his head. The others were superfluous. Casey died a couple of seconds after his companions, his chest torn open, the rounds hitting within an inch of each other.

There were screams from the crowd. People started to run in panic. A woman threw herself to the ground, her body covering her two babies. One man actually moved forward as though to threaten Buster One, but he was pulled aside by a uniformed policeman. Cars screamed down Connaught Road. Police were suddenly everywhere, throwing blankets and coats over the three bleeding corpses and hustling the SAS soldiers towards cars that had now drawn up nearby. Two ambulances screeched to a halt as the police cars bore the SAS men away, heading for the Hong Kong–Kowloon tunnel.

Less than an hour later, a Royal Air Force VC-10 took off from Kai Tak airport. It had clearance into Abu Dhabi and from there to the RAF base at Lyneham in Wiltshire.

'What happened to the girl, Boss?' the man known as Buster Two asked Buster One as the aircraft climbed away into the clear afternoon air. They all sat together, using two rows of seats on the port side.

'Flew out with one of the funnies first thing this morning.' Buster One sipped the stiff gin and tonic. WRAF stewardesses quietly moved around in the galley, forward. He would lose no sleep over the men he had helped to kill, even though it would later be revealed that the targets were unarmed. Nor did they carry any button device for exploding the bomb which was not in the missing carrier bag. The four hundred pounds of Semtex, found the next day in the hotel where the Irishmen had been staying, had not even been placed under the dais.

5

The girl they spoke of was Kathleen Fagin. Two weeks before, she had telephoned the Metropolitan Police at London's Scotland Yard. There were things the police would like to know, she said. Things that might have a bearing on the royal visit to Hong Kong. She wanted immunity, a new name and life far away from Europe. She also wanted to be with her lover, Danny Musgrove, who was serving a ten-year sentence in the notorious Long Kesh Prison for being a member of the Provisional Irish Republican Army, and having bomb fuses in his possession.

Ms Fagin was also a member of the PIRA, and she had a tale to tell – once the deal had been done. She gave everything to the authorities: names, method, time, for Kathleen Fagin was also a member of the Provo 'Active Service Unit' sent to kill the prince and princess in Hong Kong on that pleasant spring morning.

Now, she would have quite a lot of explaining to do, though the authorities had a notice out for her arrest. Police combed Hong Kong, the New Territories and Kowloon for her. Kathleen Fagin's photograph dominated newspapers and television screens for a week. Nobody, especially the authorities, wanted anyone looking for her with a contract. It was essential that she should simply disappear.

'You know what the papers'll say by the time we get back?' Buster One turned his head, speaking to the whole team.

'Another Gibraltar,' muttered Buster Two.

'Shoot-to-kill in Hong Kong,' Buster Four laughed.

Buster Six, the lieutenant, grinned. 'Bet seventy per cent use the word Gibraltar on the front page.'

On a Sunday in March, 1988, four SAS men had gunned down three members of the Provisional IRA – one of them a woman – in a Gibraltar street. The act sparked one of the greatest controversies in the long history of violence between the British authorities and troubled Northern Ireland. It was fuel to the fire of a long standing accusation that successive British governments had condoned a shoot-to-kill policy, on a tactical level, in dealings with the PIRA.

The loony left, good and honest human rights groups, and the media – always ready to stand up and be shocked – proclaimed that the shoot-to-kill policy was abhorrent. The government denied that such a policy existed at all. Privately many people thought it would be no bad thing, for there is a long collective memory concerning Irish politics – a memory that goes back to the time of Elizabeth I. At intervals, since then, the Irish, under many guises – the Fenians, Sinn Fein, the IRA and the PIRA – have fought against the British presence in that beautiful, green and bitter land.

There was a sigh of relief in the 1920s when everybody thought the matter had been settled once and for all, with the bulk of Ireland becoming a self-governing republic. The surviving, so-called, six counties of Ulster squeezed into the north, became Northern Ireland, remaining part of the United Kingdom, peopled mainly by staunch Protestant loyalists – Orangemen, Ulstermen. Then the North had finally erupted and for almost three decades the Catholic Provisional IRA had fought a guerrilla war against the British who were there to reinforce the mainly Protestant police – the Royal Ulster Constabulary. The shoot-to-kill policy had become the Provos' latest political weapon. All pretence that this was a holy war – Catholic against Protestant – had long since disappeared.

Buster One closed his eyes, thinking for a brief moment that he would not even put it past the PIRA to have set them up: sacrificed three of its men to gain more world support in the propaganda war.

After the aircraft landed in Wiltshire, the six SAS men were whisked away, in two unmarked cars, to a safe house debriefing outside Oxford. Buster Two nudged the captain as they drove past a newsagent's shop. A placard shouted, black against white – DEATH IN HONG KONG! ANOTHER GIBRALTAR!

Buster One looked bleakly from the car window. A brother officer had been one of the Gibraltar quartet. 'The killings were easy,' he had told him. 'It was the bloody inquiry that was murder.'

TWO

– 1 –

Phillip Tarpin first heard about the Hong Kong shootings when Peter Palestino took him for lunch into Dooley's, an Irish bar and diner in the East 20s, between Madison and Park.

You could all but touch the nervous, angry atmosphere, and Palestino casually asked what was wrong as a waiter showed them to a corner table.

'You've not heard?' The brogue had not been overcome by the nasality of a New York accent. 'The bloody Brits've killed three of the lads. In Hong Kong. Shot them out of hand. Unarmed they were, so. It's criminal. Just shot 'em like dogs. It's bloody Gibraltar all over again.' He threw menus in front of them and disappeared. By the bar men talked loudly, their arms moving, hands chopping the air as if to kill invisible Englishmen, their faces twisted in anger and their eyes anxious.

'I'm sorry. I should have realized. I was wrong to bring you here,' Peter muttered.

Phillip shook his head. 'No, it's okay. Don't worry about it. Their propaganda machine works well on this side of the Atlantic. Let's not get into an argument though.'

Palestino smiled, his kind, leathery face crinkling, somehow making him look younger than his forty-three years. He was a tall man with a thick bush of unruly, greying hair that sprouted upwards from his scalp, adding the illusion of an exra three inches of stature. The height gave him great presence; while his manner always remained calm and unflurried. In business, he was a natural delegator, had vast experience in the world of books, and so was

8

well fitted to be Chief Executive Officer of J. B. Pudney, Sons, one of New York's oldest and most respected publishing houses.

Three months before, Pudney, like so many American publishers, had made a successful takeover bid for Hosier & Whitehead, once the strongest, most esteemed of British publishers, bastion of Bedford Square with a list of best-selling authors designed to make the competition drool. It was the time of the accountants, and the sharp line between publishing books in New York and London had greyed out. Slowly matters were polarizing, with the wealthy New York houses swallowing London's old established firms, taking the best and cutting away the dead wood in the ruthless scramble for profits, measuring the value of books not by merit but by the number of weeks they stayed on the best-seller lists, and how many libel suits they were able to avoid. Pudney had acquired a reputation for giving its reading public a good mixed list. People said the profits were enormous.

After the takeover of Hosier & Whitehead, Phillip had gone through several anxious weeks. At forty-six he fell within that dreaded age of the borderline unemployable in a profession that was already rethinking and retrenching. He had been in publishing for twenty-five years. Straight from his achievement of a first-class honours degree in modern history at Oxford, into a small publisher with headquarters in Ludgate Circus, and a good list of social and historical books that sold in their thousands to schools and universities the world over.

He had been seduced into Hosier & Whitehead after a big party for some forgotten masterpiece, and was happy, for a couple of years, as a junior editor. Then he served, for a time, as Promotions Manager before taking on non-fiction. When the balloon went up, he was in his tenth year as Senior Editor (Non-fiction). He knew everyone in the business, was on happy terms with most of the great modern historians, and knew a huge, varied, number of authors, agents, movers and shakers on both sides of the Atlantic.

When Pudney blew into town, they also blew a lot of people out of their jobs. The axe fell heavily and was no respecter of persons. Then, six weeks after what some viewed as The Bloomsbury Massacre, their new parent company summoned Tarpin to New York.

On the previous morning, Bernie Blackthorne, Chairman of what was now The Pudney Group, had offered him Senior Editor Non-fiction for the entire organization. In terms of power and avarice it meant he would have complete autonomy over the hardback non-fiction output in both New York and London, plus the final veto in the soft cover operations, which meant Tern and Black Bear in London, with the Ritz, Emmet and Chipmunk imprints in the US. He also got a seat on the board – something he might never have attained within the old family-controlled London firm. There was a not-to-be-sneezed at $185,000 a year, rising to $250,000 over five; a handsome expense allowance; a rent-free apartment high over Fifth Avenue; use of the firm's apartment in London, just up the street from the Dorchester; eight months of the year in the US and three in the UK; a month's vacation each year, plus five days at Easter and Christmas; all medical insurance and a handsome pension at age sixty. An offer hard to refuse.

Thank heaven he got on well with Palestino, he thought as they ate cold ham and salad washed down with ice-cold Guinness in Dooley's. The tall American was younger than him, yet he felt none of the barbs of jealousy he would certainly have experienced in London had a similar situation arisen. Already they had talked for two hours in the CEO's office with all calls blocked. 'I'm not in today, Fran,' he had told the little grey-haired lady, who nodded with a smile, and had called Phillip 'Mr Tarpin' the moment he walked in.

'She's been with me for twelve years now, through thick, thin and anorexic. Knows my ways.' Palestino had the kind of laugh that made him fun to be with. It was said he had turned down at least three prime publishing jobs since he took on Pudney, and could walk out any day, with seats on a dozen boards if he wanted them.

Now, at the corner table in Dooley's, Palestino gave his most charming smile. 'So, you come at the end of the month. We'll all look forward to that. Haven't had a really first-rate guy looking after our non-fiction since I've been with the house. Is your wife going to enjoy it?'

Tarpin raised his eyebrows, cutting his eyes away for a second, then giving a small sigh. 'Not my wife, Peter.' He could see Sukie

Cartwright in his head – the deep brown eyes, hair teased up into a bundle of curls, flared nostrils, wide mouth and wicked sense of humour. He even heard her voice, and especially her laugh. Meeting Palestino's eyes he said, 'Lived together for six years. I honestly don't know what's going to happen.'

'She doesn't fancy New York?'

'I called her last night. She wasn't particularly wild about the idea. Maybe she will, maybe she won't. She's half of a literary agency, so there are mighty problems.'

Her voice had stayed in his head. 'Oh, darling, I don't know. I think we should talk when you get back.' When Sukie refused to discuss something on the telephone the omens were not good. At least she was straightforward. God knew, she had to lie on the telephone enough. Part of her business. If there were unpleasant things to say, or difficult decisions to be faced, she always liked to do it up front – *mano a mano,* as she would say, mixing her genders. *Mano a mano* was even her soubriquet for sex.

Palestino sighed, chewing a mouthful of ham, then shifted in his chair, putting his right shoulder towards Tarpin. 'Appreciate you being frank with me, Phillip. I'd truly like us to be friends as well as colleagues.' He paused as though weighing the next words. 'I'll go out on a limb. It's not all champagne and roses at Pudney. The money's good, but some of our mutual colleagues are, how can I put it? Not the smartest brains in the world. I've needed someone in the firm – for a long time now – who could be my father confessor.'

'I'm the new kid on the block.' Tarpin kept his eyes on Palestino's face. Certainly there had been a very special rapport with this long-boned, relaxed man. 'New kids need friends. They also need advice. Sure, I'd rather work with you on a basis of trust and friendship. But I really don't know what the job's going to do to my private life. I might even have to come over with a long-standing relationship dead in the water.'

Palestino nodded. 'I guess we've all had to take risks like that. You're not alone. My first marriage ended seven years ago. The lady who was what you might call the other woman, didn't marry me until last year. I think you'll get on with Patsy. I'll tell you, we went through a long and elaborate choreography before things were squared away. Very difficult. *She* wouldn't say yes or no, and she's also in the business.' His lips curved up in that wide, attractive smile. Must be murder among the secretaries, Tarpin thought. 'Matter of fact,' Palestino continued, 'she's also part of a literary agency. Maybe we could work something out.'

Over by the bar, a slightly drunk American Irishman began to sing 'Danny Boy'.

'I think they're having a wake for the three lads who got iced,' Tarpin said softly.

They walked back to the office through the warm spring streets. It was probably imagination, but Tarpin thought New York smelled fresher than London. Secretaries, PAs, people from the mail room, sat on the steps of buildings, brown bagging, laughing and talking. At the corner, an ice cream cart was doing good business, and the girls were out in spring dresses, swinging along the sidewalk, earnest, confident, their eyes saying that they owned the city and could go anywhere.

'I'm afraid we Americans are notoriously ignorant when it comes to other countries. We're bloody insular, I suppose.' Palestino walked slowly, as though wishing to spend as much time as he could out in the sun. 'The Irish business, for one thing. I hope I didn't embarrass you by taking you in there. It's typical of a New Yorker. I just didn't think. What's the real picture? Tell me. Pretend I know nothing.'

Tarpin glanced towards him. 'To tell you the truth, Peter, though it's a terrible thing to say, the whole Irish business bores the arse off me. I suspect it's the same with ninety per cent of the population, and it's probably our loss.' He searched for the right words. 'Sure, we're jolted out of it when the bastards bomb innocent people. When there's something horrific, with kids and women, you know. But, for the rest of the time, I think most of us pack it away into some little attic in our heads. It's bloody complicated, and we get brutalized: numbed by it.'

As they strolled, he went on talking of the impossible situation: how the British were under an obligation and were forced to keep troops in the North of Ireland. 'Sinn Fein and the Provos want us out, and we can't get out. Under international law we're stuck, so the fight goes on.' A spectacular blonde in a smart, black power suit swung by, clutching a briefcase. He caught her eyes as she went past. They held a kind of challenge that made him catch his breath. 'We're obligated to keep the peace,' he continued. 'Nobody else wants the North. The Republic can't afford it, and if we left, the loyalists would go berserk. Some say it would be a blood bath, with probably the loyalists becoming the winners. They'd certainly carry the fight to the mainland, just as the Provos've done.'

'This shoot-to-kill business? The Hong Kong thing? Is that for real?'

'Who knows? You can only make educated guesses. Certainly a lot of unarmed Provos've been killed. But so have a lot of armed ones, and they've blown away their fair share of innocent men, women and children. I suspect it *is* the policy of the cops in the North – the Royal Ulster Constabulary.' Tarpin told him of the famous inquiry about a shoot-to-kill policy. How senior police officer John Stalker had been sent over from England, and how the RUC had blocked him at every turn, so that he was finally taken off the investigation. 'There were trumped-up charges against him. He was relieved of his duties, then reinstated. It was oddly unpleasant, and strangely un-English, if you understand that. In the end he left the police. Wrote a book. Began a new career. I guess he found out too much. Yes, I think they have an unspoken policy. If you know the guy's definitely a Provo, you kill him. Maybe it's as simple as that. Don't know about the government, or our troops, though.'

Palestino stopped walking. 'There's a lot of feeling among Irish Americans. We've got a couple in the firm. You should know about them.'

Tarpin nodded. 'Yes, the problem over here, in the States, is that there are a lot of old memories. Fathers've told sons of the gallant way the IRA forced the British out.' He shook his head. 'That's a battle long won, and they were right to win it. But the Provos today, well, they're not fighting the same fight; they're not the same army.'

'Maybe there's a book in it.' They waited on the sidewalk, pausing for the lights to change. The figure of a hurrying man, almost bent against an unseen wind, changing to green. The colour of the shamrock, the colour of Ireland, Tarpin thought.

'I doubt it. Once an Irishman is bitten with the idea that the British should get out, and the Provisional Irish Republican Army are fighting a true war of virtue, you won't convince him by books, or even logic. It's gone too far for that.'

Palestino smiled again, then gave a short nod. 'It's an idea, though. Let's see when you settle in.'

They crossed the wide street, heading for the gold and glass doors of the building from which J. B. Pudney, Sons operated. Tarpin thought he was probably being silly, but he had a feeling that this was where he belonged.

– 2 –

The safe house was situated just off Boar's Hill, on the outskirts of Oxford. The SAS Buster Group arrived at lunch time, were fed and then allowed to rest until the following day. Colleagues in plain clothes and a smattering of funnies – as they called MI5 – ringed the place, which was shielded from the road and any prying eyes.

On the following morning their colonel, who had flown back only a few hours earlier, conducted the debriefing in the presence of two dull young hawk-eyed civilians from the Home Office, and a senior member of the Metropolitan Police.

They went through the entire operation, from arrival in Hong Kong to the target acquisition and the final moments when the three PIRA men had died.

'The usual stink's going on,' one of the Home Office men told them. His name was Dacre and he had an accent more suited to the Stock Exchange than the corridors of power. 'There'll certainly be some kind of inquiry in Hong Kong and we'll have to get the story straight.'

'We shall resist the appearance of my men at any inquiry.' The SAS colonel did not even bother to look at Dacre.

'And they'll overrule you, just as they did in Gibraltar.' The other civilian – Basington – was a snappy young man who looked, and acted, like a bad-tempered whippet.

'Possibly.' The colonel could bite as well as any government lackey. 'But we'll hold it up for a few weeks.'

'The government's under pressure.' Dacre, though not as pushy as his colleague, sounded as though he, as they used to say, would brook no argument. 'They'll have to agree, and set the thing in motion. The press are howling, just as they always do. Braying about the morality of the operation.'

'They also get a touch moral when the lads kill children with a badly timed bomb.' The colonel regarded the Irish problem as war, and all was quite fair and above board. 'The Provos send these people out to kill, then everyone gets top-heavy with guilt as soon as we take them out. The bloody kissing's got to stop somewhere.'

'They weren't armed. They hadn't even set up the bomb.' Basington's tone had turned contemptuous.

Buster One, sprawled in a soft easy chair, smiled. 'The intelligence was duff. What about the bloody girl? How much did she really tell you?'

'As far as the press, or any inquiry is concerned, we're still looking for the girl.' Dacre seemed to wince, and the senior police officer, who looked as though he did not want to become involved, made a tutting sound.

'I simply obeyed orders.' Buster One looked calmly into the icy eyes of the Home Office men, glancing from one to the other. These buggers, he thought, always want to distance themselves from the reality.

Basington made some kind of noise, from the back of his throat. It was the sound of disgust. 'Just obeying orders'll get you nowhere. The press and, I imagine, the inquiry will quote it back at you. That was the standard answer given by every SS concentration camp commandant at the end of the Second World War.'

'Then we won't tell them that.' Buster One went on smiling, knowing he was infuriating the civilian. 'We'll let the evidence from Buster Leader speak for itself.' Buster Leader was the senior officer on the spot. The one who had allowed them to proceed by ramaining silent on that Hong Kong morning.

After the civilians had gone, the SAS colonel lunched with the six men. Before he left he told them that, whatever else they said, it was essential that any inquiry believe they really thought the PIRA trio was about to explode a device already primed under the saluting dais. 'Nobody's going to stand up and say you were ordered to kill them, whatever the situation,' he said, looking hard at Buster One.

'And nobody here's going to admit those were our orders, sir.' Buster One did not even bother to smile. 'As far as we're concerned, they were about to hurt a large number of civilians. There were still upwards of a hundred people milling around the dais. We were there to save lives. You can count on it, sir.'

He would never tell anyone that the orders had been very clear. 'Take the buggers out. They are the enemy. Your job is to kill the enemy, unless Buster Leader countermands that order, okay?' That is what the colonel, who had been Buster Leader, had told them before they left the Peninsula Hotel in Kowloon on the morning of the incident. Buster One knew then that at no time would the colonel even hint that he was there, at the heart of Operation *Eradicate*. In fact he had at least nine people who would come forward to say categorically that he was in Hereford all that week.

<h2 style="text-align:center">– 3 –</h2>

Tarpin took the British Airways red-eye back to Heathrow from New York. It was Saturday morning around nine-thirty by the time he got back to the flat. Sukie was on the telephone, talking to an author who had been unavailable all Friday afternoon.

'I tried to get you, David, but you didn't even leave your machine on,' she was saying. Then, as he closed the living room door, 'David, be a love and hang on a minute, Pip's just got in from New York.' She covered the phone with a hand and leaned out towards him. He bent down and kissed her. 'David Devon, being bloody indecisive as usual,' she mouthed. 'Great to see you back. Love you.' She smelled of soap and bath oil. Her lips were as tasty as a fresh pear.

As he went through to the bedroom, she was off again. 'No, David, there'll be nobody in the office today. It *is* Saturday, and there's no way I can get back to them until Monday . . . No, no, I *do* understand, David, but we both think you should take it even if it isn't as much as we expected . . . Times is hard, lovey, and they're making a meal out of it like they always do . . . Yes, I know Geoffrey got a huge deal. There are separate rules for people like Geoffrey . . . Yes, even in a recession . . . ' and on and on, and so and so.

He hated her calling him Pip. It was one of the few things that jarred. Also, his heart had sunk when he heard her soothing a client. Sukie was an agent with scruples and, unusually for a literary agent, she really did care about her clients. David Devon was, as they said in the trade, a good earner – the author of half a dozen best-selling, sharp, witty, brittle novels which ably dissected current lifestyles and mores. He was clever, funny and sold very well. If she was doing a deal for him, Sukie's mind would be on that all weekend. She had once called him 'the British Tom Wolfe in sheep's clothing', and a reviewer on the *Sunday Times* had picked it up and used it. She thought Devon had never forgiven her.

Tarpin unpacked, throwing dirty laundry into the basket and putting unused clothes back in their drawers and cupboards. He would shove the dirty stuff into the machine later. He hung the last suit and peered at himself in the bathroom mirror. He did not look as tired as he felt, and his thinning straw-coloured hair would manage today without a wash. Opening one drawer, he came across a photograph, tucked under some shirts. It had been taken a year ago when he had grown a beard. Sukie had made him shave it off – 'Darling, you look like a stained-glass Jesus,' she had told him. 'It makes me uncomfortable in bed. I feel like Mary Magdalene all the time.'

Slowly he stripped, took a shower, and shaved.

She came into the bedroom just as he was rubbing lotion into his cheeks.

'Jesus, talk about Devon, glorious Devon,' she called out from her dressing table. 'He's got a thing about Geoffrey. Very cold about *him*, and doesn't listen when I tell him he isn't in the same league. That's something an author just has to accept.'

'What's the deal?' he shouted back to her.

'Oh, Random House have offered eighty thousand dollars. Not huge, but it's generous. There won't be much profit at the end of the day.'

'He's better than Geoffrey.'

'My darling, everyone's better than Geoffrey. Geoffrey splits his infinitives, begins every other sentence with 'And', has plots you can drive six London buses through, line abreast, and his heroes always look at a woman and say to themselves, 'She was the most beautiful girl he had ever seen in the whole of his life'. He also spends no time on description. Takes short cuts and describes people by saying they look like this or that movie star. But he sells millions of books and the public love him.'

'What do they know?'

'That's a publisher's remark, darling. They know what they like. You look good.' She came into the bathroom, behind him, wrapping her arms around his chest. 'Missed you,' kissing the back of his neck. 'So, how was it?'

'You know how it was, Sukie. Chance of a lifetime. With all the lay-offs here God knows how long I'd last. Offer I just can't refuse.'

'Oh, hell.'

'What've you been doing in there?' He cocked his head back towards the bedroom.

'Playing with my jewels, as Elizabeth Taylor is supposed to have said.'

He turned. Christ, those eyes could swallow a man whole. 'You're the most beautiful girl I've ever seen in my life,' he chuckled. 'You also reek of *Bal de Versailles*.'

'Because I like it. I love the old "Dance at the Palace".'

'We really have to talk, Suke.'

'I know we do, but not now. I think you should get over the lag first. You know what you're like flying West–East. You walk ten feet off the floor for a couple of days, and you don't think straight. It's like living with a prima donna, and I spend most of my days with prima donnas.'

'I know you don't want to come to New York, but . . . '

Her hand came up, covering his mouth. 'I didn't say I wasn't coming, but we *do* have to go through things, Pip. I have a career as well, and that's important.'

'Mmmm.'

'Take me to bed.' She pushed close to him. 'Make a dishonest woman of me. Take me to bed, then sleep. We can talk tomorrow.' She was urgently moving her groin against his leg and, despite the fatigue, he responded.

It was wild, as usual, and possibly even more inventive than it had been for a while. As they made love, Tarpin was conscious of what she was doing. Sukie Cartwright was reminding him of how it was between them. In some ways she wanted him to make the decision for them and turn down America. He had not had the heart to tell her he had already accepted.

For six years now Sukie Cartwright had meddled with both his mind and body. Rarely did she stray far from his thoughts, and, if he had his way, they would be married tomorrow. He knew she agreed, even though she said she needed space – whatever that meant. Anyway, the male chauvinist part of him could not bear the thought of starting the hunt all over again at his age. Yes, indeed, and the sex was the best ever. He knew a lot of people thought he was rather staid and dull. They should see him now, that old gang of his.

She brought him coffee – 'Just how you like your women, darling. Hot and black' – but he did not even finish drinking it. Sleep overpowered him, and he slid into the darkness without fighting, as though his mind wanted to blot out the difficulties of life. He woke to the urgent ringing of the telephone.

It was five-thirty and he cursed at sleeping the day away. Now he would not sleep tonight and that would wipe out tomorrow. Sukie had picked up the phone in the other room. He swung his legs on to the floor and, bleary, floundered to the cupboard to get his terry towelling robe. He had bought two of them last Christmas. One for Sukie and one for himself. Their respective initials were worked in blue on the white pockets.

Blundering out into the living room, he found Sukie laughing and just ending the telephone conversation.

'You're awake.' She put down the telephone. 'I hoped you'd go right on till morning.'

'No such luck. I'm not bloody Peter Pan.'

'No, you're bloody Garry Essendine. Pure Noël Coward, darling. You're lagged.'

He smiled. She always joked about him going into what she called his 'Garry Essendine mode' when there was a difference of opinion. Garry Essendine was the temperamental actor in Coward's *Present Laughter*. 'Who was on the phone?'

'Pat, with a gorgeous story.' Pat Patton was her partner. The agency, Patwright Associates, had twenty-five solid clients, and a turnover profit of almost a quarter of a million a year. He understood why she did not want to give it up.

'It would seem,' she began, 'that Jemma had some friends around this afternoon – Alexandra and Nicholas, can you imagine?' Jemma was Pat's six-year-old. 'Well, they got to talking about what they wanted to be when they grew up. Jemma said she was going to be a scientist, Alexandra said she wanted to be a vet, and Nicholas, aged four, declared he wanted to be a sheepdog.'

Phillip laughed aloud, realizing it was the first time he had done so in the past week.

'Jemma said that he meant he wanted to be a farmer with a sheepdog, but he was adamant. Said, no, he just wanted to be a sheepdog.'

'The boy's got sense. I wouldn't mind being a sheepdog.' He switched on the television, ready for the news, and asked if there was any chance of some tea.

He saw her bridle and then think better of it. Normally he would have got tea for himself. They lived together on a basis of sharing. Unless they planned otherwise they did domestic things for themselves. If he had people to dinner, Suki would act as hostess, but he would cook the meal, and vice versa. It worked well.

She made tea then came and sat beside him as he watched the news. The lead story was still the shooting of the three men in Hong Kong. Statements from the Home Secretary and the SAS declared there was no shoot-to-kill policy. It had been a necessary surgical operation. The men on the spot had used their initiative. The prince and princess, not to mention the many hundreds of civilians, had been in danger. They had information that the Active Service Unit had already placed a bomb under, or near, the reviewing dais. The reaction of the IRA men left them with no alternative.

A boring Labour Party MP stood outside the Houses of Parliament, the equestrian statue of the Black Prince just behind him, and angrily told an interviewer that it was this kind of thing which devalued Britain in the eyes of the world. Then the Leader of the Opposition spoke calmly about the necessity for a full inquiry. 'The government must stand in the court of the world, with its sleeves rolled up, and show categorically, once and for all, that there is no shoot-to-kill policy when dealing with the sad problems of Northern Ireland,' he said. 'The British people have the right to know the truth. There must be an open inquiry. I would like to think there is proof that our police, and the armed forces, do not behave like gangsters.'

'Silly sod,' Tarpin muttered. 'If the government has to stand in the court of the world – whatever that is – then so have the Provos.'

Then they went back over the events, with tape of the scene just after the shootings, cross-cutting with similar footage saved from the 1988 Gibraltar scandal.

Just as they were moving to the second story the doorbell rang. Sukie said she would get it, and Tarpin wondered idly who the hell would drop in at this time on a Saturday evening.

'It's a couple of policemen, Pip.' She was white and unnerved, as though she believed Tarpin had done something dreadful.

He got up and took a pace towards her.

'They want to see you,' she said. Then shook her head, eyes filled with suspicion.

He went out into the little passageway.

There were two of them. Both in uniform. One a sergeant and the other a police constable.

'Mr Tarpin?' the sergeant asked.

'Yes.' He flapped his hands, running them down the bathrobe. 'Sorry about this. I've just got back from New York.'

'Mr Phillip Andrew Tarpin?'

'Yes, what is it?'

'Your mother, sir. Your mother is Mrs Vera Tarpin of 12 Princess Mansions, Hammersmith?'

'Yes. What . . . ?'

The sergeant nodded at the constable who took over. He was young and it was obviously his first taste of doing a job like this.

'It's very bad news, I'm afraid, sir. Would you like to sit down? I think we should come in.'

'Bad news? What bad news?'

'Your mother, sir. I'm afraid she's dead. I'm sorry, sir.'

'Oh, Christ.' He was not rocked by the fact that his mother was suddenly dead, but by a gout of guilt. He had not seen, nor spoken with, his mother for almost three years.

'We have a car, sir. We'd like you to come down and make sure nothing's missing. A neighbour's already identified her.'

For a full minute, Tarpin stood there, not knowing what to do or say. Sukie had one hand on his arm. She looked puzzled.

'We have a car outside, sir.' The sergeant left no doubt that he was not asking Tarpin to come with them, but demanding it.

THREE

– 1 –

Kathleen Fagin was a short neat-figured girl with the face of a young nun, giving an impression of paradoxical worldliness and vulnerability. Since bringing her back from Hong Kong they had kept her holed up in a house they used for such purposes, near Regent's Park. They had not allowed her to see any newspapers, nor watch television, though they had been kind and considerate in other ways, even giving her the latest Jeffrey Archer novel to read. Jeffrey Archer was, they felt, her speed.

There were three people looking after her: two men and a woman. The woman's age was indeterminate, and she appeared to regard Fagin as some kind of a threat. Both the men were young and friendly.

'Oh, Kathleen, you've been a wicked, wicked girl.' The interrogator with clear blue eyes and long hair sat down in the chair opposite her. His face showed humour, the eyes twinkling and lips slipping and sliding in a series of quick smiles which eventually blended into one long, friendly beam.

They were in a room which looked out onto a small stretch of garden, surrounded by a brick wall and trees. The house could have been somewhere in the country from the view. Kathleen Fagin only knew the location was London because the sound of traffic came from behind the trees, and also from the front of the house. She had not seen out of any front-facing windows, and had been brought to the place at night, in a closed van with no windows.

'A wicked, wicked girl,' he repeated.

A look of fear flickered across her face, there for a millisecond then gone, as her right hand moved upwards across her face to smooth her hair. The inquisitor saw and noted it. He considered she had probably done the anti-interrogation course, for Kathleen had remained very much in control throughout the time they had been with her. Promises had certainly been made, though nobody had set a time frame, and the interrogators had not really started work yet. Her automatic action of running a hand, palm down, over the long blonde hair was one she made often – a way to shield her face for a second, or to gain time when questioned. It was the kind of body language they taught people who were likely to be put to the question.

'Why?' Her voice had only the slightest undercurrent of the original Belfast accent. Kathleen Fagin was a natural for the PIRA, having lived in England since the age of sixteen. She had especially worked on her accent, purging all traces of the harsh vowel sounds, and choosing a vocabulary more consistent with England than Ireland. It was still not quite right, but she had been getting there. 'Why am I wicked? For being a traitor to the cause?'

'No, you've shown common sense about that. It's a question of the information you gave us about the Hong Kong job.'

'I gave what I knew.'

'Ah.' Now he started to pause. The technique was to leave blank spaces in the conversation. If you did it often enough, the subject might just feel that she was obliged to fill the spaces with words. Silence and words are the stock in trade of inquisitors.

'Well, either they didn't tell you enough, or you kept something back, Kathleen. Or, and this is what worries those who instruct me, you deliberately misled us. It was all rather tragic, what happened in Hong Kong.'

'Tragic?'

He gave a little nod. 'Tragic. As in catastrophic.'

'Oh.'

He left her to stew on that one, taking out cigarettes, offering one to her, asking if she minded if he smoked, lighting up, then waiting, nodding and occasionally looking up at her from under his eyelids. Outside, the daylight was fading. How long. Oh Lord, how long? the inquisitor wondered. His name was Michael Bailey and he knew his partners – Ruth Daubney and Richard Cearns – would be arriving any minute. They were listening in and waiting for the moment. Then they planned to act out their little drama.

He counted one hundred and forty-eight before she spoke. 'What hapened?' The voice was small, low and edged with a tremor.

'You care what happened?'

'Of course I care. I've seen enough killing and maiming. It's become stupid, a nonsense. The cause doesn't mean anything now. The time's passed.'

'What time's passed?'

'Oh, what's the Bible say? – That bit about a time for living and a time for dying? There's been enough young people killed for nothing. I just want out, because I don't believe in it any more.'

'You don't believe what any more?'

'I don't believe the North will ever be a part of any united Ireland. You only have to look at the economics.'

'Is it only the economics that count?' Richard Cearns stood just inside the door, with Ruth behind him. Both of their faces were set in a kind of shock, just as they had planned.

Little Kathleen Fagin turned her face. She spoke with poison daubed on her words. 'Not just economics. You only have to look at the number of people. Take a tally on the role of death over the past thirty years and more. Then you add that to the economics. The South can hardly afford to keep itself, let alone the North. The entire question of rule would have to be changed.'

Ruth had walked past Richard, to stand looking down on the girl. 'Can't the others do their sums? If we walked out of the North tomorrow, how many good Ulstermen would shout that their heritage was going to be taken away from them?'

The girl nodded, fast, a series of little bobs of her head, turning into small negative shakes.

'And if you're so concerned about the killing,' Richard said softly. 'If you're really concerned, why did you tell us the bomb would be in place, and that the prince and princess would be blown to kingdom come within seconds of getting to the reviewing dais?'

'That was the plan.' Her eyes opened wide. Horror lunged from her face. 'What happened?'

'There was no bomb under the dais . . . '

'There was. Christ, I saw the stuff, and the electronic fuses. We

24

had it there, in the hotel. They were going to do it with three carrier bags. They went out the night before. Did a dummy run. God, I was with them.' The last words were paced, a count of two between each word.

'Well, Kathleen, someone's not telling the truth. Your three lads didn't plant the bomb. It stayed in the hotel, and your three friends just went out and left it there. Now how do you explain that?'

'You mean it went off . . . ? The hotel . . . ? Oh my God!'

If that was what she wanted to believe, it was okay by them. Already they knew she had truly reached a point where she wanted no more killing, no further massacre of the innocents.

Kathleen Fagin began to weep. 'There were tourists in that hotel. Women, children. I played with some kids in the pool . . . How many? . . . How many were killed?'

It was convenient for her to believe it. Nobody told her anything different.

– 2 –

Number twelve Princess Mansions sounds a grand address. It conjures an elegant building with a marble foyer and, possibly, a uniformed concierge with all the bells and whistles. The reality was somewhat less than inspiring. A building erected circa 1910, originally red brick, now grimed and dotted with those strange yellowish oblongs you find in edifices which had been repointed between the two world wars.

The ambulance was just leaving as they arrived, and Tarpin asked, for the twentieth time, 'How did it happen?' Receiving the same answer from the sergeant: 'Best see the inspector, sir. He'll explain.'

What in God's name? Murder? His mother? Well, he would never blame a murderer, for she was the most difficult woman ever to walk the earth, but there was something seedy and depressing about the place where she had died.

Sukie looked in shock, and she had only met Vera Tarpin once. That was the last time Tarpin had spoken to his only parent. He had never known his father – killed over Germany only weeks before he was born.

His mother had always seemed to inhabit poky, tiny places, and Tarpin's abiding memory of growing up with her was of never having enough room. Certainly never having any privacy. She had lived that way right to the end. He could tell the moment they arrived at the door of number twelve, via a clanking, dirty, utilitarian lift. During his boyhood there was a lift, but, compared to this, it was luxury – all rattling gates and brass fitments.

A man in plain clothes was coming out as they arrived. He carried a strange, oblong, box-like black case and grinned at the sergeant. 'Nothing here for me,' he said, as though it explained everything.

A crumpled man in his late fifties, with tired eyes, greying, badly combed hair, and the nose of a drinker, seemed to have commandeered the main room which became very crowded once Sukie and Tarpin entered. The sergeant and his constable remained outside, and the crumpled man looked from Sukie to Tarpin as though making up his mind who they were. His eyes were small, almost porcine.

'Mr Tarpin?' It was tentative.

'Phillip Tarpin. Yes. You are?' He stuck out a hand.

'Detective Inspector Rainbow. Gerald Rainbow.' He looked at Tarpin's hand, then seemed to realize he was supposed to shake it. His palm was clammy and, close up, you could smell the beer.

'And your good wife, I presume?' There was an unctuousness about the policeman, and Tarpin had a strange feeling he had met the man before.

'No,' said Sukie firmly. 'I am neither good nor Mr Tarpin's wife. We simply cohabit.'

Oh Lord, Tarpin thought, in the midst of death we have Sukie trying to shock the law. She would never have used the word cohabit under normal circumstances.

Very quickly he stepped in. 'Inspector, I gather my mother's died. Your sergeant wouldn't tell me the circumstances of her death, perhaps . . . '

'Little Phil.' His smile showed yellow and irregular teeth, and as he spoke so the inspector probed an ear with his finger. 'Little Phil. Good Lord. I never would've recognized you.'

'I beg your pardon?'

'Well, you might not even remember me. You were only a nipper after all. You don't remember your Uncle Gerald?' He removed the finger from his ear and flicked a morsel of wax from the nail, where it had adhered. 'Little Phil,' he said again. 'No, of course you don't remember me. I was only with them for a year. But I bet you remember my guv'nor, your Uncle Ben. Detective Superintendent Ben Willis.'

'Ohmygod!' Tarpin blurted, so quickly that Sukie gave a little laugh. Uncle Ben. Nunkie, he used to tell his friends, and they would laugh about him. Come to think of it, Nunkie was the one who finally put the boot in and tore apart his already fragile relationship with his mother. Nunkie was the beginning of the end, the last in a long line of uncles who had peopled his childhood, well into his teenage years and beyond.

Vera had never married again. He always thought she harboured a strange idea that Edward Percival Tarpin, Flight Lieutenant, Royal Air Force, might suddenly return. He had been posted as 'Missing' – MIA as they called it now in this enlightened age of acronyms. A father he never had. Uncles came by the boatload.

In the space of a few seconds, about three decades of taped memories unwound in his head. He remembered Uncle Clive who bought expensive toys; Uncle Roger who took him 'up West' as he always called it, and bought him clothes. He remembered waiting for hours while Uncle Roger bought his mother clothes as well. There was Uncle Bernie, who brought silk underwear for his mother; Uncle Harold, with the bottles of gin; Uncle Bill, who always arrived with books – he liked Uncle Bill. Then there was Uncle Rick who eventually had to go away for a long time, but he knew what that was all about because Uncle Rick's enforced stay in one of Her Majesty's prisons heralded the arrival of Uncle Ben, who, he later figured, had put Uncle Rick away.

Ben Willis had remained with Vera Tarpin – on and off – until about eight years ago, long after he had retired. The reason of his going was cigarettes, whisky, weight and, presumably, Tarpin's mother's requirements. Long before Phillip Tarpin reached his teens he had figured out that Mum was a bit of a one on the side. As a child he had thought the noises that came through the thin wall, between his bedrooom and his mother's, betokened some terrible kind of night illness. Only later did he first suffer disgust, and then embarrassment. He had told Sukie about it during the long and wearying post mortem following that last meeting – 'I suppose you can never think of your parents at it,' he had said. Sukie simply laughed and told him she had long discussions with her school friends about it, and maintained her parents only did it once because she was an only child. 'We rather looked down on Amanda Gibbs' mother and father. She had five sisters and two brothers. It was at that stage girls go through – you know, "I'm never going to let a man do that to me".'

As the memory tape containing the inventory of uncles sped through his head, Tarpin even vaguely recalled Uncle Gerald, the copper who now stood in his dead mother's apology for a living room.

'Promised Ben I'd keep an eye open for Vera.' Gerald Rainbow put on a sad expression. 'I had to cover things up a bit when he died.' He looked at Tarpin with a small wince of uncertainty. 'You weren't at the funeral, were you?'

'No. Ben Willis was not my favourite person.'

'Phil, he was damned good to your mum. Stuck by her. We had a terrible time, between her and Ben's wife at the funeral. You should've been there to support your mum, you know, Phil.'

Sukie could not resist it, 'Yes, Phil, you should have been there. Support your mum.' She put on her Goody-Two-Shoes look and told Rainbow that it was before her time, indicating that she would have seen to it had she been around.

'Inspector Rainbow.' Tarpin was getting tired of the reminiscing. 'Inspector, you should know that my mother was my least favourite person next to Ben Willis. My mother fucked up my life, and Ben Willis aided and abetted.'

The inspector looked at Tarpin as though he had been struck across the face. 'He was a bloody good guv'nor. Taught me more than any other copper. I wouldn't be where I am today without Ben.'

The room was modestly furnished, which was an understatement. He recognized the worn easy chairs and the small table. Also the two pictures which seemed top-heavy for a room of this size: watercolours, landscapes. They would have been attractive in the right setting. Here, they just clashed. 'What happened?' he asked.

'Very humdrum, really.' Rainbow shuffled, looking at his feet. 'Her neighbour, a Miss Williamson – small, bossy sort of person. She'd been away until this morning. They had planned to go to bingo together. Rang the bell when she got back. Thought Mrs – your mum – was out. Came back late afternoon. Rang and knocked. Telephoned. Then late this afternoon she talked to the other people on this landing – nice people, retired, business people. Your mum had good friends here. Her class, you might say. Except those in twenty-six, just upstairs. A bit above themselves. Checkits, that's their name. They'd pushed a note through the door, complaining about the telly being on all day and all night. Anyhow, none of them had seen her for a couple of days, so they rang the nick. The beat copper came down. Broke the door in.'

'And?' Uncle Gerald seemed to be overcome with emotion. Phillip Tarpin wanted to push him along. He had noticed the odd, unpleasant musty smell and knew it for what it was. He would like to get out as soon as possible, and he found the idea of his mother going to bingo and being with her own class of people at the end, all rather revolting. Vera Tarpin had been the snob of all time. 'Snob of ages, cleft for me,' ran through his head, sung by a male voice choir. He thought it was probably the jet lag.

'They found her on the floor in the kitchen. Quite a lot of blood. She'd been dead about two days. Nobody knew what had happened and I was in the nick when the word came through. As it turns out, the doc thinks she probably had a heart attack and cut her head open when she fell. Definitely no foul play.' He shuffled his feet again. 'We got your address from her book.' He pointed towards a small green address book on the table. 'I thought you should hear the details from an old friend, so to speak.'

'Yes. Yes, thank you.' He realized, with some alarm, that he really did not know what to do next. 'I'm not sure what I should . . . '

'Do?'

'Yes.'

'I should imagine she has everything arranged. Very punctilious, your mum. After all, she did work for a solicitor for the last ten years before she retired. You know who . . . ?'

'Cox, Russ & Pembeton, yes.'

'I'd take a look round now, if I were you. Go through any boxes. Take away any papers. Then you can ring Mr Pembeton – he was the one she worked for – first thing Monday.'

Tarpin nodded.

'I think there are some things in the bedroom. I didn't touch anything,' he added, rather too quickly. 'But there's a cupboard in there, neat as you like. A couple of suitcases and some shoe boxes. Seemed to have filed stuff in the shoe boxes. You'd best take a look.'

Tarpin nodded and asked about the keys to the flat. Rainbow handed them over. 'Though they won't be no good,' he said. 'We've got a man coming over to fix the lock. How long will you be here?'

'Just as long as it takes.' Tarpin explained that he had only arrived back in London that morning.

'I'll gee up the locks chap.' The copper helped himself to the telephone as Tarpin looked at Sukie, indicating they should go into the bedroom.

It was as small and sorry as the living room, but there were telltale signs of his mother on the dressing table. A bottle of Booth's gin, and a half-full tonic. The glass was empty, set down on the only available space, for the dressing table was a clutter of make-up and the usual paraphernalia. She had a framed poster for *Les Miz* over the bed, and a copy of *Shogun* on the tiny bedside table. The cupboard was a built-in affair with hanging space for half a dozen dresses. Three suitcases were piled up behind the dresses and, on top of the suitcases, a pile of eight shoe boxes. He reached in and pulled the first one out.

'You should've been there to support your mum, you know, Phil,' Sukie said softly, grinning at him.

He sighed. 'You know what's really terrible, Suke?'

'Surprise me. Sorry, Pip, but I couldn't stand the old bat.'

'That's the terrible thing. I cannot remember one day when I was really happy with my mother. Not a single bloody day. There must have been birthdays or Christmases. But I can only remember what a super, overbearing bitch she was. People are devastated when their mothers die. I don't feel a thing.'

'It's not surprising.'

He opened the first box which contained neatly stacked photographs. On the top was a snapshot of his mother, taken around 1954. No denying she was a looker – trim figure, high breasts, a face with a come-hither smile. He glanced towards the dressing table again. When Vera got a little older her looks began to fall apart. The hair was always a shade too brassy, and if she tackled her make-up after six in the evening there was always too much: more rouge over more foundation, and the lipstick gashing her face in a crimson scrawl. Very few people realized that, as the years climbed upwards, Mummy became a bit of a lush. A nasty lush at that.

Sukie took charge. She wanted to get out of this tiny flat. Vera Tarpin's unpleasant ghost hovered over everything. 'Let's put all the papers in one of the suitcases. You'll have to go through them, but it can wait. Let's just concentrate on getting out of here.'

He nodded, and they began to transfer the contents of the shoe boxes to a large battered case, littered with fake stickers from hotels like the Omar Khayyam, Cairo, and Raffles, Singapore. The stickers summed up his mother: brash, showy, snobbish. He could hear her voice as he stacked papers and photographs into the case: a drawl, high-pitched and affected, as though nobody was quite as good as her. She did not seem to have parents, for she always spoke of them as her people.

'Don't think I don't know what's going on,' she was saying in his head. 'I'm never wrong about things like this.'

She had *actually* said that when the real rift began. It was around 1968. He was desperate to get out of the flat he shared with her and – on about four nights a week – Nunkie. He had suddenly blurted it all out, over lunch with Ray Hacking, best seller, writer of amazingly good crime fiction and doing a non-fiction book on famous murders for Tarpin's first employers.

'If it's as bad as that, Phil, you can always stay with me for a couple of months.'

'You mean it?'

'There's plenty of room, old cock, and we have running hot and cold birds.' Ray was a devil with the women and it was the sizzling sixties.

When he told his mother that he was going to move in with a

friend, she blew her top. 'If it's a woman, I forbid it. I don't approve of that kind of thing.'

'You mean the kind of thing you've been doing since I was a babe in arms?' That made matters worse. Then, when she found out that he was moving in with a man, rich and famous at that, she invited herself to dinner. Ray had been very good about it, though not pleased when she turned up with Nunkie in tow. Nunkie even managed to drag Ray off and get a grand tour of the Belgravia mansion.

Two days later, he got in from work to find Ray annoyed and irritated as a wasp. 'Phil, I'm sorry. This isn't working out. I'm really sorry, but can you find somewhere to go within a week? Ten days tops?'

'Sure, but . . . '

'Your mother rang me this afternoon. She accused me of being a gay drug addict and said her friend – the revolting Superintendent Willis – was looking into it.'

'But that's laughable.'

'You know that, and I know that. But she was very unpleasant and is, I believe, about to lay siege. I can't handle the publicity and I don't want to sue her. Too much time and too much money.'

'But, Ray, she's crazy.'

'As a loon.'

He could hear Ray saying it as he put the last papers into the suitcase.

'Where've you been?" Sukie asked.

'Watching an old movie.'

'Any good?'

'Disaster.'

'Ah, starring Vera Tarpin . . . '

'And Nunkie Ben Willis, yes.'

She put a hand on his arm, shaking her head. 'Don't even think about seeing it again. It's too bloody depressing.'

He nodded, then became aware of movement in the other room. A new voice, soft, cultured and amused, said, 'What ho, Gerry. How's things in this part of the woods?'

'Jesus, Jack. I thought you were the locksmith.'

'Not today.'

'What're you doing here?'

'Slow night, old sport. Thought I'd take a look-see.'

'Nothing here for you, surely?'

'Who knows? They've removed the corpse?'

'Yes.' Rainbow dropped his voice slightly. 'The son and his lady're in the bedroom, getting all the deceased's papers.'

'Ah.'

Tarpin snapped the locks shut on the case and walked back into the small living room.

'Mr Tarpin, I presume.' The man was slim, bronzed, with clear blue eyes, sharp features and well-groomed hair. He could have been any age between forty and sixty. He had that kind of face. He also dressed like a successful bookmaker or a long-term Conservative MP – a brown double-breasted overcoat with a velvet collar; trilby hat to match and what you could see of his trousers proclaimed a very sharp dresser indeed. The shoes were probably Gucci. You could have shaved in their shine.

'Yes, Phillip Tarpin.'

The stranger smiled: open and friendly as he extended his arm. The handshake would have broken any unwary fingers. 'Chilton,' he said. 'John Chilton. My friends call me Jack.'

'Ms Cartwright.' Tarpin introduced Sukie.

'Delighted to meet you.' He sounded as though he had been wanting to meet Sukie for the best part of his life.

'And you are?' Tarpin thought he could detect something not quite right about the newcomer. In his head, some old parson from his youth said, 'And Jacob was a smooth man.'

'I used to know your mother slightly. I'm with the Home Office, Mr Tarpin. Nothing grand, I fear. I liaise.' As though that explained everything. 'Heard about your loss, when I called into the local station. In the area, know Gerry here. Thought I'd look in. Condolences, that kind of thing.'

'Well, thank you.' He turned to Rainbow. 'The locksmith?'

'Not arrived, I fear.'

'I think we'd like to get going. Can you advise me about where I could pick up any new keys? When the locksmith's secured everything? We might want to come back tomorrow.'

'Pick 'em up at the nick, Phil. You really can't wait?'

'I'm pretty tired.' He was also filled with an insistent need to be out of this place. Alive, his mother had disgusted him. Dead, she did not even have the power to make him sorry for her. Yet she drenched this place with her peculiar brand of obnoxious madness.

'Quite a character, your mother.' Chilton sounded as though he would like to chat the night away.

'I suppose she was. To be frank, Mr . . . er Mr Chilton . . . '

'Jack, my friends call me Jack. Your mother used to call me Jackie.'

'I wouldn't know. We didn't get on.'

'Yes, she mentioned it. Very sad about that over the last couple of years.'

'We really must be going. I wonder if . . . ' He looked helplessly at Rainbow.

'Oh, transport. Yes. I'll get the sergeant to drive you home. Can I take the suitcase?'

'We'll manage. Nice to have met you, Mr Chilton.'

'Jack.' The man had a charming smile.

Woman killer, Tarpin judged.

– 3 –

They did not correct Kathleen Fagin. She was simply allowed to go along with her presumption that the bomb had exploded in the hotel – The Regent on Kowloon side. She had known how much Semtex was there, so figured that the death and destruction had been huge. Indeed, if the four hundred pounds of explosive *had* erupted within The Regent there would have been carnage, but they did not correct her.

She wept, then cursed, then began to talk. She gave them the alternative plan, which was to blow the prince and princess to hell and gone, together with a large number of other influential Hong Kong figures, at a dinner party which had been arranged privately. It was not even on the official schedule, and it would certainly have been a softer target.

She gave them the names of the back-up team, and the way in which the explosive had been smuggled in. Then she talked a great deal about the General Staff – the Intelligence Officer, the Battalion

Commander who had planned the operation, and the political leaders who had condoned it.

In all, they had two hours twenty-five minutes of very valuable stuff on tape – and there was no coercion.

When they told her the truth, Kathleen Fagin went berserk.

– 4 –

Detective Inspector Rainbow went back up to number twelve, once he had seen Phillip Tarpin and Sukie Cartwright safely tucked into the car. He even waited until they had been driven away.

Jack Chilton was wandering through the flat, opening drawers and looking into other meagre hiding places.

'Did you really know Vera?'

Chilton did not even bother to turn around. He was examining the inside of some tins which he had dragged out of a wall cupboard in the matchbox of a kitchen. 'Knew *of* her, Gerry. Knew *of* her. Never really met the lady, of course, but she was a bitch by all accounts. Son didn't seem upset. You certain it was natural causes?'

'One hundred per cent, but, if you're that interested we can send you the forensic's report.'

'Could you do that? I would appreciate it very much. I'd be much obliged.'

'There *is* something in this for you?'

'Ask me no questions and I'll tell you no lies, Gerry. Pity I got here after the son and his lady. I wouldn't have minded a peep at her papers. Incidentally, that lady of his is a corker, what?'

'Very rompworthy, Jack.'

'You have their address?'

Rainbow gave it to him; and Jack Chilton wrote it down, carefully in a black leather notebook. He did not mention that he already had all the details in a file back at his office. Chilton was a very devious person. 'Good of you, Gerry. I'll be on my way. I might even call on Mr Tarpin.'

'You know what they called him at school?'

'I can guess, and I presume you had this from the late lamented Ben Willis.'

35

Rainbow nodded. 'They called the poor little bleeder Tampon. Imagine that, being called Tampon.'

'Children can be very cruel,' Chilton smiled as though he had suffered similar indignities during the happiest days of *his* life.

Mr John Chilton moved like a ghost. He never advertised his presence, took great pains to keep his daily itinerary secret, and rarely arrived anywhere by a direct route.

On the street outside Princess Mansions, Hammersmith, he stood for a moment, then sauntered away, walking for two blocks, turning into a side street where his nice gleaming Rover had been parked.

He drove with great care, heading for Whitehall where he parked again before walking a considerable distance to the grace and favour apartments in St James's Palace.

The man he had come to see was not identified outside his door, like the other occupants of the grace and favour houses. The white painted sign simply said *General AGM*.

General AGM's official name was Daniel Scarecrow, though he did have other aliases. He was big and almost as smooth as Chilton, but he had ex-military written all over him, from the shining grey hair to the way he carried himself.

'Well?' he asked, once they were seated, with a large whisky for himself and a gin for Chilton.

'Missed it by half an hour, I fear.'

'Damn.'

'Quite. The son has everything. I can arrange a small unnoticeable burglary. During the funeral would be the best time.'

'Perhaps you'd better do that. Only the best, mind you.'

'I only use the best, as you well know.'

'Every scrap of paper. Make them photograph the lot.'

'Of course.'

'You think the son'll put two and two together?'

'I very much doubt it. He'd have to dig all over the place, and I don't think he has the time. Bit of a publishing whizz. Just accepted a new job in New York. I should imagine he'd find the research difficult, even if he did smell a rat.'

'Good.' Scarecrow nodded, looking into his whisky as though he could see the future floating in the amber liquid. 'And the lads?' he asked. 'Will they put it together?'

Chilton looked at the ceiling. 'Very doubtful. The name's so different. You'd have thought they would have caught up with him years ago if they had known. After all, they did remove his father. As far as they're concerned, he was the last of the line.'

Scarecrow frowned. 'Amazing, isn't it? Over all the years they've taken everyone out. Every last one.'

'The Irish have long memories.'

'Yes, but it's been over a century. It's mindless. Vengeance for the sake of vengeance.'

'It's the name of their game. They did not like what happened all those years ago. Don't worry, we'll keep an eye out for the son.' He lit a cigarette with a gold Dunhill. 'What interests me is that the experts know we've hidden something, filleted the files, but they always imagine it's because of something quite different. Which reminds me, there's a fellow called Clifford – Tim Clifford – who's been ferreting around. Taking a different tack. New look as it were. He has a name for exploding myths.'

Scarecrow fixed his eyes on Jackie Chilton. They were hard, unfeeling eyes. 'I presume you can head him off if he gets too close.'

Chilton gave his master a benign, almost pitying, smile. 'There's nothing for him to find. We all know that. Anyway, we have more important things to worry about.'

FOUR

– 1 –

He was a short, fat, jolly-looking man who did not in any way look funereal. 'I haven't seen you since you were in nappies.' He spoke loudly. Some people turned their heads, frowning at the lack of respect so near to the grave, not yet closed. 'At the age of forty-something that's the last thing you want to hear, eh? Nay, lad. It's the last thing I really want to think about. Reminds me of my age. Tempus fugit and all that.'

Tarpin had seen him in the church. In fact the stranger was the only one there whom he could not place. Six of his mother's old friends. Three of them, he thought, were from Princess Mansions, the other three were vaguely known to him: old Mr Pembeton, from Cox, Russ & Pembeton where Vera had worked until retirement, and a couple of ladies of uncertain age who were probably still in the solicitor's employ. Gerald Rainbow represented the police, and presumably the long gone Nunkie. He ostentatiously wore a black armband and an expression of supreme sadness. Tarpin thought of Oliver Twist as the undertaker's mute.

As he walked back to the car from the graveside, with Sukie holding his arm, Tarpin could have sworn that he saw the man Chilton in the back of Rainbow's parked car. Then he was distracted by the jolly fat man.

'You won't remember me, lad.' For a second the laughter went out of his eyes. 'I'm Vera's brother, which I suppose means that I'm your Uncle Bob.'

'Good grief!' Tarpin had heard his mother speak of his Uncle Bob, but, as far as he knew, she did not possess a photograph of

38

him, nor did they keep in touch. 'I didn't . . . Well, I thought . . . '
Why piss around, tell him straight out. 'I didn't think there'd be any
family here. To tell you the truth, I didn't think there *was* any
family.'

'Ah!' Uncle Bob grinned and stuck his hand towards Sukie. 'Bob
Bates,' he said. 'You must be my nephew's wife.' His accent was
firm, unashamed North country. Vera Tarpin had rid herself of the
same accent as a snake sheds its skin. Only when she became angry
did traces bubble to the surface.

'No, 'fraid not.' Sukie took his hand. 'Though there is a slim
possibility that I will be his wife one of these days.' She introduced
herself.

'I've made no arrangements for . . . ' Tarpin began.

'For the cold ham and baked meats? For a wake?' Bob Bates
chuckled. Tarpin was desperately trying to remember what his
Uncle Bob had done for a living. He looked and sounded like a
retired butcher. 'You needn't worry about that, young Phillip. I'm
treating myself for a few days in town. I don't often get to London
these days. Not at my age. I got tickets for *Miss Saigon* last night,
and the escort agency provided me wi' a very nice young lady to
talk with – well, there's nowt much else I can do wi' a young
woman at my age. They can unlock their daughters when I come to
town now, eh?' He slapped his thigh gently. 'I had thought of
asking you, and your lady of course, to supper at my hotel. They do
a good supper at the Inn on the Park. Can you come? About eight? I
like to eat about eight.'

Tarpin looked at Sukie who nodded, then answered for him.
'We'd love to, Mr Bates.'

'Oh, call me Bob. Everybody does. In Burnley you're considered
a bit stuck up if you insist on the Mister business all the time.
Especially if you've come up from nothing, like me.'

He grinned and added, 'We've a lot to talk about, Phillip. Quite a
lot.'

Tarpin mumbled something about looking forward to the
supper and watched, with a certain incredulity, as Bob Bates
waddled off to a handsome chauffeur-driven car.

'Where there's muck there's money,' Sukie said brightly. 'Isn't
that what they say in the North? Your Uncle Bob seems to have

made his way in life, in spite of humble beginnings.' They were in the car now, and heading back to the flat.

'Probably why my late unlamented mum didn't like him. He would certainly have reminded her of the humble beginnings – something she wouldn't be ecstatic about recollecting.'

'What did he do for a living?'

'Been trying to remember since he introduced himself. Mum didn't talk about him much. Now I've seen him, I know why. Tonight should be interesting.'

'Aye,' Sukie mimicked Bob Bates. 'Coom to sooper, lad. I thought it'd be high tea.'

Tarpin smiled, put on his own North country accent and said, 'Dinner's what you have in't middle of the day. Supper's what you get at night. High tea on Sundays. Right?'

It was Wednesday. Tarpin had not waited until the Monday to get in touch with Mr Pembeton. The solicitor's home number was in his mother's address book and he called almost as soon as they got back from Princess Mansions on Saturday night. Pembeton sounded quite shocked at the news, but took control immediately. 'Your mother left all her affairs in our hands – the firm, I mean,' he told Tarpin. 'You're not to worry about a thing. I'll make the arrangements.' He wanted the name of the hospital where they had taken the body, then said he would call back. 'Either tomorrow or Monday, if that's convenient.'

Sukie had risen to the occasion and, by the time he finished speaking with Pembeton, there were sandwiches and coffee ready. She sat quietly at his feet, one arm draped around his right leg as he grasshoppered his way down memory lane. It was unsentimental, with no hint of sorrow or bitterness. He talked of early memories, the ever-changing uncles, the unexplained taboos, of which there were many, and his mother's stubborn, sometimes irrational, way of life. 'She was always concerned about what other people thought.' He gazed at the brown leather case with its lying hotel stickers. 'What will the neighbours say? You know the kind of thing?'

Sukie said she knew. There had been an aunt once, back in the dawn of her time, who was like that.

'Yet, the stupid woman carried on in a way which must've made

40

the neighbours very curious indeed. That's the word for my mother – stupid. She really was rather dumb. Spoiled, and always wanting her own way. The only sadness I feel is that she left no mark on life. Not even a minute scratch. She gave very little and took everything. A part of her clung to the old inverted snobbery of her roots.'

'She left you, my darling. Obviously you were her scratch on life.'

'She didn't want me, Suke. That was made perfectly clear. I was a kind of accident.'

'A freak of nature. I'll go along with that.'

'I was unwanted baggage.' He sounded quite bright. No self-pity. It would have been difficult for anyone to tell whether Tarpin was serious. Sukie Cartwright knew he was only partly in earnest.

As he talked it out so fatigue began to wrestle him down on to the mat of sleep. In the end, Sukie shook him and he staggered off to bed, waking early the next morning.

It was not quite six o'clock. Sukie was deeply asleep (later she said she had dreamed of dinosaurs). He went quietly to the kitchen and made coffee, taking it into the living room, where he opened the suitcase, and began to sift through piles of papers and old snapshots. His mother's whole life, he thought, boiled down to this case full of nothing: letters, postcards, stubs from theatre tickets and the omnipresent photographs. There were even some receipted bills going back well into the sixties.

They spent the day going through roughly half the contents of the case, wasting a lot of time on the photographs. He recognized some faces – not able to put names to them. There was one studio photograph of his father. A head and shoulders in uniform, the ribbon of the DFC showing under the RAF wings. An open-faced, clear-eyed young man, looking into a future which never came for him.

'I can't relate to him,' he said to Sukie. 'For some reason my mother would never let me have a copy of this. I often asked her, but she always refused, and it's the only one she had. There are no snapshots of them together. Not even a wedding photograph. Funny, she always kept this hidden away.'

Like any child in a single-parent situation he had wanted to know about his father, but Vera Tarpin all but forbade the subject. 'He was a gallant officer. He died for his country. There's nothing served by adding to it,' she had constantly told him.

When he was older he asked probing questions, but gleaned little more. 'He flew Lancasters; went missing on a raid on Berlin.'

In his twenties Tarpin had gone to the Imperial War Museum and looked at the nose of a Lancaster displayed there. 'You can stand above the cockpit. I stood for about fifteen minutes thinking that my dad, who I never knew, spent hours sitting in one of these, flying dangerous missions night after night. I thought it'd make me feel closer but it didn't.'

– Was my father fun to be with?

– Did he have hobbies?

– Haven't I got a grandfather and grandmother on his side?

The answers were forced from his mother. 'It was like squeezing drying cement from a toothpaste tube,' he told Sukie.

– 'It was wartime,' Vera had said. 'Yes, he was as much fun as the next man. To tell you the truth we were married less than a year. That was a long time in those days – but not long in the sense that we had time to get to know one another well. And, no, his father and mother were killed in the blitz.'

'She got angry once. When I went on and on about him. She screamed at me: "His favourite song was 'There'll be blue birds over the white cliffs of Dover'. I couldn't stand it. I told him, you'll get a good job cleaning all that bluebird shit off the white cliffs when it's over."'

Sukie had put the Bruckner *Fourth* on the CD player, and it stirred something from Tarpin's past. 'She couldn't stand music. Said it hurt her ears. When I was a kid, she did read, but I don't think she had one line of poetry in her memory. Not even from her school days I don't think she ever went to a museum or art gallery.'

'Well, that's not extraordinary. Plentry of people miss out – music, art, the classics. You're liberated, Phillip. You were pulled to those things.'

'Yes,' he muttered, far away, 'Yes, I know. I listened to the radio when I was quite small. I loved radio plays, but my stupid mother called them "screaming women". "Switch those screaming women off," she would shout. It was the same with television. Stupid. She never opened her mind. Suke, she went through life blinkered.'

'You're a cultural snob, Phillip.'

'Maybe.'

They came to a fat, heavy, sealed envelope which Tarpin weighed in his hand. He was about to open it when Pembeton called to say everything was organized. The funeral was to be on Wednesday morning at eleven. Would that be convenient? He said thank you, and, yes, of course it would be convenient. The 'convenient' business appeared to be part of the solicitor's litany.

'I've been through the papers she left with us. Probate shouldn't be difficult. Matter of weeks.'

'She only had her pension,' Tarpin said, almost to himself.

'Oh, no, Mr Tarpin. You're her sole beneficiary. She left, well, somewhere in the region of one hundred thousand pounds. After taxes, of course.'

He just stopped himself saying, 'Jesus Christ!' out loud. Instead, he said, 'Of course. After taxes,' hoping his voice did not sound too eager.

'I've contacted everyone.' Pembeton hardly paused.

'A hundred? You're certain?'

'Oh, yes. It was a good sum originally, and she invested well. Dipped into it from time to time.'

When he had finished, Phillip Tarpin replaced the receiver. 'She left a hundred grand.' His voice hollow and stunned.

'A hundred grand?' The conversation sounded like something from Harold Pinter.

'That's what Pembeton says. Where in the name of heaven . . . ?'

'Nunkie? Proceeds of a life of detective work?'

'That wouldn't surprise me.' Then he repeated, 'A hundred thousand. She lived like a bloody hermit . . . '

'Except for bingo nights.'

Absently, he opened the thick envelope. There were letters, several sealed envelopes and some photographs. They were all of the same man: tall, very straight, military. He had light-coloured hair brushed straight back, and a slim face with good bones. A handsome man. There were several snapshots of him alone in some garden. Then a few taken with Vera Tarpin. In one he had an arm around her shoulders and looked down on her. The faces were relaxed, yet anyone seeing the picture would know they were a couple. The spark between them had almost burned its way into the

43

picture.

Then there was a larger print. The pair of them posed in some wartime photographer's studio. Vera wore a spotted dress and one of those rather mannish 1940s hats. He was in a suit which just fitted in the right places. They posed as though for a wedding picture and Tarpin was jolted to see what appeared to be a look of sadness in his mother's eyes. A trick of the studio light? he wondered. Never had he seen his mother look like this in real life.

'Who the hell is he?' Sukie asked. 'Looks foreign to me.'

Tarpin laughed. 'Oh, no. Mummy would never have disgraced herself with a foreigner. Haven't got a clue who it is, or where. I've never seen these before.'

'Perhaps he gave her the hundred grand.'

The telephone rang again. This time it was Bill Price, MD of Hosier & Whitehead.

'Thought I'd call to congratulate you,' he said as soon as Tarpin answered. 'You've landed on your feet, Phillip. Going to run the whole show before you're through.'

Tarpin raised his eyes to heaven. 'Bill, I hardly think you need to worry on that account. My contract is for three years, with a renewal to be negotiated; Anyway . . . ' He told the MD about his mother's death, and Price went through the usual words of commiseration.

'Not necessary. I hadn't spoken with, or seen, her in three years. I'd like Wednesday free; apart from that I'll be at the editorial meeting in the morning.'

They chatted for a little while about the books he would have to clear from his desk over the next three weeks, and when the conversation ended there was Sukie, looking innocent and wearing next to nothing, knowing that the particular next to nothing she wore would rouse Phillip even from a state of unconsciousness.

As they headed towards the bedroom, she said, 'Can I be the slave girl tonight? You can be the brutal master.'

So, now it was Wednesday evening and, what with the mounds of work to be got through in the pleasantly situated Hosier & Whitehead offices, and two lunches and a dinner party – all publishing oriented – Tarpin had not even glanced at his mother's papers again, nor had time to discuss the future with Sukie. In a way, he felt as though life had taken a cinematic jump cut to the gilded luxury of the The Inn on the Park's Four Seasons restaurant, from whence you could almost see into the Queen's back yard.

They were seated at a very good window table, and a waiter hovered around them, obviously delighted to be serving Bob Bates, who looked happy and informal, as though the dining room was his preserve alone.

'You order what you like. They know what I'll have.' He lowered his voice to an almost conspiratorial level. 'To tell the truth, they think I'm a bit eccentric here. Been coming to this place for a long time.' He turned to the waiter. 'My usual.' He grinned, and the waiter gave a little bow and a knowing wink, saying yes, Mr Bates, certainly, Mr Bates.

His usual turned out to be a plate of fish and chips, bread and butter – no decadent rolls for Bob Bates – and a pot of tea. Phillip and Sukie went for the smoked salmon, followed by lamb cutlets.

Tarpin set the conversation in motion by bluntly asking what line his Uncle Bob had been in. 'I mean you're obviously retired now.'

'What line? Eh, lad, I don't think of it as a line. It started out as almost a hobby at the end of the war. I were a Desert Rat, you know. Eighth Army. With Monty. Invalided out. Wounded at Alamein. Not permanently crippled or anything, but they gave me a small disability pension and I went on from there. Scrap metal, young Phillip. That was my line, as you put it. It were a grand time for those of us in scrap metal at the end of the war. You could buy up almost anything. I once nabbed a fleet of American Army surplus vehicles, and three hundred of them coal-burning stoves they used in Nissen huts, and Quonset huts. Got the lot for two thousand pound, eventually made a profit of six thousand pound. Those were the days.'

'Talking about money, Mother's solicitor says she's left me a tidy lot.'

'Aye, that wouldn't surprise me. Your mum had a mean streak in her. She were a hoarder. Bloody magpie.'

'She kept piles of receipted inconsequential bills.'

'That would be Vera.'

'Did you see much of her after you came out of the army?'

'For a while, yes. That's why I want to talk to you, after all, I reckon you've a right to know.' He gave Tarpin an odd look, like someone who was about to break very bad news. 'Aye, I came out of the army right after Alamein. Well, a few months in hospital first. Our tank got brewed up and both my legs were burned pretty bad. In the end it took a long time to get them right. I was in and out of that burns unit at East Grinstead for the best part of four years, but I could work in between times. Yes, came out of the army in – Oh, it would be December 1942. I saw plenty of Vera, on and off, between then and – when was it? – 1946. Yes, we had our big bust-up in 1946.'

'You knew my father, then?'

The pause was unnervingly long, and Bates finally nodded. 'Yes, lad. Yes, I knew your dad. It's what I want to talk to you about. Your dad was who? Flight Lieutenant Ted Tarpin, DFC, Royal Air Force?'

'Of course. You know he was . . . '

Bob Bates slowly shook his head. 'She said she'd never tell you. And I swore I would. Even if I had to wait till she died.'

'Tell me what?' Tarpin had a terrible sense of *déjà vu*, as though he had lived this moment before – several times, in many lives.

'Tell you that Vera's husband, Ted, was not your dad, Phillip. He was her husband, yes. She was his widow. But he didn't father you.'

– 2 –

In all, Kathleen Fagin gave them a great deal of information, including a few tiny nuggets which concerned individuals. Names they already had on file, but not placed definitively within the PIRA hierarchy. One of them – a name she mentioned a number of times – was Connor Murphy.

Ten years previously, Murphy had been a bomber. A member of the movement since childhood – his grandfather was a hero of the old IRA, and his father was a man marked by the Brits, though only arrested once. Murphy had done a course in Syria, and knew his way around the dangerous world of explosives. His trademark was the horrible anti-personnel bomb, stuffed with old nails and bits of metal. They were pretty sure he was responsible for a dozen explosions in the North, and had made at least one bomb which caused death and destruction on the mainland.

But that was a decade ago. Since then, Connor Murphy had disappeared, thought to be undergoing instruction at the feet of the General Staff. This, according to Kathleen Fagin, had been correct, for she now marked him as assistant to the Intelligence Officer. 'He's in charge of what they call Special Projects,' the girl said.

'And what exactly are these Special Projects?' Michael Bailey, the inquisitor, asked in the neat little back room looking out on to the trees and brick wall.

'It's not what it sounds.' She took a deep drag on the cigarette she was smoking. They had told her she smoked too much, and she said it was only until the present problems were over. 'Once I'm away, it'll be a good healthy life. No booze and no fags.'

'And what *does* it sound like?'

'Special Projects sounds like the Hong Kong business, but I doubt he'd even have known anything of that. No, Special Projects is something pretty mysterious, and I can't say I know the details myself. Some of it's to do with old scores that have to be settled. Men and women – like me I suppose – who've somehow betrayed the cause at one time or another.'

'He's a kind of enforcer?'

'Maybe. Maybe something like that. But the old fellas talk about this thing they have – the oral tradition. You ever hear of the oral tradition?'

'I know exactly what you mean.' Ruth Daubney had lectured, at the intelligence school, on what she called the myths and legends of organized freedom fighters. Those who worked in a clandestine environment against the Provos were never allowed to forget that one man's terrorist is another man's freedom fighter, however warped the aims and motives had become over the years. 'We should all bear in mind,' she would say, 'that the Provisional Irish Republican Army is an extension of those gallant men and women whose *rightful* struggle goes back a very long way. The Provos are the natural descendants of those who fought for rights that were theirs from the last century. The problem is that the ultimate objective of the Provos is *not* the same as the goal of their forefathers.' She would go on to talk of the myths and legends, the

47

long memory which invests men, women, battles and skirmishes, and the events surrounding them, with almost mystical powers. 'In the communal memory of the Irish people there is a bitterness which festers, and regenerates a hatred of wrongs already put right. All popular movements require heroes, even if they have to invent them.'

She would then talk about Wolf Tone and his revolution in the eighteenth century, and of Robert Emmett's revolt in 1803; the Young Irelanders of the 1840s; the Fenians of the 1860s. She even quoted Kipling –

> Believe, we dare not boast,
> Believe, we do not fear –
> We stand to pay the cost
> In all that men hold dear.
> What answer from the North?
> One Law, one Land, one Throne.
> If England drive us forth
> We shall not fall alone!

Not everyone would agree with her, particularly Connor Murphy who, even as they talked with Kathleen Fagin, had made his way, secretly, across the border into the Republic of Ireland. He was a man with the ability to move like a spectre across borders, putting on a different name and personality like a suit of clothes, as though he had power to reproduce himself, in new identities which knew no frontiers.

On this occasion he made his way into Dublin, becoming Patrick Hagan, complete with an Irish passport, driving licence, and address which authorities would have a great difficulty in proving false.

From Dublin he went to Galway and there met an old, honoured member of the original IRA. A man respected and steeped in that secret lore which is passed from mouth to mouth down all the years. They talked for half a day and all night.

When he left Galway, Patrick Hagan became Fergus Downey, a British citizen with a London address. He flew to Heathrow, and walked calmly past the watchful eyes of Special Branch and the Security Service. No alarms were triggered. No bells or whistles clanged or shrieked, for Fergus Downey had a different eye and hair colour to Connor Murphy. He was also a good three inches taller than the wanted ex-bomber, thanks to the lifts in his shoes.

He brought a death warrant into England, and checked into one of those thriving little hotels in the Marble Arch area, just behind Selfridges. Connor Murphy, who was now Fergus Downey, ordered ham and salad from room service, then stretched out on the bed to watch the nine o'clock TV news. The Home Secretary was getting all hell thrown at him by the Opposition who were again demanding that a public inquiry should be held to examine the facts behind the Hong Kong shootings.

'I challenge the honourable gentleman,' a puffy-faced MP was shouting. 'I challenge him to state the government's position on what is becoming increasingly obvious: that a shoot-to-kill policy exists in Northern Ireland, and against any Irish people, men, women or children, who are suspected of being members of the Provisional IRA.'

There was uproar, with jeers and catcalls: the Speaker reciting the toneless, 'Order! Order!'

'Bloody Mother of Parliaments. They're nothing but uncontrolled schoolkids,' Murphy spat.

'I can assure this House,' the Home Secretary finally said. 'I can assure this House, as I have assured it many times in the past, that Her Majesty's government does not – I repeat *not* – support any so-called shoot-to-kill policy in Northern Ireland.'

'You can tell that to the Marines. *And* the fecking SAS,' Murphy muttered.

It was five minutes past nine, and, less than a mile away, Phillip Tarpin had just been told that his father was not his father.

FIVE

– 1 –

Coffee and brandy had been served, and the restaurant was filling up. Bob Bates still drank tea. He also told the waiter to 'Take away those silly little cups. My guests need proper cups of coffee, not a thimbleful.' Then he began:

'Our Vera liked men. Liked 'em from the age of fifteen when she first discovered sex, behind the bicycle sheds at school. I only know about that because it was a mate of mine that first felt her up, and he told me she went crazy, wanted the lot. It frightened him.' He looked up from under his lids at Sukie. 'I hope I'm not shocking you, luv.'

'I've heard all the words and seen all the pictures, Bob.' She was not being arch, just plain honest. 'I also went crazy at fifteen, the first time I got felt up . . . '

'You . . . ' Tarpin began, then saw her smile and the lifted eyebrow.

'Any old how, Vera, your mum, was – not to put too fine a point on it – the school bicycle. That wasn't much fun for me, being her brother. That went on through school, and after, when she had the job at old Joe Clegg the Chemist. Eventually Ted Tarpin came along. She were just eighteen and should've known better. She went overboard for the uniform and the glamour. You know, in those days it was quite something for a girl to be seen out wi' a bloke wearing his pilot's wings.' His fingers traced a little curve above his breast pocket.

'But, she should have known better. So should he. He worshipped the ground our Vera walked on, and she ran him

50

ragged. Loopy about her. Lived for her. I remember talking to one of his crew at the wedding. His navigator it was. Said they all liked to fly with Ted, 'cos they knew he'd get them back in one piece, and all because of Vera. He probably didn't know at the time that Ted Tarpin had knocked her up.'

'That's slang for putting her in the club, darling,' Sukie said, low and daring, trying to lighten her lover's heart because he looked as though he had seen the ghost of Hamlet's father.

Within the centre of his mind, Tarpin knew what was coming: he could feel it, almost taste it, the bitter, salty irony and the stench of death.

'She only married him 'cos she were afraid of what people might think. There's a lesson for you, lad.'

'I know all about *that*.' He did not sound as though he really savoured the knowledge.

'Aye, happen you do, Phillip. You can probably guess some of the rest. She lost the baby at three months. She hadn't even begun to show. Lost it in the middle of the night, and with it went any feelings she had for Ted Tarpin. I've often wondered if he knew everything. I'm afraid your mum wasn't really a very nice lady, Phillip. She wasn't going to be the one in the wrong, so she treated him like something foul. She really wanted *him* to break from *her*.

'He were on leave once – the one long leave he had before his second tour of ops. I went down the pub with him. *In vino veritas,* isn't that what they say? He told me, "Bob," he says, "she treats me as though I've grown scales like a lizard. It's as if she finds it revolting to touch me."' He shook his head and the light caught his cheeks, making them look the colour of a ripe apple.

'Soon after that he goes back on ops, and by then Vera'd met the love of her life – and I mean that, Phillip. He *was* the love of her life. If things had been different, I think she'd have been okay. A couple of years after you were born she told me that Ted went missing soon after she wrote asking him for a divorce. For all I know she told him she was having someone else's baby. Right at the end of the war and all.'

He saw the look in Tarpin's eyes and, gruff, bluff old North countryman that he was, Bob Bates stretched across the table and laid a hand over the younger man's clenched fist.

'I never told her this, but I swore I'd tell you. Ted Tarpin's crew came out of it alive. They bailed out over Germany and spent the rest of the war in a prison camp. Being a nosey old bugger, I made it my business to see that navigator, the one I'd met at the wedding. Tracked him down, though that wasn't hard because he lived not far from Burnley. He told me that Ted could've saved hisself. They all got out. Ted rode the Lancaster right down into the deck.'

Tarpin cut his eyes away, turning his head as though looking for somebody across the room. Dead Ted Tarpin, perhaps.

'I'm not bein' mawkish, Phillip. We're all old enough and ugly enough to live with things like that now. It was a long time ago.'

'My father?' His eyes were clear, and he spoke as though there would be a need to prise it from his uncle.

'Was a man called Paul Bartholemew. Half French, half English. Lived most of his life in England. He told me his father had died when he was quite young. His mother – the English half – brought him over here. Vera had some story that his father was murdered, but she told me that when she was half out of her skull with grief.'

'He was killed as well.' Not a question, but a simple, unemotional statement.

The older man nodded. 'I've no doubt, had he lived, he'd have married Vera, and things would have been very different.'

'Bob, this comes . . . '

'As a bit of a shock? Happen it does, lad. Did you never suspect anything?'

'Maybe I was slow on the uptake. Yes, it *was* odd. She'd never talk about him – Tarpin, I mean. I've gone through life thinking my father died over Germany. A hero. Now . . . ' He gave a gigantic shrug. 'It's going to take a while. To adjust. Tell me about . . . What was his name?'

'Paul Bartholemew, and I don't think you have to worry about your dad not being a hero. Paul was in SOE. You know what SOE was?'

Tarpin nodded.

'He was a spy?' Sukie put a hand on Phillip's sleeve.

'I don't know about that, but I suppose you'd call him a spy.'

SOE was the Special Operations Executive, formed by Winston Churchill in 1940 to 'set Europe Ablaze' after Hitler's legions had conquered the bulk of the continent. Men and women were inserted into France, Holland and Belgium to assist the underground, to sabotage, to glean information and prepare for the invasion four long years later.

'He was a natural, being half French. She met him at Ringway; she went to a dance there with a crowd of other girls. He was doing the parachute course.' He explained that RAF Ringway – now Manchester airport – had been the parachute training school during the war.

'Vera said he went into France three times. On the last occasion he didn't come back. I never tried to find out what happened. It wasn't like Ted Tarpin. Oh, I got on okay with Paul, but I can't say I liked him, even though he changed Vera for a while. Once he was gone, well, she sort of reverted to type. It's bloody sad, Phillip. I promised myself I'd tell you. Now I have.'

When Tarpin did not speak, he continued: 'Maybe I should've kept it to myself. Maybe not. I'm sorry if I've upset you. I thought you had the right to know.'

Tarpin finished his brandy, fast, like a man tossing back hard liquor for the sake of it. Just to get drunk. Then he signalled for the waiter to pour more coffee.

'Have another?' Bates indicated his glass.

'No. No, I'm sorry, Bob. That was no way to treat a good brandy. This is weird, but I somehow feel cheated. I've lived without a father all my life, yet . . . '

Bates looked distressed. 'It's a right shame about your mother.' It was difficult to know whether he was talking about her death or the way she had lived.

'If she had only talked about it.'

'She were past talking about it by the time you were old enough. Let it rest now, Phillip.'

Quietly he said he could never just let it rest, and after that the conversation went downhill.

Back in their elegant little flat, Sukie made coffee, then disappeared. Tarpin had hardly spoken on the way home and she knew there was only one way to pull him from gloom.

When she came back she was wearing a navy blue tennis skirt, that could have doubled as a hair band, and white knee socks.

'Father, I have sinned,' she said softly.

It did the trick and they were soon engrossed in the virgin convent girl and the lecherous priest. That one always worked wonders.

– 2 –

Connor Murphy, who was Fergus Downey, had breakfast in his room. When he woke the message light was blinking on the telephone. He called the desk. There was a package waiting for him, delivered by courier. He went down and signed for the carefully wrapped box. In his room he opened the package, put the contents in a briefcase and dropped the box and wrapping into a Selfridges carrier bag, first removing the label addressed to himself – tearing it up and flushing the pieces away in the tiny bathroom. Then he left the hotel, taking the Underground to Camden Town. He changed lines at Tottenham Court Road and dumped the carrier in a waste bin.

From the Underground station he walked down Camden High Street and turned into the little cul-de-sac where they had the safe house for an Active Service Unit. Whoever had organized the safe house knew what he was doing. You could drive into the cul-de-sac, but there was hardly any room to park and only the one way back for vehicles. It could be approached from two directions by foot, but it would be the very devil to watch without tipping your hand. They had told him that this group of three men, who were there to carry out a short bombing campaign towards the end of the summer, had got in completely undetected. He did not doubt that as he sauntered past the mews house, then through the narrow alley that took him, in a circle, back to Camden High Street.

He did things by the book. Checking that he was not followed, pretending to look lost, consulting a map as he walked. There were no vehicles in the mews that could belong to any surveillance team: no vans, or long antennae; only an old Rover, circa 1987, and a clapped-out grey Ford.

On the second circuit he rang the bell next to the little blue door of number five. Paddy Flanagan answered the bell through the speaker:

'Who is it?'

'I've come about the advertisement. The car.'

'When did you see that?'

'Last week, in the *Standard*.'

'Well, the Austin's gone, but there's an old VW if you'd be interested.'

'I'm interested.'

You could never be too careful. The intelligence people in Belfast were adamant about sticking to the rules.

Flanagan opened up, looking bleary-eyed and wearing a gaudy dressing gown. He had not shaved and his hair was all over the place. 'You look like a bloody unmade bed,' Murphy told him.

'I'm on nights.' Flanagan was a hard young man who had been brought up in the midst of turmoil and sudden death in the Falls Road, the Catholic stronghold which had been the site of many horrors in west Belfast. A tall man, with the broad shoulders of a labourer and calloused hands, he had already killed without showing squeamishness. He had the steady, icy eyes of violence, and the restless habits of one who spends a lot of time waiting to be exposed to danger. Flanagan also knew guns and had no fear of explosives, though his besetting sin was women. They were his weak point, and the Battalion Commander had read him a long lecture on the subject before sending him to London.

'Coffee?' he asked with an edge of contempt in his voice. It was not personal, Flanagan's tone was locked in contempt for everything except the job he did best. The voice and manner only altered when he talked about life and death – especially death.

Murphy nodded, sitting in the small living room and watching the young man through the open arch which led to the kitchen. From what he could see the kitchen was neat and clean, which was a good sign. He looked around him. The furniture was shabby, the woodwork scratched and gouged, the heavy armchairs and sofa ragged and worn. There was a Green Lady picture on one wall, and a hideous reproduction Constable across from it. A girlie calendar hung near the kitchen. May was a busty redhead who looked worried about the stability of her silicone implants.

'You really on nights?' Murphy asked.

'I go out around eight. Keep to a routine. Get back about three in the morning. I'm going after a job next week. Jacko works the bakery. Night shift so he's free in the day. He's sleeping now.' He cocked his head towards one of the two doors off the living room.

'And Martin?'

Flanagan came back into the living room with two mugs of coffee. He gave a quick, humourless smile. 'The Post Office took him on. Would you believe that? He's doing a delivery round. This area. Goes on at five, gets back about noon. He'll be of real use when they give us something to do.'

'I've brought you something to do. You. Not any of the others, so keep it to yourself. Just a hit. Quick, no heroics, and no getting seen.'

Flanagan made a little movement of his head, as if to say he understood. He sat on the shredding sofa, across from Murphy, taking up his mug from the cheap low oblong table that stood between them.

'I thought we just had to blend in. Establish ourselves for some bangs later in the year. Nobody said anything about people being hit. It could compromise the unit.'

'Not if you do it properly, Paddy. That's why they chose you. So you could do it, then melt away. It's non-attributable. Nobody's going to be looking for any of us after it's done. There'll be no backstops, and no comeback.'

'So who is it?'

Murphy slid a photograph across the table and gave him a name. 'It's very low profile.'

'Why this fella?'

'You know better'n that, Paddy. You don't ask questions. You just do it. The man doesn't even know he's a target. It'll come as a great surprise to him, and his friends. The movement just won't be suspected, believe me.'

'I believe you. After all you come straight from the Holy Spirit, don't you? And the Holy Spirit is never wrong.'

'The man lives a routine. Leaves home the same time every day. Goes to the same office by the same route. Leaves for home again at different times in the evening. Sometimes works late. Until nine or ten. Goes out a lot in the evenings, and at weekends. You could get him as he starts his day, or watch and catch him in the evening.

There's no hurry.' He went through times, addresses, the target's background.

'What am I to use?'

Murphy smiled, took the large black automatic pistol from his briefcase and placed it on the table. It had been in the package delivered only a few hours ago, by courier, to the hotel.

'That's one of those Austrian pistols, eh? The Glock?' Flanagan hefted it in his big right hand. Even unloaded, the weapon immediately became an extension of the man's arm.

Murphy nodded, placing the noise reduction unit and one magazine next to the pistol. 'It would be perfect if the safety wasn't iffy. Play with it, unloaded, for a while. A man could shoot his balls off with that thing. Normal magazine, not the big one. The rounds are soft kill. They peel off inside the target. Don't shoot-through, okay?'

'I heard some fella say you could take this right through an airport metal detector.'

'Almost. We split them up. The plastic comes in by air, the metal by the soft sea route. It's very accurate, but watch for that damned safety.'

'Consider it done.'

'Evening might be best.'

'Leave it with me. I'll probably do a little recce tomorrow. Just follow him around, then set it up for Monday. Monday morning's always a good time. The first of the week. They're all dozy as hell from the weekend.'

Murphy gave him contact numbers, and they went through a quick exchange of buzz words to use on any insecure line. It was almost midday when Murphy walked back to the Underground station. So he strolled straight past the Post Office van, parked illegally. Inside, two men continued to watch the video being fed to them, by electronic wizardry, directly from a camera with a huge wide-angle lens, hidden in the boot of the elderly Ford, sitting almost directly opposite the little mews house being used by the Provo Active Service Unit. Fibre optics were wonderful things.

One of them spoke into a walkie-talkie, instructing a footman to pick up the visitor who had just left the mews house. The other watcher was on a secure line, talking to his superior.

57

Late that afternoon, Jack Chilton took a call from Scarecrow.

'Jackie, we think the lads in Camden Town have been activated. They had a visit from a highly disguised Connor Murphy this morning.'

There was a lengthy pause, for Chilton had just been reading the take from Kathleen Fagin. 'We sure it's Murphy?'

'They've analysed the video. It's him. He's staying near Marble Arch, bold as you like, in a hotel. You want a word with him?'

'You haven't lifted him?' Quick, concerned.

'No, but . . . '

'Please, leave him where he is. I think the three lads should have a closer watch on them, though.'

'Assigned. We've got good people out. All controlled from the van.'

'Kind of you to let me know, sir. I'd appreciate it if I could be alerted to any unusual moves.'

'Naturally, Jackie. That's what we're here for.'

Chilton leaned back in his chair – the tall leather one with the padded high back. He liked listening to music in that chair, but the music he had just heard was both sweet and scary. The arrival in London of Paddy Flanagan, Jacko Reilly and Martin McManus had been tipped via an informer, working quite close to the centre of things in Belfast. They called the girl Shallow Throat because she was highly selective in what she gave to them. Chilton believed that Shallow Throat was motivated by her love life. Woe unto any of the lads who crossed her in love, for their whereabouts were signalled to counter-intelligence at the speed of a bullet. Paddy Flanagan, who was a likely lad with the ladies – plausible, good-looking in an obvious way, and with a taste for the chase – had taken a ride through the park with Shallow Throat and found he did not love her in the morning. When he was sent to London with the Active Service Unit, the watchers were waiting. Bad luck for Reilly and McManus. There had been a video watch on the safe house since they had taken up the two-year lease. They also had a very informative telephone, and the Technical Branch were well on the road to inserting a probe so that all conversations could be relayed on the BBC World Service if necessary.

Chilton did not look like a worrier, but he cared deeply about his job. What the woman Fagin had said about Connor Murphy concerned him. After ten minutes' thought, he picked up the telephone and called the Director General of MI5.

– What can I do for you, Jackie?

– Lend me a team of very silent watchers, sir. Short-term job.

The DG usually gave Chilton anything he wanted. The team of four men and one woman were briefed that evening.

– 3 –

On that same Thursday morning, Tarpin dealt with the messages waiting for him at the office, before he did anything about his private life. Three years before, he had edited the now-standard two-volume work on Special Operations Executive 1940–1945. The author – William Shepherd – had become a friend.

'I don't want to talk on the phone, Bill,' Phillip said when Shepherd answered. 'It's a little delicate. If I give you a name, could you look him up in your records?'

'Of course.' Shepherd was always wary of telephones at the best of times. His research into the history of SOE had in many ways affected him in a bizarre manner. Bill Shepherd had a tendency to go through life as though he were operating under cover in a foreign country sometime in the 1940s.

'Could we meet this evening if you have anything?'

'Yes. What's the name?'

'Paul Bartholemew.'

'I have him. I'll call you some time this afternoon to fix a place to have a drink, okay?'

'Right.' He had hardly said it before Shepherd closed the line.

Phillip Tarpin went through the day with a tiny part of his mind circling the name Bartholemew.

Shepherd called back and said six o'clock at a wine bar in Charlotte Street, an easy walk from the office. Then, at four-thirty, just as Tarpin was settling down to a short session with an author – Graham Belcher, doing the biography of a very newsworthy actor – his secretary buzzed through to say there was an important call from New York. Peter Palestino.

'Phillip, I'm sorry,' the dry, half-amused voice said in his ear. 'I need you over here sooner than I thought. It's all just been cleared with your people. We've fixed a flight out on Monday morning . . . '

'Christ, Peter, I haven't wound up half the things here.'

'I know,' soothing. 'I know, Phillip, but it *is* essential. We've had to make some unexpected management changes over here. We'll keep you for about three weeks, then let you go back to London for a couple of weeks to tidy things up at your end.'

'Jesus, Monday? Does it have to be that quick?'

'Yes. See you Tuesday morning. Eight-thirty. The apartment's all set up for you. I'm having you met with the keys and everything. See you Tuesday, Phillip.' Palestino's strength lay in his friendly firmness. Nobody putting a telephone down after hearing his 'See you Tuesday' would think, even for a second, of cutting the appointment.

The rest of the afternoon was chaos, and he felt loaded with all sorts and conditions of worry as he set off to meet Bill Shepherd. Uppermost was the fact that he *had* to pin down Sukie within the next couple of days.

Shepherd was already sitting in a dark corner of the wine bar. He had chosen a place which allowed him to have his back against the wall and with the sight lines clear to the door. Tarpin ordered a glass of red and waited.

'Paul Bartholemew,' Shepherd began. Even in conversation, he used the minimum number of words. He also had the infuriating habit of talking as though you were very familiar with his subject. It had been one of the things that Tarpin had found difficult when they were editing the books. He had to push constantly for more detail.

'Paul Bartholemew. French father, English mother. Father died June 1931. Mother brought him to England where she still had family. Bedford actually. Joined Section F in 1942. Did three trips into France – one in 1942, then, again in the autumn of 1943. The last time was just before D-Day.' He named the networks, and the places, people called Vény, Monk, Gaspard and St-Paul. 'They gave him a posthumous Légion d'Honneur. Did wonderful work. Odd death.'

'How odd?'

'He'd finished. He got out of France. March 1945, just before the end. There was nothing left for him to do. I never had all the details, but the military flight bringing him back diverted to Belfast. He had one night there.'

'Yes?'

'Went out on the town by himself. Someone shot him in an alley. A .22 in the back of the neck. They thought it was some Pro-Nazi group. Vengeance. But nothing was ever proved. He was due out the next day. Macabre. Shot in Belfast. Expect it nowadays of course, but in 1945? Strange.'

'Very.' An elusive butterfly of concern flitted through Tarpin's mind.

'There's another thing . . . '

'Yes?'

'His father. He was murdered. Poitiers 1931. Disturbed a thief, who shot him. The gendarmes never arrested anyone. Like father, like son. Strange.'

The butterfly in Tarpin's mind turned into a rabid bat.

SIX

He had anticipated a difficult time with Sukie. She swore when he told her of Palestino's call, and his imminent departure on Monday. 'Oh shit!' Then, once more with feeling, 'Oh, shit, Phillip. Just when I was getting used to you being back. How can I get through another – how many weeks? Three? Three whole weeks!'

He began to plead with her to come to New York, not whining, but forcefully, trying to sound as authoritative as Palestino. 'Damn it, Sukie, I want to marry you.'

'You do?' The wicked smile. 'Well, let me tell you what I've done.' She crawled to him on all fours, purring like a cat, entwining herself around his legs, rubbing up against him, using her whole body as she told him of the plan concocted between herself and her partner, Pat Patton. She would leave the London agency for three months, and come with Tarpin to the United States where she would investigate the possibilities of opening a New York office, which, if it made sense, she would run.

'I've always believed that you should swim against the current.' She was swimming against more than Tarpin's current now, her hands massaging him so that he became too distracted to ask any sensible questions about the proposed New York office. He had arrived home tired, and emotionally washed out. Now the fatigue vanished under Sukie's probing, stroking, tickling, brushing, fondling fingers.

She talked on. 'Publishing always figured it was recession-proof. Well, now we know it isn't. Everyone's drawing in their horns – except you, my darling. Oooooh, Phillip, that vein is huge and it's throbbing. What I mean is that publishers, on both sides of the ocean, are retrenching – you fancy some retrenching of our own, Phillip? It isn't the time to start new publishing ventures – you want me to take my top off? One second, my darling. So, for us, that's exactly the time for opening a New York office. We'll be all set up and ready to go when the recession reverses itself. Yes, there you go.' Half naked, she buried her head at the crux of his thighs. 'Yes, I know, Phil. I know your mother wouldn't have approved of this, but I'm a good little lap dog.' She was not able to talk after that for a full ten minutes. When that was over they changed roles and, an hour later, he asked her what she was doing about a visa.

'I can come in for three months on my normal one.' Naked, she snuggled against him.

'And if we get married you can come on mine.'

'Ooooh. I've just . . . '

'Yes, Sukie, I know. But we can have a joint visa if we're man and wife.'

She twisted on to her back again. 'But that way I can't work. I've had a long talk with a nice helpful man at the embassy this afternoon. I know all about the visas, and what to do. Can we play trains?'

They played trains, an erotic fantasy which, like all lovers, they thought they had invented before anyone else. Then she wanted to go out to dinner. 'A celebration,' she said. 'Because we'll be together in New York. Though not straight away. I'll come back with you after you've done this three weeks' stint.'

'You really want to eat out?'

'Mmmmmm' which meant yes, 'I won't wear any pants, and you'll be the only one in the restaurant who knows.'

They went out to dinner at the Trattoo in Abingdon Road, a short walk from their service flat in the old, refurbished building behind Kensington High Street. On the way in they met a world-class best-selling author of fiction, who knew them both well, and that was a big deal for the *maître d'* so the service was splendid – they even made *crêpes citron* specially for Phillip.

During the meal they talked. Or, to be more accurate, Sukie talked. When Tarpin had first met her, over six years ago, one of the many facets of Sukie Cartwright's complex make-up that had

63

appealed to him was her knowledge of publishing.

He lived for the profession. It was the best game in town and he was good at it. Only rarely did he find a woman who could eat, sleep and live for the same reasons as himself, though he quickly discovered that they were on opposite sides of the fence.

Later he realized that, while he had always known authors were suspicious of publishers, he had never realized exactly *how* suspicious until he began trading confidences with Sukie. They had fallen in lust first, but within a month they had reached that stage of mutual trust and respect which was the harbinger of something more than merely a physical relationship. Indeed, he had asked her to marry him after a six-week courtship and her reply had been typical – 'I'll live with you, but I want my independence,' she told him. 'At least for now. Maybe there'll come a time when that'll change, but you're a bit of a porker, Phillip, and I'm a paid-up, card-carrying feminist. Let's see how we go.' They had gone exceptionally well, and he now had high hopes of legalizing the situation.

This evening, Tarpin had come home with Palestino's news uppermost in his mind, though the conversation with Shepherd constantly intruded, and around these two items a million other problems buzzed, a wasps' nest of urgency. Everything had been pushed to one side by Sukie's physical demands – and who was he to grumble about that?

So now, over the smoked salmon and chicken Kiev, he let her talk, for she had that greatest of all assets in the agenting business – intuition, born of her knowledge of publishing. That day – after three weeks of bartering – she had pulled off two major deals with London publishers. By the next morning she would know about one particular deal with an American house, and there was a nailbiting situation developing with a TV mini-series in the States.

Sukie talked with wit and enthusiasm about her day, the authors with whom she was dealing, the idiocy of some publishers, and the crass stupidity of one particular copy editor who had taken a client's book and turned the dialogue into strict, grammatical English, thereby removing the subtle nuances of speech patterns he had built in to delineate character. 'Out of Oxford with a third in English and she hadn't learned the first lesson of writing fiction,' she giggled. 'You wouldn't believe some of the idiots they're employing these days. None of them seem to really *care* about selling books.'

Then she became passionate about the possibilities and plans for a New York office, so it was only towards the end of the meal that he was able to turn the conversation around to the news that his real father had been murdered in Belfast, and that his grandfather had also been done to death, in France.

'Jesus, darling, why didn't you tell me?'

'Because you were having a good time talking. I like listening, Sukie.'

'Are you going to follow it up?'

'Don't know how. His mother was English, and she brought Paul Bartholemew back here in 1931 after his father was knocked off.'

'That the only date you have?'

'At the moment, I'll probably go through that package of letters and things . . . '

'The Bartholemew file. Make a good title.' She wrinkled her nose. 'On second thoughts, it wouldn't make a good title. Too glib.'

Tarpin told her he would probably read the stuff during the flight to New York on Monday. The conversation swung between business and the strange revelations concerning his parents, then, as they walked home, marriage came up again. She started to tease him which brought a glow of hope. The question of marriage was usually turned off by deathless lines such as, 'When I'm ready, I'll tell you.' Now she was flirting, like a coy girl in the first flush of a romance, holding out on him. 'Maybe it is time,' she said finally as they reached the doorway, turning to kiss him, long and hard. 'When I've got the office set up in New York, how about that?'

'I can think of nothing nicer. Does that make it official, at last?' He unlocked the door.

'Yes.' It was her small voice, slightly breathless.

'Then I'll open the champagne we've had in the fridge since Christmas.'

She held on to him very tightly, as though the step, after so long, frightened her.

'Hey, this is a time to be happy.'

'I know, Phillip.' She pulled away slightly. 'I've been so happy for the past few years. We've kept our pact, haven't we?'

'Yes.' Soon after they met, Sukie and Tarpin had made an agreement. They would never talk about anyone else with whom they had been in love before their meeting. The idea was that it would contain any jealousy.

'I want to tell you something about my past, now.'

'Tell me now and I'll get it serialized in one of the low-grade Sundays.'

'No, don't joke.' She looked very serious.

He tried to kiss her again, and once more she pulled away. 'When I was very young – around eighteen – I fell in love with this married guy. You know him, in fact. He's in publishing, but I'm not going to tell you his name. I lived with him for three years – wonderful years. I didn't think anyone could be that happy. I know it sounds sentimental, romantic, slush, but that's how it was. Then he just walked out on me. One day he was there, the next back to his wife and kids. He never explained why and I was really wiped out. I was an emotional basket case when we met, Phillip. That's why I've held off. I didn't think it could last; I didn't want to go through a thing like that again. Until this last year, I really thought that, one day, I would lose this new happiness. In a way, I was frightened of happiness. As though, somehow I didn't deserve it. I didn't want to risk a complete commitment.'

'And you're ready now?'

'Yes. I know we trust each other, and, yes, I love you, Phillip.' Almost immediately, her mood lightened. 'Now, tell me if you've got any skeletons in your cupboard.'

'Only my mother and this strange father I never knew about. I don't think I should tell you about Grace Poole, who's locked away in the family country house.'

'That would be Wuthering Heights, off the M4?'

'Got it.' He kissed her again and, entwined, they went into the main living room. The message light blinked on the answerphone.

'You know who this is.' Bill Shepherd's voice came, very formal, from the tape. 'A small piece of extra information about the historical character you were interested in.' He meant Paul Bartholemew, and was cloaking everything in his World War Two paranoia. 'It seems he was born in England. Brighton, 10 February

1920. They went back to his father's country in 1922. Nine years later, the papa died. Just thought you should know.'

'Well, there's a turn-up for the book.' Sukie nuzzled against Tarpin's face. 'Your dad came into this vale of sorrows via Brighton.'

'I bet my mother wished it had been Hove. Smarter end of Brighton, Hove.'

Sukie gave a sound of mirth, half-laugh, half-giggle. 'How would you like to come via my smarter end?' she said.

Tarpin, who had gone through a little trouble in the restaurant trying to forget that she wore nothing under the little cream and beige number, moved in for the *coup de grâce*.

They slept very peacefully after that. As Sukie said, the evening should have got them on to the Olympic sex team.

– 2 –

Paddy Flanagan woke early on the Friday morning. 'Your man leaves the flat at eight o'clock sharp,' Murphy had told him. 'Well, around eight. Never before, sometimes five or ten minutes past. But he's out and running at eight as a rule.'

Flanagan took the Underground over to the target's building, and, sure enough, he came out at two minutes past eight. Not a care in the world. Looked like he had rested well and was ready for a hard day's work. He followed the target to his office and, by a series of devices known to all good street men, kept an eye out all day.

The target went out to lunch. An indian place up the Tottenham Court Road. A good Indian place, a really four-star curry house in an area noted for its two-star restaurants. His man was out for almost two hours. Flanagan even knew what he ate: Madras Bhoona Ghosht, with a vegetable curry and chapatis. He drank beer, and had three men and a woman in tow. The woman had a Khorma and the other men raised the stakes by opting for the Chicken Vindaloo. They talked seriously and constantly through the meal.

Around four, the target went out for an hour, and Flanagan tailed him, there and back.

After that, the Irishman had a long wait. The target was in his office until nine. He got back to the building at nine forty-five. At least he earned his daily chapati – Flanagan thought that was quite amusing.

He rang Murphy from a public telephone box so the call was not monitored, though Chilton's people, press-ganged from the Security Service, had Flanagan under a microscope all day.

Neither the target nor Flanagan knew they were being watched.

When Murphy answered the telephone in his hotel room, Flanagan told him that everything was arranged. He liked his mind to be neat and orderly before he did any kind of job. 'Monday morning,' he said. 'Either as he comes out or on his way home. I'll play it by ear.'

'As long as you do it, friend.'

– 3 –

Tarpin had the hell of a day, cramming in almost a week's work. He dictated a letter to be sent to all the authors with whom he had dealings, then he called his bank manager, made arrangements for a dollar account to be opened at the Allied Irish Bank in New York – he had been introduced to the Allied Irish in London, by a waspish, shrewd, personality in the business who maintained that relatively small was beautiful in the world of banking. As well as opening the account he asked them to ring old Pembeton and check on his forthcoming legacy, on the strength of which he borrowed money. Then he held a long and concentrated meeting with his junior editors, assigning books that, up until then, he had been working on.

Similar meetings took up the bulk of the afternoon, following a long lunch with his more senior colleagues.

Later in the day he telephoned some of the authors with whom he had been working, talking to each of them for around half an hour. Somehow, mixed in with all this, he had taken a taxi to Piccadilly, walked into the Burlington Arcade and visited a jeweller he had done business with on a couple of occasions before. He came out with a superb ring – diamonds and sapphires – which set him back the entire bank loan of fifteen thousand pounds.

This prize he carried back to Sukie. She cooked dinner that night, and over the splendid *crème caramel*, which was one of her specialities, he made a romantic proposal of marriage, on his knees, and slipped the ring on to the third finger of her left hand.

It was a very happy, and moderately lazy, weekend. On the Sunday night he packed enough for three weeks, filled his briefcase with work that would still have to be done for the English end of the operation, then added the bulky envelope containing what he now thought of as the Bartholemew File.

On Monday morning all the newspapers carried variations on the same theme – GOVERNMENT SET DATE FOR HONG KONG SHOOTINGS INQUIRY. A taxi picked up Tarpin, just after seven in the morning, and he was already ticketed and checked in for British Airways Flight 175 when Flanagan called Murphy.

'The man's disappeared.'

'What d'you mean, disappeared?'

'Didn't go to work.'

'Could be off sick.'

'Damn it, I had everything going for me. There was hardly anyone around at eight o'clock.'

'You didn't miss him? You weren't late?'

'No way.'

'Call the flat.' Murphy gave him the number.

Half an hour later Flanagan was back. 'There's a fecking answering machine on. I'm going in. See what's what. Might be a clue as to where he is.'

'Don't do anything stupid now.'

'Don't worry, friend. I know my job.'

– 4 –

In another part of London, Chilton was talking to Scarecrow.

'I understand you've removed the watchers the DG of Five so kindly loaned us.' Scarecrow smiled, unctuously, as though he had caught Jackie Chilton out in some monumental blunder.

'Our interest's been called to New York, sir. There was nobody on him. We still have the surveillance in Camden Town, and we know where to pick anyone up when he returns. I can't see them following him to the Apple.'

'Who knows? Who can read their minds? After all, the whole damned thing's mindless. Has been from the beginning.'

'There I agree with you, sir. But, for the time being, it appears he's out of harm's way. I can get on with some of the other stuff. Have you anything for me?'

'As a matter of fact . . . ' Scarecrow always looked embarrassed when these things came up unexpectedly. 'Yes, there is a little thing that has Her Majesty concerned. It's to do with a television personality and young – ' he lowered his voice to name the prince who had been a shade indiscreet with a lady news anchor called Kate Crochette, known in the trade variously as the *Casse Noisette,* or Golden Crotch.

Chilton nodded understandingly. He would certainly bring all his astute, if dubious, powers to bear.

– 5 –

Sukie Cartwright cursed long and loudly. It was the middle of the morning when she discovered that the draft contract, which she had to take across London to have vetted by their lawyers, was not in her briefcase. At the moment of discovery she had a clear picture of it lying on the table back in the flat. She had read it during her lonely breakfast after Phillip had gone.

There was only one option. The taxi, ticking over and waiting to take her to Grey's Inn, would have to detour into Kensington so that she could pick up the wretched document.

Half an hour later, with the taxi clocking up waiting time, she rode the elevator up to the third floor and left the gates open, so that she could grab the papers and run, without anyone else having a chance to tie up the lift.

She took one pace towards the door of the flat then stopped. The door was open, the lock prised halfway off the jamb.

She stood, silent for a second, her heart thumping, trying to make up her mind whether to go on or send for the police. She decided to go in, and took another step forward. The man came out when she was only a pace away.

'What the hell . . . ?' she began angrily.

She heard a curse and saw his hand come up. She did not hear the shot, but her mind grasped at the gun in his hand just as she felt the burning wrenching pain which threw her back towards the lift, and sent her sprawling into oblivion.

SEVEN

– 1 –

Three months later, in the hellish boiling cauldron which is New York in high summer, the events of those terrible days remained, to Phillip Tarpin, a swirling muddle of images. A nightmare of blurred faces and conversations. His numbing grief mercifully buffered him from any clear memory.

He could see Peter Palestino standing, with a BA official, at the top of the jetway at JFK, his face a mask, his lips moving and no sound reaching Tarpin's ears because his brain did not want to accept what Palestino was saying; the laughter around him, business conversations and the smell of wealth on the Concorde back to Heathrow. Then the solemn faces waiting for him; the repaired lock on the door of the flat; the hastily-cleaned carpet by the elevator door; the new paint slapped over the walls to hide the blood; the consideration of people like the tall, dark and leggy Pat Patton who had been to the flat and removed all of Sukie's things, so that the memories might be less.

But the flat was redolent with Sukie on that first night back and forever after. Even Derek Morrison, his oldest publishing friend, who stayed with him for a week, until he moved out, could not take away the smell of Sukie Cartwright and her laugh which seemed to be trapped within the walls.

There were other sharp-focused pictures from that time: Sukie's younger sister, Hilary, hugging him, her face stained with weeping; her mother, white under the badly applied make-up, her eyes seeming not to comprehend the facts, and her father being the brave, stiff upper lip, ex-soldier that he was.

He could remember the funeral only in flashes, touched by some of the well-known publishing faces who were there. He recalled the faces quite clearly, though not the coffin. Freddie Forsythe, Jeffrey Archer, Geoffrey Balley from Hatchards, Patrick Janson-Smith and Paul Scherer, from Transworld, with whom Sukie had done so many deals. Even Larry Kirschbaum, Sonny Mehta and Michael Korda were there, having flown in from New York. Names and faces not recognizable to the book-buying public, but men with enormous reputations within the profession. People, Tarpin thought, who would never be caught dead at his funeral. He was proud for Sukie, his almost bride.

The obituary in *The Bookseller* spoke of Sukie's 'energy, commitment to and passion for books'. A weekly trade columnist noted a memory, a time when Sukie had read *War and Peace* over one weekend because an author had described his new manuscript as a modern *War and Peace*.

Then it was over, and Tarpin was left with this scattered jigsaw of memories, which he packed away, sealed off, and locked into a dark strongbox within his mind, so that he could get on with work and rebuild his life.

By mid-summer his time was filled, hardly an hour wasted. There were five books he was personally editing – including the biography of a beloved, elderly movie star, a task which necessitated a trip to the coast every third weekend. Tarpin, being conscientious in all things, was also overseeing five other books which were being handled by his junior editors. On top of this there were meetings and planning sessions connected with the purchase of at least four new books from a possible ten. Life was full again. The pain and loss began to intrude less and less. Then it happened.

On that night in mid-August New York, one of the forgotten, blanked-out memories came back: suddenly, like a wolfhound unexpectedly attacking his brain, leaping from the past as though it had something to tell him.

It was not surprising that the wretched remembrance returned on this particular night, for he had lunched with Hilary. When he had seen her, a fragment of the week of hellish shock, he had not even recalled that she lived and worked in New York. In truth he had met her only once before Sukie's death, though he had heard much about her. He knew, vaguely, that she had tried to write and failed, not miserably, but in a way which made it plain she would never be able to keep herself by the pen or the word processor. Twenty-six years old, with the same enthusiastic fervour of her dead sister, she had started her own business. A research facility for authors – DataCart Associates – which had attained a moderate success, and dug out facts and figures for writers of fiction and non-fiction. Hilary Cartwright had a degree in history from Cambridge, and was a born traveller. She would go anywhere, excavate anything – from the make of weapons used in the Crimea, to the private life of some forgotten politician. The only requisite was that the author had the money to pay for her services. She had six people working full time for her in New York, and a host of part-time delvers throughout the world.

She had called Tarpin at the office, saying she would like to talk with him. A professional matter. The call had knocked him off balance because when she began to speak it was as though Sukie was at the distant end of the line. He offered her lunch, and found it even more unnerving to sit opposite her in the small French restaurant he always used to entertain visiting authors.

'If this is too painful, just say so and we'll do it by mail,' she said, with Sukie's voice, mannerisms and eyes. 'I know that I'm very like her, Phillip, and I understand.'

It was uncanny, but, surprisingly, nothing he could not handle. No, he said. It was okay. 'Let's eat and enjoy ourselves.'

She was a very clever and tactful young woman. Throughout lunch she never once spoke of England, her dead sister, or her parents. The conversation roamed the shelves of bookstores and the inner sanctums of New York's publishing houses. Who was doing what, who had slurped up the gravy, and which house had taken a pounding because of an ill-timed book, or one for which they had paid some foolish sum.

She also talked of authors, and Phillip could not be anything but impressed at the names of her clients. Most were in the mega-selling bracket. All had formidable reputations. It was not until the coffee arrived that she touched on the reason for their meeting.

'Please, Phillip, believe me when I say I didn't choose you for the obvious reason. I'm not an agent, but I have promised to do what I can, on both sides of the Atlantic. It's for something I've helped to research.'

Tarpin nodded her on. A commissioning editor never showed initial interest or surprise at some new project.

'You ever heard of Tim Clifford?'

'The historian? Yes. He did a wonderful book about ten years ago. *Richard III and the Princes in the Tower.*' It had been a quite remarkable piece of historical detective work, wonderfully written, assuming nothing, painting an accurate picture of English life in the mid-fifteenth century – particularly life at court. The book read like a novel and re-wrote a segment of English history that had always been, at best, dubious.

'That's Tim. He's incredibly thorough, and we did some heavy digging for him with this new book. I think it might probably be one for you. It's certainly going to cause controversy.'

'You *are* agenting it. Tim Clifford shouldn't have any trouble selling anything new. The Richard book was a massive best-seller.'

'Ah.' She winked, just like her sister, and Tarpin noticed how the laugh lines formed under her deep brown eyes. His heart skipped a beat, and his stomach churned. Had this been wise? It was like sitting opposite a ghost.

Hilary did not seem to notice that he had become disturbed. 'I've finally got someone in the UK to read it. It's been difficult, because the subject's been done to death, no pun intended.' She paused, taking a little breath as though about to go off the top board into an Olympic pool. 'You see, Phillip, the subject's Jack the Ripper.'

'Oh.' He genuinely could not keep the disappointment out of his voice.

'Wait!' she said, reaching across the table and touching his hand. 'Tim's turned up some really incredible new material.'

'Hilary, they all do. Jolly Jack attracts scholars and nuts alike. It's also a magnet to fruitcakes. When some new theory is pushed forward, there's always a novelist behind the theory, ready to work it over. And, when that happens, people realize it really *is* fiction. Or a hoax.'

'Please, Phillip, this is truly different. He's unearthed concrete facts – set in stone.'

'He's fingered the killer?'

'No. That truly isn't the point. He admits in the prologue that the identity of the Ripper will probably never be known. The book isn't about naming the culprit.'

Tarpin was suddenly depressed. 'As a subject, Hilary, Jack the Ripper has become passé. There've been too many books, and too many theories.'

That was true enough, yet a small part of his mind toyed with the name Tim Clifford. He was a spectacularly good historian, and an even better writer.

'Publishers can't get enough serial-killer books, Phillip. Particularly sex-killers.' She looked at him as though pleading for some gift that only he had the right to bestow. 'Jack the Ripper is the first tabloid serial sex-killer in history. Talk about Victorian crime, and people immediately think: The Ripper.'

That was true, just as it was also true that the five murders over a period of three months in sleazy London's Whitechapel, during the autumn of 1888, grabbed at the public imagination. Jack the Ripper was a hardy annual.

'And this, I promise you,' she continued, 'is *very* different. The evidence he's managed to get hold of – Oh, why be coy? the evidence I helped get hold of – is something else.'

'You want to give me a clue?'

'No. I want you to read the manuscript. I want you to have first option in the United States, because I believe you'll kick yourself if you don't read it.'

He sipped his coffee and smiled at her. 'I presume you've brought your harp to the party?'

'You mean have I got the manuscript with me? No. I never take anything for granted and, at the moment, there are only three copies. Tim has one; one is with a London publisher, and the third is locked away in a bank vault. I need Tim's permission to get it unlocked and into your hands. Oh, there're also some conditions, imposed by Tim.'

'Rules and regulations? That's an old agent's trick, Hills.'

Very quietly she said, 'Please don't call me Hills, Phillip.'

'I'm sorry. I didn't realize . . . '

'It's something from my past – well, your past and mine. I don't like to hear that abbreviation.'

He nodded, forcing the many possibilities from his mind. 'So what are the formalities?'

'You alone read it, as a commissioning editor. You undertake not to divulge its contents to anyone.'

'Not even my CEO?'

'Not to start with, no. Also, in the event of you deciding not to even make an offer for the book, you pledge not to disclose its contents until after it has been published by somebody else.'

'Why?'

'In a nutshell, because certain irrefutable conclusions, drawn by the author, are so sensitive that we believe there will be attempts to suppress them.'

'Oh, it isn't the connection with the British royal family again is it, Hilary? That's a chestnut which has not only been cracked open, but decimated by historians.'

'No,' she all but snapped. 'No, this has nothing to do with the royals!' Her anger showed, in her eyes and in the set of her mouth.

Some years previously, several authors came up with what they considered to be the ultimate answer to the infamous Ripper murders, linking them with the Duke of Clarence, King Edward VII's ill-fated son, and pinning the murders on the court physician, Sir William Gull – though the good doctor had been smitten with a stroke over twelve months before the events. In the end, the theory had been annihilated. But that had not stopped at least one novel and a movie, both based on the debunked theory.

'You really believe it's that hot, Hilary? You're not just excited because you and Tim Clifford have discovered some tiny gems that can be made to fit a new theory?'

'I've told you, Phillip, it's not a theory. We're dealing with hard facts.'

'Which you cannot tell me.'

'Right.' Again, chilly, almost unfriendly. 'Do you want to read it?'

He had no room for manoeuvre. If he hesitated, she would obviously cross him off her list, and that might not be a bad thing. Jack the Ripper books were a dime a dozen. On the other hand, Professor Tim Clifford was no historical slouch.

'Yes. I would like to read it,' he heard himself say.

'And you'll abide by the restrictions?'

'Of course.'

'We require a legal document.'

'No problem. Yes, of course I'll do exactly what you and the author require.'

'Good.' The smile came back into her face and eyes, resurrecting Sukie in a way that made him catch his breath.

'Can we have dinner some time? I mean a non-professional dinner.' He realized that he had not even thought about what he was going to say. The words came out with no clear journey from brain to tongue.

The smile died for an instant. Then, slowly it returned, and she stretched across the table again and placed a hand over his. 'Do you think that's wise?'

'Meaning?'

'I know what I look like. I would hate being second best to my . . . You know what I mean. I'm afraid you might . . . Well, you might think because I look like her that I *am* like her.'

'I'm sorry. Yes, you do look like her. But I'd still like to give you dinner, for yourself.'

'I'm not a spectre.'

'I never thought you were.'

Okay. I'll have dinner with you as long as you don't look on me as a substitute. That wouldn't be wise.'

'I'll call you.'

'No, I'll call you. In a couple of days, when I know the manuscript can be delivered. We can fix up the legal stuff, and take it from there.'

Now, waking with a start in the middle of a hot and humid night, Phillip Tarpin faced something he had pushed away, down among the dead things that crawled around that part of his mind reserved for memories he would rather forget.

He lay in the dark, remembering the scene, seeing and hearing it, just as it had occurred in London three months before.

– 2 –

Tarpin had always believed that, in one lifetime, you were lucky if you made a single friend in whom you could trust implicitly – 'One person,' he often said, 'who will get on a plane and come to you if you are in need. One person for whom you would do the same.' For him, Derek Morrison was that friend. They were of an age, and had entered publishing about the same time. When he was working at the small publishing house in Ludgate Circus, so Derek was becoming a force in publicity at another house, in Bloomsbury.

On the evening when he arrived back from New York by Concorde, courtesy of J. B. Pudney, Sons, Derek Morrison was' waiting at Heathrow, having heard the news of Sukie Cartwright's murder in his car while driving to an appointment in Reading. He had kept the appointment, then called Hosier & Whitehead, after which he drove out to Heathrow and was waiting for Tarpin when the flight arrived.

After the shock, and a general, sympathetic, interview with the police. It was Morrison who drove them both back to the flat. Morrison who cooked a meal. Morrison who made sure his old friend did not hit the bottle too hard.

It was also Morrison who opened the door to Mr John Chilton when he arrived around eleven that night, stating that he wished to speak with Tarpin immediately, backing it up with an official-looking laminated card.

'Do you *have* to bother him now?' Morrison was a forbidding figure: six feet two inches, a former rugger blue, and blessed with a face known to charm the pants off ladies, and frighten all hell out of other prospective boyfriends, board members, even authors, when required.

'I'm afraid it is somewhat urgent.' Morrison's death-ray look did not even reach first base with a cool customer like Chilton. 'Tomorrow would be inconvenient, I fear.'

'Well, the poor bugger's in shock.'

'Naturally.'

'He's also had quite a bit to drink.'

'That's a shame. You should really watch the booze. Lock it up or something. I've seen bereaved young men nearly kill themselves in a situation like this.' He marched forward into the living room and stretched out a hand to Tarpin.

'So, I always seem to be offering you my condolences, Mr

Tarpin.'

'You do?' He had seen Chilton somewhere before, but, for a moment, could not place him.

'Chilton. John Chilton. Usually known as Jack. We met on the night they found your mother.'

'Oh yes.' He had no desire to recall his mother's death.

'Yes. I have to ask you a few questions.'

'Why? The police have . . . '

'Yes, I know. But this *is* necessary.' It was certainly not only necessary, but imperative for Chilton. He had already listened to some scalding comments from the man known as Scarecrow. 'After all, Jackie, *you* took the surveillance off. I thought that was a shade risky. In fact, I told the Chief I felt it was downright foolhardy,' Scarecrow had barked, making it perfectly clear that it was Chilton, and not himself, who would carry any cans that demanded carrying.

Now, sitting opposite Tarpin, and refusing a drink, Chilton went though his personal litany of questions:

– Had Mr Tarpin noticed any strangers around the building?

– No.

– Had he been aware of anyone watching him over the past week?

– No.

– Had Ms Cartwright mentioned any suspicions?

– No.

– Did either he, or Ms Cartwright, have any particular enemies? People who were unstable enough to seek vengeance by force?

– No.

And so, and so, and so. Did . . . ? How . . . ? Was . . . ?

Chilton stayed for the best part of an hour, piling question upon question. In his mind, the cunning, smooth and shrewd Jackie Chilton only wanted the answer to one question. After all, he knew the score already. The powers that be wanted to contain things. That afternoon, the two Irishmen, Jacko Reilly and Martin McManus, had been arrested in Camden Town, and they had them bang to rights, with the bomb-making equipment stashed away in the little mews house.

Flanagan and Murphy were a different proposition, for they had disappeared as though they had never been. Happily, Sukie's cab driver, waiting for her outside the apartment block, had given them a description good enough to use an exact photofit picture of Paddy Flanagan, and even append his name to the wanted posters now being printed. Real photographs had gone out to airports, railway police and all ports of exit.

Yet Jackie Chilton needed to know one further truth. He rose to leave, and again offered his condolences. Then, almost at the door, he turned back, face blank, manner almost diffident. 'Oh, Mr Tarpin, one point. Just a foolish idea of mine. No basis really. After your mother's death? You didn't find anything in her papers that was out of the ordinary? Nothing odd, nothing anyone might want to get their hands on – that kind of thing, eh?'

Tarpin merely shook his head. His real father, Paul Bartholemew, and his father before him were none of Mr Chilton's business, and he was certainly not going to say anything about that.

Now, here, in the sleepless night in the city that never slept, Phillip Tarpin remembered the look on Chilton's face, and the casual tone of his voice.

He got out of bed, went through to the kitchen and made coffee. He unlocked a drawer of the desk, which stood between the two windows looking down on Fifth Avenue, and took out what they had laughingly called the Bartholemew File. It was the first time he had opened it since the night before Sukie had met her end.

Quietly, he sat down in front of the desk and began to go through the papers.

EIGHT

– 1 –

On that same August night, Patrick James Flanagan waited for a visitor. He sat in the living room of a small stone house looking down on the Hudson River, near the town of Rhinebeck, in upstate New York. As he waited, his mind went back, as it so often did, to the day, three months before. To the afternoon when he had killed the girl.

Even as he lifted the pistol, and his finger squeezed the trigger, he knew this was not the way. Murphy had said 'Don't do anything stupid, now.' When the Glock bucked twice in his hand, and the arterial blood began to travel from the girl, he realized this was about as stupid as you could get. But Paddy Flanagan, usually cool and careful, had fallen prey to the most capricious of emotions. Panic. The panic of being seen; the anxiety of being caught in the act of leaving the target's flat.

He had reacted like this before: in the back streets of Derry; off the Falls Road in Belfast; and in the wild open country of Armagh and Fermanagh. Killing the girl had been like the time, one moonless night, up near the border, when he had taken out two British soldiers who had not even seen him. Or worse, the child he had shot – a so-called innocent bystander – during the execution of an RUC sergeant.

There was a taxi ticking over in the street outside, and he knew the driver had looked at him. Their eyes met for a second. The driver was lucky to be alive, for the beast which drove Flanagan told him to kill again – for his safety, for the cause he served, for the simple fact that the driver was a Brit and all Brits were equally guilty. For the most part the civilians were as culpable as the army and the politicians. They had the power of protest, and few of them would stand up and demand their government should right the wrong that was the unyielding British presence in Northern Ireland.

But he stayed his hand, walked quickly towards Kensington High Street, and was lost among the people going about their daily business.

'Have you posted the parcel then?' Murphy asked, using the code they had agreed, after Flanagan identified himself, speaking from a public telephone in the Underground station.

'The postage isn't right. There's been a foul-up.'

'Is it a serious thing?'

'I'll need to take the parcel home again instead of sending it.' He heard the short intake of Murphy's breath on the distant end of the line.

'Then go. After all, your mother's a sick woman.' Murphy closed the line. Within fifteen minutes he had checked out of the hotel and was riding the Underground out to Heathrow. It would take a little longer than a cab, but the security was better. A cab driver would always remember an Irish accent, and that was the one physical aspect of his nature he could not sufficiently disguise.

'Your mother's a sick woman', they had agreed, would be Terminal Two at Heathrow. Murphy travelled light and carried the spare identities, sealed in manila envelopes in his briefcase. The documents were incriminating, but it was a small risk. His job, after all, was to assist the Active Service Unit as well as arranging to eliminate the target. To carry out his duties, the sophisticated intelligence department of the Provisional IRA provided him with documents. Over the years they had learned that an Active Service Unit on the mainland was often given away by name or the documents they carried. In recent years they had done much to put that right, by using experienced forgers and contacts within government circles.

Flanagan was waiting for him. Hanging around the W. H. Smith's bookstall area. He carried a copy of the *Standard* under his left arm, which was the sign that he could not detect any surveillance. Murphy signalled him to follow, and began the long walk up to the short-term car park.

Whenever there were 'actives' on the mainland – which was most of the time – there was a group of sympathizers who took turns at parking a car every three days in Terminal Two's short-term park. The cars were always 'clean', with the spare keys hidden in a magnetic box under the chassis. All Active Service Units, and those who looked out for them, had keys to the magnetic box.

Murphy sought out the car, always parked on the first or second floors. This time it was a grey Austin. Flanagan followed at a careful distance, only hurrying when he saw Murphy unlocking the driver's side door. Seconds later he slid into the passenger seat, and Murphy made a gesture indicating that he was to remain silent until they were out and away. Murphy paid the parking fee, and they drove, in silence, out of Heathrow, through the tunnel, heading west on the M4.

'So what happened?' Murphy scanned the mirror to be certain they had not been picked up.

'I was just leaving. A girl came up in the lift. She saw me. Saw I'd broken in.'

'Jasus, Paddy don't tell me you . . . '

'It was a reflex. I turned and she was about to scream.'

'You killed her?' The words were soaked in disbelief.

'I did.'

'Jasus, man, you'll get us all blown, and for no reason.' Connor Murphy was angry now, scrabbling around his mind for answers. No matter that Flanagan had screwed up, it was him who would have to face the General Staff and take the blame. 'Did anyone see you?'

'There was a taxi driver . . . '

'Where?'

'Outside.'

'He get a good look?'

'Enough.'

Murphy took the next exit, circling the huge roundabout, then heading back on to the M4, driving towards Heathrow again. 'You'll be on your own, Paddy. You still have the gun?'

'Here,' tapping his hip.

'Take it out and put it on the floor. I'll get rid of it. Pull that briefcase from the back.' He rattled off the numbers which would activate the brass combination locks. 'Open the one marked Frank Donovan.'

It was a fat, manila envelope, and he saw there were three others like it inside the case. Before he had even opened it, Connor Murphy was ticking off the contents and instructions. Passport, with Flanagan's photograph, in the name of Frank Donovan. All necessary visas. Five hundred dollars, cash; nine thousand in traveller's cheques; one hundred pounds sterling, cash. Visa Card, MasterCard, American Express Gold Card. All valid and each one with a limit of five thousand dollars.

'You're Frank Donovan, director of McArthur Office Equipment, 5 Fairhazel Gardens, Belsize Park. Telephone: 071-624 9764. That's as genuine as they come and they'll verify you're on a business trip to Paris and New York.' Murphy spoke quickly, slewing the car into the lane marked Terminal Two Departures. 'You hop the first flight you can grab to Paris. Then the first you can get on for JFK. If they pick you up, you behave like a deaf mute. Remember we've one hell of a long arm, Paddy. Once you're in New York call 975-8967 and ask for Billy. Just tell him the car wasn't there to meet you. He'll come out to the airport and see you on your way. Then you'll lie low. They'll look after you, and someone'll be in touch. I'll be out of here within the week.' They pulled up among the taxis and hire cars disgorging people laden with luggage.

Murphy leaned over and opened the door. 'You'll find three suitcases in the boot. Take any one. They're there for emergencies. At least you'll look like a traveller.'

'I want to go back to Belfast.' Flanagan, who could kill without felling, now sounded like a child wanting its mother.

'You'll feck off to New York, and you'll obey orders, or you'll never walk again. And pray they haven't yet got your picture circulated. Now, get the hell out.'

Within the hour, Paddy Flanagan was on an Air France A330-Airbus to Paris, where he waited for a worrying five hours before picking up a flight to New York.

The photographs of him were circulated to Heathrow security nearly two hours after he had left, and nobody recognized him as the man who had snapped up the last seat on the Paris flight.

At JFK he called the number Murphy had given him, and by the following day he was settled into the pleasant little house in the Hudson Valley. He felt at home, for the countryside he could see from his living room window reminded him of the rolling Wicklow hills near Rathdrum where he had often gone on R & R when serving with the South Armagh Battalion. They used a lot of places in the Republic for R & R. You could even get an odd night out in Dublin, which was more than they let him do here.

But, at least, he was safe, being looked after and hidden by people with a loyalty stretching back to the days of the *Clann na Gael,* the old Irish organization which flourished in New York, Boston and San Francisco. He was in no danger and there was even a girl, Mary Craig, with dark eyes and lustrous jet hair, who smelled of wild grass, and came to him three or four times a week.

She had been there that morning, and brought news.

'The man, Murphy, will be coming tonight,' she told him as they lay on his bed, smoking, when they had done with each other's bodies – a wild, exhausting bout. She liked him to play the hard man. 'It was the message I had to give you. About Murphy,' she said, then fondled him again. 'You're a lovely man. Did you know that? A fine, lovely man.'

Jasus, he thought. She should know me. Aloud he said, 'You're a flatterer, Mary. It makes me feel good, so it does.'

The message was not altogether a happy one. The killing of the girl in London had been a disastrous error. It might be that Murphy, who could be a cold iron man, would be accompanied by others with a warrant of discipline, which meant anything from kneecapping to execution. After all, he thought, it was his panic in offing the girl that had blown the whole unit and landed Jacko Reilly and Martin McManus in jail.

But, as he thought about it, Flanagan knew that it was not Murphy's style to advertise his arrival in advance, particularly if it meant some serious action. More likely Murphy was bringing orders. Murphy had a way with him, and could well have persuaded the General Staff to give him another chance. Some way to purge himself of the folly.

86

Phillip Tarpin had sorted through the little bundles of letters. With only a few exceptions they were written on flimsy blue paper, and the first packet, held by two elastic bands, contained around forty letters from Flight Lieutenant Edward Tarpin. Most were addressed to Mrs Tarpin at an address in Burnley, Lancs.

As he flicked through them, a faded buff envelope fell from the centre of the batch. Picking it from the floor, he saw the envelope had been ripped open hurriedly, and was split down one side. He recognized it, dimly, as a telegram, something long gone from the British Post Office. The form, inside, contained a stark message, written by hand:

THE AIR MINISTRY REGRETS TO INFORM YOU THAT YOUR HUSBAND, FLT. LT. EDWARD TARPIN, IS MISSING, BELIEVED KILLED IN ACTION, OVER GERMANY.

It was dated 15 July 1944, and there was a half circle, brown and yellow, at one corner where a tea cup had been placed on the form. Another two letters seemed to have originally been clipped to the telegram. One from Tarpin's Squadron Leader, the other a form letter signed by Air Marshall Harris – the famous 'Bomber' Harris, architect of the Royal Air Force's night-bombing strategy.

He shook his head, oddly moved by these little bookmarks in his mother's life. Then he began to read his 'father's' letters, finding that, after the first two or three, he could distance himself from the realities, now long gone.

They began in the late spring of 1943 when Ted Tarpin had just gone back to his squadron after the leave which had included his marriage and honeymoon. The letters told a sad, somewhat naïve, story of a marriage doomed to failure from the first day.

That young man from 1943 obviously had little talent for writing letters. The language was stilted, alien with words he recognized from old war movies. The honeymoon had been 'wizard'; Vera was a 'scorcher'; when he wrote, he gave her 'pukka gen'. There were tiny indicators of feelings, such as, 'Sometimes I cannot believe that you have chosen a dull bod like me. Take care of the little one you are carrying with so much love.' He always signed himself, 'Your loving husband – Edward.'

The letters were so far removed from life as he knew it, that Tarpin did not even feel sorry for the man. By early summer the tone had changed. The baby was obviously lost, one letter had been written after returning to his squadron from compassionate leave, but – at least in writing – he showed no emotion. Concern for Vera, of course, but no distress. The reason hit Tarpin a few letters later when he did show sorrow, but this time for fellow flyers. One of his close friends had, as he put it, 'got the chop over Hamburg', while another had 'bought it when he pranged on take-off'.

Then, the mood altered for a second time. He began to plead with Vera, asking her to 'have a heart and come to live near the station, like other fellows' wives and girlfriends'. He was off operational flying now, attached to some advanced training unit for the obligatory rest period. There was a long gap in the letters here, and one of them was obviously written soon after the leave Uncle Bob had talked of, for Ted Tarpin used words which Bob Bates had repeated – 'Vera, my dear, I feel there must be something reptilian about me. You obviously did not want to be near me, in a wifely sense, if you follow what I mean.'

Good grief, Tarpin thought as he read on, they obviously had no common sexual language. One or the other of them – maybe both – could not talk, or write, about the sexual tenor of their lives. He was to find, soon enough, that it was not his mother, for the other letters, from Paul Bartholemew, scorched the pages with vivid descriptions of their intimate lives.

The last of Tarpin's letters that his mother had kept was dated 30 May 1944 and was undoubtedly his shattered reply to her demand for a divorce. For the only time that night, Tarpin felt something for the young flight lieutenant, who had been clearly dismayed and shocked.

'Your sudden and unexpected demand has come out of the blue. I have been to see the Padre who suggests that I get compassionate leave, so that we can talk it over. You really have shot me down in flames, dearest. I had no idea that you felt this way. For God's sake let us talk. I have been ringing the flat at all hours. The station operator now knows the number by heart. Why don't you answer? Why has everything fallen apart like this? I really don't understand.

If you had only done as I suggested – come to live near the 'drome – things could have been different . . . ' And on over eight pages, lost, spiralling out of control, repeating rhetorical questions over and over again.

Tarpin, in the wee small hours, reading the faded pages, felt disbelief that his mother could have been so cold and heartless, not even explaining what was wrong. She must have given no indication until the one shattering letter. Unless, of course, the young, doomed officer had been incredibly dense. Slowly he went to the kitchen for more coffee, wide awake now and slightly dreading what he would find in the second packet of letters: these tied with ribbon, as a young girl might keep gauche notes during a teenage crush.

The first, two pages of it, was an immediate surprise, and nearly sent him rocking off the chair with laughter. The date was 2 August 1943, only a few months after the wedding. Glancing at the second page he saw it was signed Paul. It began 'Darling Fruitcake'. Tarpin could never, in his wildest fantasy, imagine anyone calling his mother Fruitcake, but there it was, and as he read on, a completely new side of his mother came, second hand, from the neat, very legible writing.

Darling Fruitcake, Paul Bartholemew had written,

You must forgive this letter. I do not usually write to strange women (strange in both senses: odd and unknown). You see, I don't really know if you exist. I keep asking myself, did I dream last night or did it all really happen? Will the glass slipper I discovered in my parachute this morning fit should I find you? Only you can tell, so let me recount what I might have imagined. After a morning of absolutely ridiculous physical stress, running around over assault courses, being shot at with live ammunition, and having large, muscular and hairy men explode guncotton charges near at hand, I thought they might give me a restful afternoon. No such luck, I had to jump from an aeroplane, from under a thousand feet – admittedly with a parachute, which was a relief. When that was over, I took what passes for a hot shower in these parts.

Having dried, shaved and dressed, I walked to the NAAFI,

which is the nearest thing here to a British Restaurant. During the untaxing stroll, I noticed that music was coming from the main assembly hall. I felt I should at least investigate lest the music led, as it so often does, to that wicked and sinful business they call dancing.

I do not usually take part in frivolous pastimes like the foxtrot, the waltz and the jitterbug, having been brought up in a somewhat sheltered environment. Dancing such jigs, shuffles and twists is not my style. Yet, as soon as I stepped inside, I bumped into a charming dark-eyed enchantress who almost begged me to dance with her.

Though I am not normally a prey to such blandishments of wanton women, her pleading finally ruled over reason and we danced. In fact, I recall we did more than dance, we floated and twirled with such abandon that soon our bodies became almost entwined. Certainly, when the band played something she told me was a piece called 'the Last Time I Saw Paris', our cheeks were actually touching. And sweating.

As you can imagine, I was a mite hot and overexcited by this, so I apologized, and excused myself, saying I would have to go outside for air. This shameless hussy insisted on accompanying me, and what happened after that – well, I blush to think of it.

Back in the hall, where the RAF dance band was lashing itself into a frenzy, we partook of some refreshment: some kind of punch, I think, and a so-called fruitcake which the lady pressed upon me. I need not add that there was little remotely resembling fruit in the cake, so we took the air again and, well, I quiver with embarrassment to think on it.

On waking this morning I found a piece of paper with a name – Vera Tarpin – and the address to which I am writing. I cannot believe that such a person exists, but if you were real, I shall be outside that cinema in Piccadilly, Manchester, on Saturday at seven-thirty. They are showing *Casablanca* which I have not seen. It has a song in it they played at the dance. My dream lady said it was called 'Time Goes By,' or some such. Oh, yes, be warned, I have a weekend pass.

All my love if you are real and not a figment.

Paul

Given the time and place, Tarpin supposed that a letter such as this would be considered more than mildly amusing. His mother – our Vera, as Uncle Bob would say – had undoubtedly spent a very pleasant, and different, kind of evening. This, he reminded himself, would be only a few weeks after she had lost the child, and seen Ted Tarpin on his compassionate leave. To Vera, a letter like this would have more than a certain rhapsodic charm: particularly when he thought of the stuffy, dull, prosaic missives which came from her husband. Paul Bartholemew must have leaped into Vera's life like a hurricane of fresh air – and it continued. The following week he wrote:

Darling Figment,
I never said thanks for that lovely weekend, or have I stolen that from some pitiful ballad which I heard sung by somebody called The Forces Sweetheart?
Well, my dear one, I suppose the world has changed for both of us. Nothing in life can ever be the same, of that I am certain. And, if you were not having me on, then your life is changed also . . .

So it persisted, with passion, some wit, and a great deal of charm, all scampering across pages of cheap, wartime notepaper.
Tarpin read, fascinated, for the letters became almost fiction for him. He found it difficult to believe that he was reading raw history: a tale of two people trapped in a passionate, incredibly caring, yet tangled love affair. The war intruded, of course, but this added an edge of excitement. Bartholemew wrote enthusiastically about the Italian campaign, now in full swing, and of the gains being made on the Russian front. There were the more mundane side effects like food and clothes rationing. It appeared that Bartholemew was able to get extra rations, and one letter alluded to parachute silk and the uses to which it had been put. They were the kind of remarks which Tarpin would have exchanged with Sukie . . . He stopped reading the passage, which became erotic in tone and nature. The memory of Sukie filled his head, and he sat, looking out of the window, bright from the glare of lights outside; his eyes moist, like those of an old man full of regrets.

The fact that the letters were one-sided, from Bartholemew's viewpoint, in no way diminished the truth and impact. The man's writing was steeped in love and total commitment, and the references to Vera Tarpin's replies showed that her response was equally involved. In a letter written some time towards the end of September, he said,

'Your last note filled me with longing, for your description of your own feelings so mirrors mine that it is uncanny. The very fact that you can put such intimate and personal reminiscences on paper answers all my questions, and proves to me your own devotion.'

They were also planning. Tarpin felt himself wince when he came upon the first reference to Vera's husband. He had detected pieces of possible code in Bartholemew's style, and now the cryptic word for Edward Tarpin was clear to anyone. They called him Old Dogear. Paul Bartholemew wrote,

'Yes, the time will come for you to tell Old Dogear; just as the day will begin when you have to move away from him, and start on the road to becoming a whole part of me. But I was alarmed by your remarks suggesting you should start proceedings now. I beg you not to do this. We both know that Dogear could cop it any time over France or Germany. If he does, you will be entitled to a pension. I am not being sly. You must understand, my darling, that I could also die, particularly in the next few months. If that happened, there would be no pension should you have already obtained a divorce.'

But Vera had been single-minded. In mid-October she moved to a London address, and about this time there were gaps in the correspondence. Bartholemew's second trip into occupied Europe, Tarpin presumed. Bill Shepherd had said he did one in 1942, then a short one at the end of 1943, before going in before D-Day and staying until the battle in Europe was over.

There were some notes, which looked hastily scribbled, and made no reference to any recent meetings, conversations or replies. He had, it seemed, left a series of notes behind, to be posted at intervals while away, underground in Hitler's Fortress Europe.

He was back by January, and seeing a great deal of Vera, in London. The neat pile of letters had dwindled, and towards the end, they were replaced by a larger envelope. It contained little notes, theatre tickets, a couple of menus – relics of the final months of the grand romantic illusion between Vera Tarpin and Paul Bartholemew. Almost at the bottom of the pile was a card with the words:

> I did not wake you.
> Better you should dream on,
> While I go out to make my daily bread
> In the dark corners of some foreign field.
> I will wake you when I return.

That was the end. There remained only a formal solicitor's letter, and he was shaken slightly when he saw it was from Cox, Russ & Pembeton – signed by old Pembeton himself – only he would have been young Pembeton in those days. It read:

Dear Mrs Tarpin,
This is to confirm the information I gave you when we met on Thursday last. The estate of your late friend, Paul Louis Bartholemew, comes to some fifty thousand pounds sterling, after tax. I would, of course, be delighted to assist you in advising a good investment plan.

If you would telephone me at the above number, I would like a further meeting as we will shortly be looking for a new clerk in this office, and I believe you would be a most suitable candidate should you wish to consider it.

So, he thought. So, that is how Mummy got the job with Pembeton. Slowly he packed away the papers, his mind a whirl of pictures conjured into his head from the correspondence. For a brief moment he wondered if he should suggest it as a subject for a book, then almost dismissed it. Almost, but not quite. He would go through the Bartholemew letters again, for they were a mine of information, a background to love in the forties. Love and tragedy. They would bear several other readings, for he had skipped some pages – including notes scribbled by his mother, and two or three poems – in his desire to get on with what seemed to be a narrative.

Tarpin was surprised to see that the dawn had come and gone. It was almost seven o'clock.

Two hours earlier, the black Ford Taurus had pulled up, out of the dark, and parked in front of the little stone house overlooking the Hudson Valley. Paddy Flanagan opened the door, and with some relief saw that Murphy was alone. There would be no scenes; no violence; no kneecapping today.

He made coffee for his guest, who refused food. 'Maybe later,' he said. 'I'm past eating. That's a long drive from Manhattan.'

Then –

'So you're a lucky fella, Paddy Flanagan. There were some that felt you should have been put out of commission, but I spoke in your defence. You know the Brits got Jacko and Martin?'

Flanagan nodded.

'Then I should tell you that you're a wanted man, Paddy. Our sources tell us they had the place in Camden Town under surveillance.'

'They'll be after you as well then, Mr Murphy.'

'Ah, I'm not so sure about that. I'm an old dog and they'd have to recognize me.'

'So, am I to come home?'

Murphy shook his head, slowly. 'Indeed you are not. The target you made a bollix of in London?'

'Yes?'

'He's here. Here in New York. Alive and strutting like a peacock, so. You'll get him this time or there'll be hell to pay.' He sipped his coffee. 'Now, this has to be different, Paddy. Very different. You have all the time in the world, but we want to play a little game. You'll watch him. You'll get to know when the man takes a leak and when he farts.'

'I can do that.'

'You'd better. Eventually you'll take him out in the way *we* tell you, and within a time frame we dictate. For the moment, you'll get his measure. Right?'

'I'll not let you down this time, Mr Murphy.'

'Indeed you won't, Patrick. Indeed you . . . will . . . not.'

In London, the day was five hours older, and Mr John Chilton sat with the Scarecrow in his neat little grace and favour apartment adjoining St James's Palace.

'So, you said there were *two* factors, Jackie.' Scarecrow had lit a filthy pipe and, for a second, his head was invisible in a cloud of smoke.

'First, there's the historian, Professor Clifford. Tim Clifford.'

'Yes, we spoke about him before, I recall. Has he made unwarranted progress?'

'I fear he's got in by the back door.'

'Meaning?'

'Meaning that we filleted everything from our records, but there was apparently some information in France which has led him to other buried treasure.'

'And he's going public?'

'So it appears.'

'Will this cause much damage?'

'Some embarrassment. Nothing that cannot be handled. Truth, as you know, sir, is stranger than fiction.'

'So they tell me.'

'We have a coincidence here which truly *is* stranger.'

'And?'

'It concerns the last of the line.'

Scarecrow said the name aloud, and Chilton's face screwed into shock, as though Scarecrow had uttered some truly offensive obscenity.

'Yes, sir.' He pulled himself together. 'It appears he'll be reading the manuscript, in New York.'

'Well, can he add two and two and make it five?'

'I doubt it, but we won't know for sure until he's actually read the thing.'

'And we cannot stop that? Cannot prevent it?'

'There is no way. That is, unless the lads get to him first.'

'They've tried once, which means *they* know.'

'And they'll try again. You'll recall the one who slipped the net?'

'Flanagan, yes.'

'Murphy was controlling him, right?'

Scarecrow nodded him on.

'We allowed him to return to the North.'

'I allowed it, Jackie. It was *me*. Remember that when you come to do the final report.'

'Naturally, sir. Murphy is, it seems, leading us to the man Flanagan.'

'The one who killed . . . ?'

'The same. We're presuming that he'll be again sent after his original target.'

Scarecrow stared at a point just above Chilton's head. Eventually he said, 'Are the Americans difficult about us operating on their pitch at the moment?'

'I can but ask.'

'Then do so. And, Jackie . . . ?'

'Sir?'

'I suggest you handle it yourself. We want this contained.'

'It will be my priority.'

So, Mr John Chilton – known as Jackie to his friends – went about his business of speaking with contacts at the American Embassy in Grosvenor Square, and choosing at least two people to accompany him to New York.

NINE

– 1 –

By eleven o'clock that morning Tarpin knew he was not going to do a full and productive day's work. Apart from the sleepless night, the letters preyed on his mind, scratching away just below the surface of consciousness. He felt like a child lying in the dark, certain that a monster lurked in the closet, ready to spring out and devour him the moment he slept. He could not quite put his finger on why the apprehension was so overpowering. Certainly reading his mother's long-ago love letters was enough to tamper with his psyche, yet there was something else: lines or phrases which he thought were some kind of code. Words that did not quite fit. Entire letters he would have to read again and again to reach the true meaning. On top of this, there was the everyday information: the peek into people's lives during a time of great tension.

At around eleven-fifteen he called Peter Palestino's office and asked the CEO if he was free for lunch.

'Just had an appointment cancelled. Who's buying?'

'Me, I guess. Just want to pick your brains.'

Since he had joined the New York end of J. B. Pudney, Sons, they had kept the pact made on that first day, when the news of the Hong Kong shootings had intruded on lunch. Now, they had swung easily into the habit of a mid-day meal, or dinner, at least once a week. Today they walked a couple of blocks to Luigi's, a quiet Italian restaurant, rarely frequented by people in publishing. It was a place they went to in order to swap confidences, and Tarpin knew that he was the receptacle for a great deal of restricted information. In the short time Tarpin had worked in New York, the CEO had shared much with him: fears, concerns, policy, whether some decisions – purchase of books, or a particular promotion strategy – would be seen as right for the house. There were also things that impinged on Palestino's private life. Information was freely given and received, in the knowledge that it would not be shared with anyone else.

'You look like shit.' Palestino's crinkled, leathery face broke into a friendly smile. 'You okay, Phillip, or are you working on a new image?' They had both ordered the spaghetti and meat balls, with side salads. It was not gourmet Italian, but the meatballs were incredibly good. As the *padrone* said, 'We make 'em from secret recipe, passed on from my mother's mother's mother. That piece a paper, he's worth Carol King's ransom.'

Tarpin told him of the sleepless night. Then talked about the letters, in a very general sense, not going into detail. 'They're raw data, Peter. If someone could put them in context, I believe they'd tell a moving story, and give a new slant on what it was like to live in the UK during World War Two. What it was like to be caught in a crippling emotional crisis, while the world burned.' He did not say the correspondence in any way invaded his own life, but Palestino was not one of the best publishers in New York for nothing.

'They're your mother's letters,' he said bluntly.

Tarpin paused. Then – 'Okay, yes. Yes, they were with my mother's papers.'

'And they've upset the hell out of you.'

'Right. Your crystal ball's operating at full strength.'

'You don't have to be a genius to figure that out. You want some kind of reaction from me, Phillip. Or what?'

'I don't really know. I guess if you're in publishing there comes a point when you believe your own story would make a book.'

Palestino frowned, took a forkful of his meatball, chewed, then said, 'Geez, these are so good. Phil, is it nostalgia – World War Two Britain, I mean?'

'Possibly.'

'Over here we're still dealing with the collective guilt of Vietnam and its aftermath. It's there, supersedes the Gulf War, even though there's a lot of fast publishing mileage in that conflict. The supposed end of the Cold War seems to be producing a lot of nostalgic words, even conspiracy theories. Look at the stuff coming out about the CIA . . . '

'Mainly bandwagon jumping. There's no substance to most of it. Ex-spooks are reaping vengeance by feeding ideas to would-be experts. Nostalgia? Yes, I think the forties are in the frame.'

'What you really need is the opinion of another good editor. Why don't you talk about it to Liz Oliver?'

Elizabeth Oliver was the most senior of Tarpin's non-fiction editors. A tall, graceful, immaculate blonde with a strange sense of humour, and that look of assurance which came so naturally to New York career women. If he told the truth, Tarpin was secretly a little in awe of her. Liz was the one who argued at editorial meetings, or pushed a point more forcibly than the others. In awe was, he thought, the wrong description. She frightened him with her abrasive personality, and at times she could be plain rude. He had held back, but there were moments when he found her offensive: a very intense young woman, with a hard outer shell and, he surmised, a huge chip on her shoulder.

Again, as though reading his mind, Palestino laughed. 'Or are you scared of her?'

'She's the kind of girl who's pretty forceful. I don't think she likes men very much.'

'Well, there you're wrong, my friend. It's just that she had one short, and very unpleasant, marriage which ended in a doozy of a messy divorce. I think she's simply immersed herself in work – like you.'

'Mmmm.'

'For Christ's sake don't ever let her know I told you. The marriage and divorce are still open sores, and she still hurts. Oh, I know she can be bloody rude: comes at you out of nowhere with an almost childish temper. But you ought to cultivate her, Phillip. You both have a lot in common, really.'

Tarpin was lost in thought for a moment. 'I'll trade you a confidence.'

Palestino nodded, and the thought crossed Tarpin's mind that a nod was not as good as a word, so he repeated, 'I'll trade you a confidence.'

'Okay. It's a trade. I spend so much time with the boardroom generals, and their accountants, that I tend to nod more than I say yes. Keeps it off the record. So, what's new?'

Tarpin told him about Hilary Cartwright and the Tim Clifford book.

'You going to take a look?'

'Of course. What d'you think?'

'If he's really on to something new, yes, we'd go for it. Hilary's right. Serial killers are in, but it's more than that with the Ripper. He really is the first notorious serial sex murderer. Of course we'll go for it, as long as he hasn't come up with a name.' He chewed another mouthful of meatball. 'Phil, I have my own publishing theory about the Ripper. People will go on reading stuff regarding those murders as long as nobody brings along absolute proof of Jack's identity. The sting goes out of it if you can conclusively name the killer. That's why Ripper books sell, because nobody can, with absolute certainly, name Jack. I should imagine one with Tim Clifford's name on it would be more than a modest success. But, beware killing the goose that lays the golden egg.'

'You didn't hear about the book from me.'

'I didn't hear anything. Come to think of it, you're not the only one to be offered an exclusive. The London *Sunday Times* Insight team are putting together a book on the Hong Kong inquiry. You been following that?'

Tarpin had not even noticed that the inquiry was taking place. 'The wolves baying for the Special Air Service's blood? Shoot-to-kill policy? All that stuff?'

'Looks like it. They're bringing the SAS people on, incognito and behind screens, like the Gibraltar inquiry. One senior officer – Officer A – and Soldiers B through G. They haven't had their say yet. Up to now, it's been eye witnesses, the Hong Kong police, and the pathologist. Usual business, with a heavy Queen's Counsel acting for the families of the victims. He's really torn into some of the eye witnesses. I guess it's going to be the same as Gibraltar, with nobody really any the wiser at the end of the day.'

The inquiry into the three Provos killed in Gibraltar had been marked as a whitewash by many journalists. Certainly there had been conflicting evidence from the eye witnesses. There were also later charges of the media rigging some of their own onlookers who were later proved not to be credible.

'A bloody circus. We going to do the book?'

'I've given them a solid maybe. We've got first refusal, and have to commit within forty-eight hours of the inquiry's verdict. I'd be grateful if you'd read everything as it comes out. I'll have the current stuff Xeroxed for you, and everything else as it appears. *Time* and *Newsweek* are topping it up and doing features when it's over.'

'And we buy it sight unseen?'

Palestino nodded, 'Yeah, but we don't pay the earth.'

As they walked back to the office, he gave his lightning grin. 'I'll be interested to hear what Liz thinks of the letters. Talk it over with her, Phillip. In spite of the brashness, she's a very sound editor.'

Back in his office there was a pile of messages waiting. Two authors needed to talk, and there was a relaxed invitation for him to call Hilary Cartwright. He finally got through to her around four-thirty.

'When can we do the legal stuff, Phillip? I'd like you to take a look as soon as possible.'

He told her that his schedule was tight and, whatever, he would not be able to even look at Tim Clifford's manuscript until the weekend. 'I want to read it as soon as I can, Hilary,' he told her, sensing her disappointment. 'But, truly, I can't clear space for it until then.'

'We've done the British deal. Six figures, even in these straitened times.'

'Are you saying that unless you have an answer tomorrow we can't do business?' He was an old hand at dealing with agents.

'Well . . . '

'Because, my dear, if that's the case I'll have to let it go.'

He sounded convincing enough because she came back with, 'Philip, I really want you to have it. Pudney would do the job properly. I know it.'

'Then let's do the legal stuff late Friday, and I'll read it over the weekend.'

There was a pause, as though she was wrestling with a difficult decision. 'We'd have your answer by Monday?'

'A week today. Tuesday. I doubt if anyone else could do it as quickly.'

Another stretch of silence. 'Okay, Phillip. Can we fix the handover now?'

They set it for five o'clock on Friday. Then she asked it he would like to have that dinner date they had talked about. It was Tarpin's turn to pause. Somehow she sounded too like Sukie, and more eager than she had done when he first mentioned it. The fatigue was catching up with him, and he felt there should be a distancing before he saw her in a non-professional environment. Eventually he pleaded a terribly tight week. 'Let's fix up something when I see you on Friday.'

Did he imagine it, or did she sound disappointed? He picked up the telephone again and rang through to Liz Oliver's office. She answered on the third ring, sounding snappy. Her PA's going to get hell for not being there, he thought.

'Liz, it's Phillip. You up to your eyes in work?'

'Aren't we all?'

'Sure, but I need to talk to you about a possible project. If it's not good today, can I fix a time for later in the week?'

'How long'll it take?'

'Initially? Oh, a couple of hours, I guess.'

'Phillip, that's lunch, or a dinner date. There aren't enough hours in the day.' Her voice carried that tone women use when they want to put up a protective wall.

'Okay, let's make it a dinner date.'

'All right, why not? When?' Sharp, almost uninterested.

'You doing anything tonight?' It came out pat, without him even thinking about it. Conscience nudged him. He was really too tired to discuss the letters tonight.

'Only reading manuscripts and doing notes for a session with Goodchild.'

Harley Goodchild was a military analyst, with a special knowledge of the politico-military link. He had a popular style, and a nose for scandals and cover-ups between the military and the establishment. He was a number-one box-office draw, and his books always ended up on the lists because of their readable quality and his knack of creating controversy. The new one was outgunning Bob Woodward in his claims of dissension between the Pentagon and the White House during the Gulf Crisis.

'Any good?' he asked.

'He's got a lot more dirt than Woodward. My only concern is the lawyers. They've flagged a dozen passages. Oh, yes, there is something else.'

'And?'

'If all he says is true, there's no way we could have won Desert Storm. Our troops would have been shooting at each other all the time; aircraft would have flown up each other's tail pipes, and every Scud would've been bang on target.'

'Can you leave it for one evening?'

'I guess.'

'Pick you up at five-thirty?'

'I'll be ready. Look forward to it,' in a tone that suggested it was the last thing to which she was looking forward. Perhaps Peter had been wrong. Maybe Ms Elizabeth Oliver was not the right person after all.

He called Le Relais, where he was just becoming known. Yes, Mr Tarpin, they said. Certainly, Mr Tarpin. We look forward to seeing you, Mr Tarpin.

She wore a high-necked silk blouse under a beige suit with a mini-length skirt which showed off her long legs. How in heaven, Tarpin wondered, could such an elegant girl look so damned severe? Then he saw it was her hair: short, styled with a tight curving wave at the front. It would have taken hundred-knot winds to knock that out of place and it did nothing to soften her face. The hair style was lamb dressed as mutton.

She gave him a tight little smile that travelled nowhere near her eyes, which was a shame, because they were clear blue, the lids long-lashed. She could have eaten most men with one bat of an eyelid, like a Venus flytrap.

They rode down in the elevator and she stayed firmly on his left, with a bag slung over her right shoulder, like some kind of barrier, to make certain they did not touch. In the cab they made small talk all the way to the restaurant.

'What d'you think of Brandt's new manuscript?' she asked, not looking at him. Cyril Brandt was proving to be a headache. After a huge success with a book on the FBI during the Hoover years, he had come up with a tough, take-no-prisoners assassination of the Kennedy dynasty, and was asking the earth for it.

'He's not telling us anything new.' Tarpin studied her face. He presumed that a popular novelist might have taken the easy way out and described her as a blonde Jamie Lee Curtis type: she had the same bone structure and could be really something if she loosened up on the severe hair style.

She met his eyes, then looked away, as though disconcerted. 'I'm advising that we turn him down. It'll only make that kind of money if we pour in a massive publicity budget.'

'I'll back you on that.'

'Good.' She sounded as though it was his duty to back her.

They were settled in the restaurant and had ordered when she asked about the project. 'I really haven't got all night, so if we could get on with it.' Her attitude was really unpardonable, and her personal dislike of him showed like a rash.

For a moment he wondered if this was her problem. Had she expected to take over the non-fiction? 'Okay, Liz,' he said, willing himself to remain calm. 'How do you view World War Two?'

'From this table, or in front of the TV watching the late Duke Wayne storming the beaches of Iwo Jima?' She did not even crack a smile.

'From your not inexperienced place in the world of publishing.' Liz Oliver, he considered, had big problems. The humour was there but it stayed deadpan. Even seated, her body seemed tense, as though she expected Tarpin to, at least, mug her at any minute. 'What I'm asking is does World War Two still play?'

She gave a little nod. 'The Battle of Britain played in 1990 – the fiftieth anniversary – and last year there were six one-volume histories which all sold well. We did one of them, and it did very well. Book club and everything. Why?'

'I'm thinking about the social history of the time. What it was like to live, love and lose in wartime Britain.'

She frowned, was about to say something, then stopped as the waiter placed the *Coquilles Saint-Jacques* in front of her.

Tarpin had settled for the smoked salmon. Sukie used to say that, as far as food was concerned, he was the most unadventurous man she had ever known.

'The social history of wartime Britain,' Liz began, then gave a little mirthless laugh. 'That's rather like asking about the humorous aspects of the Holocaust.' He could almost taste the bitterness, and she cut her eyes away.

Her attitude was so belligerent that he could not let it pass. 'What happened, Liz?' he asked, his voice dropping, even soothing.

'I don't want to talk about it.' Then a little sniff. 'I'm sorry. I must seem very rude.'

'Just a lot. I think you should talk about it. I think you owe me some explanation. I ask you about the social history of the UK during Big Two, and you look like you would be pleased to see me flayed alive.' He spoke flatly, with no rancour. 'Liz, I'm asking you as a friend, not head of the department.'

'Beware Brits offering friendship,' she muttered.

'We're not all the same, you know.'

'You might be wrong about that. Lightning doesn't strike twice? You could have fooled me.'

'Do we have a problem, Elizabeth? If so, I've a right to know.'

'It's my problem. I do my job. If you don't like the way I work . . . '

'You're the most intelligent and skilful editor we have.'

'Then that's okay. As long as I do my job to your satisfaction . . . Look, Phillip, let's just talk about this project. I really don't think we know each other well enough for me to . . . '

'Come on, tell me, Elizabeth. I asked you out to discuss something which is pretty personal, though you had no way of knowing it, and you behave rather like a child in a tantrum. You *can* trust me, you know.'

'I can? My father thought that. Then I followed in Daddy's footsteps and made the same mistake.'

'And that was . . . ?'

She told him. Quick, short, caustic sentences, some tinged with the acerbic humour he had come to recognize as her trademark. Her father had been a B17 pilot with the Eighth US Army Air Force in World War Two. Like so many of the young men who faced indescribable danger in the skies over Europe during the early forties, he had fallen in love with an English girl – 'From Lincoln where they're not as green as you'd think.' They were married – 'He said that, in retrospect, the ceremony was more like the ritual for hara-kiri.'

She was adamant that her father had tried to make the marriage work. 'He stayed with her for fifteen years, and life was a battlefield. She loathed America, and, I think, loathed my father. She treated him like shit, but he tried, and she never attempted to leave him. Me? My childhood was lived out among their rages. When the marriage fell apart – he left, taking me with him – I found it difficult to adjust. I had no guidelines against which to measure a normal life.'

'A difficult lady, your mother. So was mine.'

'Difficult? She was certifiable. In the end they did put her away. Then she committed suicide. I've been in analysis, Phillip, and I know I'm scarred for life.'

That was the least of it, he thought. He also felt it was sad that an intelligent, brilliant, beautiful young woman should be so marked by her childhood. He could see them in the way she told of the loveless, skirmishing marriage that became, to her father, an extension of the war.

Then, in the same, clipped, uneasy way, she told him of her marriage. To a British journalist: a drunk and a womanizer who gave her little peace of mind, and less security. 'Thank heaven there weren't children. I eventually got out and began to build a career for myself.'

'And a good one.' Tarpin looked straight at her, knowing she was probably an emotional time bomb. A woman who, in moments of depression, could wrap her mind in a shroud of self-pity and rail against the world, 'Why me?'

The main course arrived, and she began to attack her food, using little, violent gestures, spearing meat as though she was cutting out the hearts of her mother and the husband who had betrayed her. Her behaviour had been quite appalling, but Tarpin had already started to think of her as a victim. He had always been a sucker for victims.

'Let me tell you my story,' he began.

'Must you, Phillip?'

'If we're going to deal with the possible project, yes, I must.'

She looked up at him from her plate. 'You asked me to tell you, and I did.'

'Yes, but I also asked you here to discuss a possible book.'

She lowered her eyes again, like a child caught out in some taboo activity. 'Oh, Lord,' she said, and this time she smiled. 'I'm sorry. It's been a particularly bad day. I get low sometimes and spit everything out. You must think I'm a basket case.'

'No more than I am.' He started to tell her everything, from his mother's death, to Uncle Bob's revelations, through Sukie's murder, and on to the letters.

Elizabeth Oliver stopped eating when he got to Sukie's death. By the time he started to tell her about the letters she was listening, her eyes moist, and her perfect white teeth gnawing at her bottom lip.

Tarpin thought he could just detect a small movement of shame in her eyes.

– 2 –

They had finished with Kathleen Fagin, but she was jittery and withdrawn. She had also become hostile, even though they were sticking to their part of the bargain. Later, the evidence became tinged with suspicion, but those charged with her security were able to explain everything. She had asked to be resettled in Australia, and they agreed. She would go first to somewhere out of England – Spain, they said.

Arrangements were made to spirit her lover, Danny Musgrove, from Long Kesh to Wormwood Scrubs in London. From there he would be taken to Spain and they would be reunited. Nothing would get into the press. Fagin had been allowed to speak by telephone – a very secure line – with Musgrove. They had a done deal.

It appeared that had it not been for the tricks they had played to ease more information out of the girl, things might have been different. There was no doubt that she had become a liability. Nobody suspected that she would work out the means to make contact with the Provos. That is what they stated, under oath, later.

According to the evidence, she managed it in a particularly simple manner. A letter to her mother, she said. That was not really wise, they told her, but she insisted. Surely they had ways of posting it in the North? They could read the letter. She would be careful.

There was talk of waiting. Posting the letter when she was well away. But, in the end she prevailed, playing on what conscience was left. They had performed the dirtiest tricks in the book. Now it was over they should keep the faith with her.

Neither of the two officers who screened the letter picked up any telltale signs. Luckily they kept a copy of the long, seemingly innocent, three pages which began, 'Dear Mam'. For some reason, nobody bothered to check if her mother was at the address on the envelope. Both of the security officers were very shaken when it later transpired that Kathleen Fagain's mother had died four years ago. But the words she scribbled appeared innocent enough. Later, the investigating officers did not think it was odd that the copy of Fagin's letter had not been Xeroxed but laboriously typed. This, it was explained, was a formality. Kathleen Fagin's handwriting was difficult to read, and they merely wanted a clean copy for the files.

At the inquiry, a very senior man from GCHQ – where they knew about such things as codes and ciphers – said only an expert could have unbuttoned the hidden message. He also swore, under oath, that the words would be far from innocent to the people in the North who might have read them.

Again – too late, it seemed – they realized they should never have mentioned the scheme of flying her to the American base at Rota, arranging to keep her off base in a safe house in the small Andalusian town.

They made the move by night, and everything was very relaxed because the whole operation was so secure and watertight.

Nobody queried the car, latching on to them as they came off the base. Nobody paid any attention when it overtook them as they stopped in the side street, in front of the house, which had been arranged by the Security Service.

The two men emerged from the darkness, taking everyone by surprise. There were several plops and flashes. One of the security detail flung himself across the girl, but it was too late. The gunmen were obviously professional. Nobody had time to give chase.

Kathleen Fagin just lay on the cobbles with seven 9mm bullets in her chest. Nobody else was even scratched. The police were alerted about twenty minutes later. Naturally the security around her had attempted to resuscitate her first. That explained the delay. The ambulance arrived after the police, and the body was quietly moved back on to the base. That was the official story accepted by the court of inquiry after the event. Nobody questioned it. Just as nobody questioned the suicide of Danny Musgrove, in his cell in the Scrubs. Things like that happened all the time.

The only fact that threw any suspicion on the events, as told at the inquiry, was the Provos neither confirmed nor denied killing Fagin.

– 3 –

Paddy Flanagan had been put on the job straight away. 'It's best you learn the New York streets in your own way,' Murphy told him.

So, he had seen the couple emerge from the office building. He liked the look of the girl. Tall and rangy. Sexy in a subtle way. He was so close to them that he even heard the target tell the driver to take them to a restaurant called Le Relais on Madison and 63rd. He found it easily, though he had a long wait. Just over three and a half hours.

When the couple came out, they looked much more friendly than when he had first seen them, leaving the office building.

Paddy Flanagan was unarmed, but he followed them home just the same. The trick, Murphy had advised him, was to become part of the everyday scenery. There would be many other long waits for Flanagan.

On the next night, he picked up the target again. He was with the same blonde woman, and they were laughing as they came through the big doors, surrounded by other men and women looking tired and grey after a long day's sweat at the treadmills of international commerce.

This time, the girl accompanied the target back to his apartment.

And the best of luck to you both, Flanagan thought. Make the most of it. Youse haven't got long to go.

TEN

– 1 –

Once she accepted the fact that Phillip Tarpin had been a victim – like herself – Liz Oliver's whole attitude changed. It was not an overnight conversion. Not any Paul on the road to Damascus sensation. Her hard shell was still there, and her self-involvement would take a long time to disappear completely. Yet, over dinner that first night at Le Relais, she started to regard Tarpin as a friend.

They ended up talking. Not of the possible project concerning his mother's letters, but about their separate pasts. Before the meal was over, he had her laughing for the first time.

'I didn't speak to my mother, didn't even see her for the last three years of her life. But I was lucky, I had Sukie then. However unpleasant it seems now, we simply laughed at her eccentricities. Laughter's a good healer, Liz. It's often a mistake to view your own life too seriously. As someone once said, you're not going to get out of it alive.'

If asked, at that point, why he used precious time and energy in an attempt to transform Liz, he would have admitted that he had no idea. Yes, she was very attractive, but, emotionally, she was a wreck. An accident waiting to happen. The last thing he wanted was any close involvement.

Later he was to realize that it was inevitable. Yet, to begin with, he simply reflected on the curious paradox that was Elizabeth Oliver. Her work as a non-fiction editor, he had to admit, was much better than his own. She had an encyclopedic memory, spoke four languages, and turned out to be the best-read woman he had ever met.

She could look at a difficult page of manuscript and immediately see what was wrong or clumsy about the way an author had presented a theory, or laid out facts. She also had that wonderful gift, rare in editors, of making notations, so that when the author went through the pages, doing the rewrites, he, or she, would end up thinking the changes were his alone. Elizabeth never claimed the credit due to her as the editor.

This professional side of her life was very much at odds with the woman who could wallow in self-pity, and become suddenly unbalanced by events. Even as early as the first dinner together, Tarpin realized that anyone close to Elizabeth had to beware of the spectres that lurked in her head. An innocent, possibly unthinking, remark, could throw her into a blaze of anger, often ending in tears.

Over the dessert, he made a comment about the dedication true editors had to maintain towards their authors. 'It's sometimes like being a doctor,' he said casually.

Elizabeth flushed and exploded into a tirade – he did not have to remind *her* what it was like. She had wanted to be a writer and found she could not do *that* job, so she had gone into publishing as an editor. He did not have to tell her how much of a vocation *that* was. She had worked with authors until the early hours of the morning: in her apartment, or in a hotel room, or the office. *She* had given up weekends to books; she had even left a party – 'My party. My *birthday* party' – to sit with an author who had hit a difficult patch There was nothing, she said, that Phillip Tarpin could tell *her* about the vocational life of an editor.

He learned, from that spat alone, to be very careful not to say anything she might misconstrue as a reflection on her work, or even her lifestyle, which was, he soon discovered, a pretty lonely existence.

She thanked him when he finally dropped her off at her apartment, leaning forward and kissing the air next to his cheek. 'I'm looking forward to seeing the letters,' she smiled, and was off, long leggy strides, with the breeze whipping at the mini skirt, pushing it into a mould of her thighs. The breeze did not even move a single hair on her head.

His office telephone rang almost before he had seated himself at his desk the following morning.

'Phillip, when can we look at those letters?' She sounded a trifle breathy, he thought, though it might have been his imagination.

He told her he had no time today, and she immediately suggested the evening, after office hours. 'I got to thinking about them last night. The sooner I see them, the quicker we can make some kind of decision.'

He told her they were in his apartment. If she would like to take pot luck with him, they could look over them tonight. She sounded delighted. 'I can be ready by six. Not before, I'm afraid.'

'Six'll be fine.'

Then, at five-thirty, Palestino sent down a pile of cuttings on the SAS/IRA Hong Kong shootings inquiry, together with a note asking if he could let him have his first reactions by the morning.

When he picked up Elizabeth at her office, he said his evening was going to be shot to pieces, but she could still come around and start reading. 'I've got to do some homework for Peter,' he added.

'That'll be fine.' She was smiling, and he noticed, with a tiny double-take, that the hair had lost its lacquered solidity, and was combed into a little, blonde cap. The wave had gone, and he had been right: her face *was* softer.

He called for a cab, and they decided to pick up a bottle of wine and some subs to eat while they read in his apartment. Going towards the cab, Tarpin saw someone out of the corner of his eye – a man, tall, casually dressed, with rumpled hair and a vaguely familiar face: the features of a man who, when younger, might have been described as elfin. He even turned, in the back of the cab, and saw the man trying to flag down the next taxi.

The image disturbed him, and he could not say why. There was something recognizable about him. Publishing? An author he had once known? A long-forgotten friendship?

'You okay, Phillip?' Even her voice was less edgy than on the previous night.

'Just thought I saw someone I used to know.'

'Oh, who?'

He gave an embarrassed little laugh. 'Stupid. Can't put a name to him.'

'You want to go back?'

'No. But I wish . . . Never mind.' He stopped quickly because part of the uneasy feeling came from a thought – nothing definite, just an obscure, clouded, memory – that he had seen the man on the previous evening. Not outside the office building, but as they were leaving Le Relais. If his life had depended on it, he could not have sworn it was the same man. But the image flitted in and out of his mind for the rest of the evening.

They called at a liquor store and a Subway on the short journey back to his apartment, and arrived there with two one-foot subs, stuffed with ham, cheese, tomatoes and all the trimmings.

'This is fun.' Liz looked around the apartment and, for a second, he wondered if she was thinking it could have been hers if only the board had given her the job instead of handing it to Tarpin – the Brit. But, when he looked again, there was no trace of jealousy in her eyes. Just a pleasant, almost comfortable, smile.

They ate the subs, drank the wine, and then Tarpin made coffee, settling Liz on the couch with the piles of letters. She took off the jacket of her suit – it was similar to the one she wore on the previous evening, though black this time – and curled up with her legs under her. The skirt rode very high, displaying her thighs, almost to the junction. He was sure she had caught him looking at her, but she showed no embarrassment or unease. She merely glanced at him, then leaned over to pick up the first bundle of letters, her head bowing and the short hair falling free, towards her face.

Tarpin sat at the table and began to read the clippings on the Hong Kong inquiry. It was all very familiar. The coroner made an opening statement, saying they were not here as a court, to find guilt or innocence. Rather, they were to hear the evidence and decide whether there were any grounds for further investigation by police, or any other agency appointed by the Crown.

Then, the bystanders were led through the incident, by the QC appointed by the Crown, and cross-examined by the Counsel appearing for the families of the three deceased men. This last, Sir Archibald Wedding, was a formidable, well-known figure at the bar, considered eccentric, yet brilliant when it came to getting at the truth – or at least the truth as he wanted the court to understand it. His cross-questioning had at least three of the bystanders tied up in knots, contradicting themselves and looking like idiots with no real powers of observation, by the time they left the stand.

He did similar things to the pathologist whose evidence was clinically brutal, in the way of most pathologists. Archie Wedding actually got him to admit that each of the dead men could well have been killed by the first bullet to hit him: thereby establishing in people's minds a condition of overkill.

'Doctor,' he had said, with what one reporter described as a friendly smile, 'you have told us that any of the bullets you found in these unfortunate men could have killed them? Yes or no?'

'Yes, but . . . '

'Thank you. If this is the case, can you in any way point to the one bullet – in each victim, of course – that actually killed?'

The pathologist had produced a chart of each of the corpses, showing exactly where the bullets entered the bodies.

'I've already said, any of them would have killed.'

'Quite; and these bullets, they are known as Splat rounds are they not?'

'Yes.'

'An unpleasant name for a bullet – Splat. It sounds almost obscene, does it not? Like something from a particularly violent comic book. Splat! Wham! Crunch! Why, Doctor, are they called Splat rounds?'

'I am not responsible for the naming of military equipment, sir. I was simply made aware that the bullets are known by that name.'

'Oh, come, come, Doctor. You've seen the results of these Splat rounds. You've examined them – the results, I mean. Going on what you saw at the post mortems, you can surely hazard a guess at why the British military refers to these bullets as Splat.' According to the reporter, each time he said 'Splat', he spat out the word, as though conjoining the word with the sound of metal hitting tissue.

'I rarely allow myself to guess, sir. I am a pathologist. That is a science. There is no guesswork involved.'

'Ah, I see. Yes, Doctor, thank you for a definition of your work.' He had paused, seemingly for effect. 'Let me put it another way. From your examination of the bodies, would you say that the bullets all behaved in a very similar way? Yes, or no?'

'Yes. Yes, all the wounds were similar.'

'Good, then am I not right when I say that the Splat round is designed to make the same kind of wound? Is it not true to say that one of the purposes of this type of ammunition is to prevent what is known as shoot-through?'

'I believe so.'

'And negative shoot-through is what, exactly?'

'As I understand it, the ammunition is constructed in a way which prevents a bullet from passing through a human body and travelling on to hit a second person – an innocent bystander perhaps.'

'Yes, good. Doctor, am I right in saying this ammunition is designed with yet another purpose in mind?'

'I couldn't say.'

'I'm surprised, but tell me if I am wrong. I understand that the actual bullet, when coming into contact with flesh and bone, peels off a layer or two of its jacket. This peeling off achieves two objectives – correct me if I'm wrong – it slows the bullet down, so that it will not pass through the victim, and it also spreads out inside the target, thereby inflicting a terrible wound. Am I correct, Doctor?'

'That seems to be the case, sir. Yes.'

'And all the wounds you examined in the bodies of these unfortunate men *were* terrible wounds, were they not?'

'It depends, sir.'

'On what?'

'On what other terrible wounds you use as a yardstick.'

'Doctor, please don't treat me like an idiot. They *were* all terrible wounds, correct?'

'Yes.'

'And, from what you have already said, any one of those bullets would have killed. Any one of those terrible wounds could have been fatal.'

'I suppose – yes.'

'And any one of these wounds would have "stopped" the man who was hit? I believe "stopped" is the technical term used by law enforcement agencies, and the military, is it not?'

'I believe so.'

'Then wouldn't you agree that there was some considerable overkill here? If one bullet would have killed, or even stopped, one man, there was no need to add further bullets. You've told us that each body was penetrated four times. Twelve bullets in all entered the three men. Correct?'

'Correct, sir.'

'In military terms, have you heard the expression "soft-kill option"?'

'I've heard it, sir. Yes.'

'It means the use of this kind of ammunition, does it not? Splat and similar types of bullets?'

'I believe so.'

'And when you look at those riddled corpses, with their terrible wounds – four in each body – would you say that you have seen the results of a soft-kill option? No, you need not answer that, sir. I think we can judge for ourselves. Four bullets in each man, where one would have been enough.'

Sir Archibald had made his point, Tarpin thought, turning to the most current reports which dealt with the first questioning and cross-questioning of the SAS man called Soldier B.

'Phillip?' Elizabeth spoke softly from the couch. 'Can you explain something to me?'

'Sure, what?' He pulled himself back from the Hong Kong courtroom, to the present, rising and going over to Elizabeth, leaning against the back of the couch, to look over her shoulder.

'This letter.' She held up a page of flimsy paper. 'There's a long paragraph that seems to be a kind of code, or it's something peculiarly English that I don't understand.'

'I think they used a code some of the time.' He took Paul Bartholemew's letter and began to read:

You remember the subject we talked about – the one we agreed to call 'millstone'. I was a little concerned. No. that isn't true, I was very worried when you joked about it the other night. 'Millstone' is truly what I told you: a weight around the necks of my family. We've traced it back a long way – over three generations. My dear love, you must *never, never* treat this subject lightly. The other night you said it sounded like one of those stupid horror films – *The Curse of the Bartholemews*, I think you called it, like *The Mummy's Curse* and other such titles. My darling, it really is the curse of our family, and you *must* take it seriously. I cannot stress this too strongly. I learned about it from my father when I was not even in my teens, and you know what has happened since. So, please, Vera dear, never joke about it again. I'll tell you more when we next meet – and that can't be too soon for me.

'Does it suggest anything to you? Am I missing something?' she asked.

Tarpin shook his head. 'Millstone,' he said quietly. 'Not immediately. In any case, Paul Bartholemew, my father, wouldn't use a word through which you could trace anything. He was a trained clandestine operator.' He explained Bartholemew's position in the Special Operations Executive; then he had to explain what the SOE was.

'You think this is for real?' she asked. 'I mean the guy's a bit of a joker. You think this thing, "millstone", is to be taken seriously?'

'Looks that way.' He said he had not noticed the passage when going through the letters. 'Mind you, I did skip a lot. Maybe it's an idea to keep your eyes open for any other references to – what was it? Millstone?'

'As in round your neck, yes.'

He went back to reading the Hong Kong reports, and half an hour later, having been through all the clippings with reports of the first day's questioning of Soldier B, he arrived at the beginning of Sir Archie Wedding's cross-examination.

'Soldier B. Soldier B. Will you come and have some tea with me?' Sir Archie was being his usual obtuse self.

'I beg your pardon, sir?'

'Just musing, Soldier B. Musing. As in Soldier, Soldier, won't you marry me, with your musket, fife and drum. You married, Soldier B?'

'I don't think I have to answer that, sir.' He appealed to the coroner who said it was not necessary.

'Very well. Here's one you *are* allowed to answer, I'm sure. We have heard you were in charge of what was called Buster Group. Correct?'

'Yes, sir.'

'Then I think we can all take it that you are a commissioned officer. Correct?'

'I am Soldier B, sir. I was in charge of Buster Group in Hong Kong, on the date in question. I am not obliged to give you any further information about my military status.'

'Especially not your name, rank and service number, eh, Buster Leader?'

Soldier B did not reply, so Sir Archibald asked him again. 'Eh, Buster Leader?'

'I am Soldier B, sir. I *was* Buster Leader on the date before this court. I will answer to the name Soldier B.'

'For a trained soldier you're a mite squeamish about things, Soldier B.'

'In what way, sir?'

'Well, you and your comrades in arms seem to be in hiding. You like to hide behind the skirts of authority, Soldier B? I think it's very unsoldierly myself.'

'With respect, sir, I think it unlikely that you have ever been involved in anti-terrorist operations.'

'You are calling the Provisional Irish Republican Army terrorists, Soldier B?'

'I am, sir.'

'But you'd agree, I'm certain, that this depends on who you are, and where you are . . . '

'If you mean that one man's terrorist is another man's freedom fighter, yes, sir. It is something brought home very clearly to all military personnel engaged in operations against the PIRA.'

'Is it, indeed?'

'Yes, sir.'

'Well, Soldier B, what did you think these three men were, on that morning in Hong Kong? Terrorists, or freedom fighters?'

'They were both, sir. But to us they were unequivocally terrorists.'

'Who told you this?'

'I don't follow you, sir.'

'Who actually told you that the three men you shot to death were terrorists?'

'It was inherent in our briefing, sir.'

'And who briefed you?'

'An SBO, sir. A senior British officer.'

'Just you? Did you have to pass on the briefing to the other soldiers – let me see, I have their names here – yes, they also seem to be incognito. Soldiers C, D, E, F and G. Did you have to brief them?'

'No, sir. We were all briefed at the same time.'

'By this senior officer?'

'Yes, sir.'

'Anyone else present?'

'Yes, sir.'

'Would it be too much trouble for you to say who else was there besides yourself, and the other brave, but shy, soldiers C through G?'

'There was a senior member of the Hong Kong police, and a member of the Security Service.'

'Ah, the Security Service. That would be MI5, wouldn't it?'

'I have no way of knowing, sir.'

'But the Security Service *is* known as MI5, is it not?'

'I've heard the term, sir. But I know it simply as the Security Service.'

'I see. What were your orders, Soldier B?'

'We were to keep the men – O'Brien, Casey and Flynn – under observation.'

'Just under observation?'

'No, sir, we were to apprehend them, if it became obvious they intended to harm the royal personages who were about to land from the royal yacht.'

'Isn't it more correct to say you were ordered to kill them, Soldier B?'

'No, sir.'

'Then why did you?'

'Why did we what, sir?'

'Shoot to death Sean O'Brien, Kevin Casey and the man Flynn.'

'Because, when we tried to apprehend them, they made threatening movements, sir.'

'Threatening?'

'Yes, sir.'

'What did they threaten you with, Soldier B? A water pistol? A rubber dagger?'

'From their actions we believed they were about to detonate a bomb under, or near, the dais from which His Royal Highness was to review the honour guard. I also thought they were about to open fire on us.'

'But they had no weapons, Soldier B. They were unarmed.'

'They gave the impression of being armed sir. They also gave the impression of trying to explode a device by remote control.'

'Really? I think we should go into more detail about that a little later. Soldier B, when did you first learn these three men were in Hong Kong?'

'The night before, sir.'

'The night before.'

'Sir.'

'And when did you arrive in the Colony?'

'The night before, sir.'

'Ah. So you learned about the men – O'Brien, Casey and Flynn – after you arrived in Hong Kong?'

'We learned who they were, sir, Yes.'

'You mean you had been told something before you arrived?'

'We had been briefed by an intelligence officer in London, sir. The information was that a Provisional IRA Active Service Unit was in Hong Kong.'

'And you were sent to destroy that unit, weren't you?'

'No, sir. We were sent to contain it.'

'Did you know where the men were staying?'

'We were told where they were staying, yes.'

'And where was that?'

'The Regent Hotel in Kowloon.'

'So, you were told that a dangerous Active Service Unit of the PIRA was in town, staying in the Regent Hotel – which is a pleasant place. I am staying there myself. You were told all this?'

'Yes, sir.'

'Then why did you not simply proceed to the Regent and take charge of these three desperate, unarmed, men at the hotel, instead of shooting them in cold blood, in public?'

'We . . . ' Soldier B began, but Sir Archibald Wedding stopped him, suggesting to the coroner that they should break for the day as it was almost four-thirty.

Tarpin glanced at his watch. 'Good grief, it's almost midnight, Liz. I must get you home.'

'Why?' She raised her head from the papers strewn around the couch.

'Because we both have work to do tomorrow.'

'So? I've been working quite happily here, tonight, I can stay, can't I?'

He took a quick deep breath. 'Sure, if you want to. I'll take the couch. You can have the bed.'

'No, Phillip. We're friends. I can sleep in your bed, surely?'

'Elizabeth, I don't really think that's . . . '

'Just for the cuddle, Phillip. I'm not suggesting we get further entangled. Not yet anyway.'

'Look, Liz. Perhaps you haven't looked in the mirror lately, but you're a highly desirable young woman. I don't know if I can be trusted . . . '

'Let's see,' she smiled, then dropped her eyes, almost modestly. 'How about some more coffee? These letters are fascinating, but what a terrible way to find out about your father, Phillip.'

He hardly heard her. Phillip Tarpin was more concerned about how he could possibly share the same bed with Elizabeth Oliver without touching her.

As though reading his mind, she repeated, 'Just a cuddle, Phillip. I didn't get many cuddles when I was a kid.'

– 2 –

He was walking down a long passage, and it was dark. From far away he thought he could hear a whimpering cry. It frightened him, but at the same time made him try to hurry. Someone was in danger. He thought he knew who it was, but his feet seemed to stick on the thick, heavy carpet. It was like trying to walk in treacle.

He put his hand out, and felt a wall, then something damp. At that moment he broke into light and could see, and recognize, the corridor. He was in London. He looked at his hand and it was covered in blood.

The walls were also covered in blood, and he saw that the

stickiness, which made walking so difficult, was also blood. It was up to his ankles.

Then he started towards the door, and saw the man come out and look him straight in the face, smiling, like an old elf.

'Phillip! Philip! It's all right, honey, you're only having a bad dream.'

He woke, to find Elizabeth Oliver cradling him in her arms. It was dark, but he clung to her, for he was still half in his nightmare. Half in and half out, for he had seen the man last night. He had been outside the Pudney building. Before that he had only seen his picture, on the Photofits and the grainy snapshot they had blown up and put on the posters. It was the man they were looking for. The one they wanted to question about Sukie's murder.

In the dream, the man had given him a hideous smile, and blood had run from his mouth. Tarpin knew it was his blood bubbling from between the man's teeth.

'He killed Sukie,' he said, and Elizabeth just went on hugging him, telling him it was all right.

ELEVEN

– 1 –

He tried to reach for her, but she had him in a tight grip, soothing him like a child, one hand stroking his head, the other around him, pinning his hands. When her grip relaxed she asked if he was all right, and he half sobbed, realizing he had never truly wept for Sukie.

After a while he kissed her on the lips, his tongue penetrating her mouth. She responded, then stiffened, drawing away. Tarpin realized that she was the first woman he had kissed since Sukie's death.

'Just for a cuddle, Phillip,' she whispered with a trace of admonishment. 'You've had a lousy dream.' Then she released him and slid from the bed. Her body, in the half light of dawn, was every man's fantasy – smooth marble, curves and valleys, the skin glowing. Tarpin closed his eyes and willed his shrieking body into passivity.

He heard the shower running, but in his mind the reflection of his dream remained clear, then the word millstone came into his head, and he remembered last night – the section of his father's letter which had so puzzled Elizabeth. He was consciously making a connection between the dreamed terror and the word Millstone, though there could not possibly be any link between the two.

She came back into the room, half naked, and Tarpin wondered at her lack of embarrassment as she dressed, for she radiated a sexual need, as though she were performing some weird reverse striptease.

Again she asked if he was okay.

'Yes. Now, I'm okay.'

'You sure?'

'Absolutely, Liz. I'm sorry.'

'You want to talk about it?'

'No, it's to do with Sukie's death.'

He took a breath, changing his mind, on the verge of talking about the dream and the man he had recognized, when she said, 'I think you'd better try to get your grieving over, Phillip. This kind of thing isn't healthy. Maybe I shouldn't have stayed after all. I'll see you in the office.' Her coolness was complete, and he did not know how to answer her.

She did not look at him again. Her face, turned away from him, had a closed, tight expression, as if he had caused her great offence.

'Liz, I'll . . . ' he began, but she was gone, gathering her things together and walking quickly from the room. He heard the front door close, not with a slam but quietly, firmly, as though she were shutting him from her life.

He gave a mental shrug, recalling her quick changes of mood when he had first given her dinner. Again he thought of her need for help. Then he wondered if all this had been wise, deciding he would be better off not getting involved with her. Easy to think. Hard to do.

She had talked about being in analysis, and her mood swings were only part of a complex unbalanced psychology. Her actions disturbed him, almost as much as the nightmare, and the knowledge that Sukie's probable killer was here, and now, in New York.

After showering, shaving and dressing, he called Hosier & Whitehead in London to get the number of Hammersmith police station. He dialled the police number, and a calm voice with a South London accent answered. He asked for Detective Inspector Gerald Rainbow, and was told he was not in. Could he leave a message?

He gave them his office number, pausing to work out the time difference and saying he would be there within the hour and could Rainbow call him collect before ten-thirty tonight, London time – five-thirty in New York. The policeman, sitting in Hammersmith over three thousand miles away, asked what it was in connection with, and Tarpin simply said Rainbow would know. Then he gave his home number. 'If my office is closed, I'm usually here. It is urgent,' he said, and the police operator told him Mr Rainbow would get the message the moment he came in.

In his office, Tarpin called Palestino and said he had not been able to do a written memo about the Hong Kong inquiry, but if it was up to him, he would make an offer for the book on the evidence so far. 'They're obviously going to cross swords over the shoot-to-kill policy.' Then he corrected himself, saying 'the *so-called* shoot-to-kill policy.'

'They already have,' Palestino drawled. 'Knock-down drag-out shouting match. All very unpleasant, but good journalism. You don't need to write a report, Phillip.' He was sending down the latest clippings, but Tarpin could tell he had already decided to bid for the *Sunday Times* book which was obviously going to be highly controversial. The British press had made up their minds long ago that, however much the establishment denied such a policy, it existed, and was seen to exist.

He called Elizabeth's office, and her PA – a quiet, mousy girl called Emma – said she was not in. 'She's working at home today, Mr Tarpin. I'll be speaking with her later on if you've got a message.'

'Just tell her I'd like her to call me, okay?'

'Sure will, Mr Tarpin.'

Ten minutes later Rainbow called from London. 'Young Phil? What can I do for you?'

'That liaison man, Chilton?'

'Yes?'

'Can you get hold of him?'

'Maybe. What you want?'

'Well, possibly I don't want him at all. Maybe I should tell you.'

'Just as you like, Phil.'

'The man they were looking for after Ms Cartwright's . . . '

'Murder. That's the word you want, Phil. Never be shy about it. Like you should never be shy about using the word death. Better to say it out, straight off. People cover it up – they say someone has passed on or passed over. Death is a clean word.' He sounded a little drunk.

'That man's here, in New York. I saw him last night, and I think the night before as well.'

'You're sure of that?'

'Sure as I'll ever be. The man from that Photofit and the snapshot. I've seen him.'

'Really?'

'Yes, really, Gerald. I want to know what I should do – tell the cops here, or . . . ?'

'Don't tell your local police, no.' Rainbow seemed stone sober now. 'I have your numbers. Someone'll be in touch, and, Phil, don't have a go. Don't tackle him yourself, right?'

'Why not, Gerald?'

''Cos he's bloody dangerous, that's why not.'

'You know the man?'

'*Of* him, Phil. I've seen his file . . . '

'Then what's he doing lurking outside my office?'

'Someone'll be in touch, Phil. I promise you. Just watch how you go.'

When the connection was closed, Tarpin felt even more uneasy. How could it have been the same man? Yet, if it was, why would he be in New York? And why would he, Phillip Tarpin, see him? There was only one logical explanation, and he did not like to dwell too deeply on that. Sukie had been shot dead on her way into the flat. *His* flat as well as Sukie's. No, it did not make sense. Why should anyone want to kill him? A thief, disturbed by Sukie, he could understand, but someone, having killed once, coming across the Atlantic to dispose of him? No. Yet there would be logic in it. But who would want to . . . ?

He ploughed through the day. A lunch with a Harvard professor – a former adviser to the CIA – whom Palestino had been wooing to do a book on the future of the intelligence communities in the nineties. It was heavy going, and when Tarpin got back to his desk, he had decided he preferred fictional intelligence officers to their rather dull counterparts in the real world.

He had an editing session for the rest of the day, working with Fergus Frances who had produced a wonderfully amusing and illuminating book on the old burlesque theatres and artistes of New York.

Frances was a garrulous, entertaining man, and by the time they had finished, the working day was well over. Elaine, his PA, had left a stack of letters for his signature – they would be picked up by the mail room which stayed open until after eight. There was also a new batch of clippings from Palestino, and a note which said that Liz Oliver's PA had called to say that Ms Oliver would be working from home for the rest of the week, but would call him at some point if it was an urgent matter.

The inexplicable ghost of the man wanted in connection with Sukie's death prowled around his mind, leaving him jumpy. Uneasy. As he walked through the deserted editorial offices he felt a cold apprehension. Intimations of mortality? He looked at faces on the street as he walked to Luigi's, which he and Palestino used for their quiet lunches. He found himself pausing, glancing back over his shoulder, as though certain the familiar figure was behind him. There was no sign of anybody. Nobody behaved oddly or seemed to be in the least interested.

At the restaurant, the *padrone* broke into a broad smile. How nice, they didn't often see the *Dottore* in the evenings. How was Mr Palestino? Would he be joining the *Dottore*?

Tarpin chatted with the *padrone* and ordered a simple meal: *pasta fagiole* and the *scallopine Bolognese*, with a half bottle of the house white.

He had intended to begin reading the clippings over dinner, but the restaurant was not busy and the *padrone* was talkative, wanting to put the world to rights.

It was nine o'clock before he was through and out on the street, where the anxiety hit him again. He walked back to the apartment building on Fifth Avenue. Nothing unusual. Nobody behind him as far as he could tell. The night doorman had already come on duty. Like the *padrone* at Luigi's, he was talkative. Nice to see ya, Mr Tarpin, How ya doin'? What's goin' on? So, it was almost ten before he sat down to go through the continuation of the cross-examination of Soldier B by the caustic Sir Archie Wedding.

– 2 –

From his vantage point, in the doorway of a famous old book store on Fifth Avenue, Flanagan watched the target chat with his doorman, then go into the building. He walked a block east, found a public telephone and called the number, as he had been instructed.

Connor Murphy answered with a curt, 'Yes?'

'He's in and looks cosy for the night. Alone.'

'Go home then, my boyo.'

'I thought I was to . . . ?'

'You are, to be sure. Your day will come, but before he goes I'm going to play with him. I told you that already. See me tomorrow. Usual time, usual place.' Murphy plunged Flanagan's voice into oblivion, putting the receiver down.

'Well, Stoker, and what time did you say you had to be back on your ship?'

Stoker Gallagher. Six feet four in his bare feet, rake thin but with muscles never intended for a normal mortal, gave a cockeyed smile. His grey dead fish eyes had been known to scare even a hardened man like Connor Murphy, indeed as they did now. 'Half one in the morning. We sail at six.' Stoker Gallagher was dedicated to the cause: a man who had done terrible things to other human beings in the forty-five years of his life. Deep inside his brain he drew power and satisfaction from the crude images of pain which roamed a mind sick with brutality.

Gallagher was a useful member of the Provos, if only because he worked for a British-owned shipping line which took him from Liverpool to New York with the regularity of the lunar phases.

'You have something for me, Connor?' His voice had the same flat unfeeling quality as his eyes.

'I do, Stoker. The kind of thing you're good at. You might say you're even cut out for it.' Connor Murphy could conjure up the devil's laugh when he had a mind to do so. 'Now you do only what I tell you. No taking matters further, or embellishing the work. There's a fella we want to play with a little. Now, here's where you come in . . . ' As Murphy talked, Gallagher's smile remained, twisted on his lips. A student of the dark side of the mind might just have noticed some terrible, hellish worm stir deep in the grey eyes: there for a moment, then gone.

All the clippings took up the cross-examination as soon as it had resumed on the following day. Sir Archie was on the finest of sarcastic form.

'Now, Soldier B,' he began. 'Yesterday we talked a little about the three men you, and your comrades-in-arms, shot to death on the streets of Hong Kong; and I was asking why you didn't just march up to the Regent Hotel and take them from their rooms, without any violence. They were seen as a threat to the visiting royalty, yet, I gather you followed them through the streets, and then gunned them down. Why?'

'I've already answered that, sir.'

Sir Archie consulted his notes. 'Oh, yes. You were ordered to apprehend them, instead of which you shot them to death, because you imagined they were threatening you with no weapons, and menacing the royal couple with a bomb that was not there. That is basically what you said.'

'No, sir. I said their actions, after we told them to stop, gave us the impression they were about to detonate a device by remote control, and also exchange fire with us.'

'I've already pointed out the fact that they were unarmed, and there was no device for them to detonate.'

'With respect, sir, the means for that device were discovered in their rooms at the hotel. We'd been well briefed. The intelligence all pointed towards an attack on their royal highnesses – almost certainly with explosives – as soon as they stepped ashore.'

'You've said this before, Soldier B. And I've shown that the facts, which emerged following the killings, are not borne out by the intelligence briefing you say you were given.'

'The intelligence briefing we *were* given, sir.'

'As you wish. Tell me, Soldier B, have you seen service in Northern Ireland?'

'I'm not sure that's a pertinent question, sir.'

At this point, the coroner interrupted. 'Sir Archibald, *is* this line of questioning pertinent? Does it have a direct bearing on the incident?'

'Oh, indeed, sir. It has a very direct bearing.'

'Very well. Soldier B, you will answer the question.'

'Could Sir Archibald repeat the question, sir.'

'Yes, of course I can, though I must say for an officer of the Special Air Service you do not appear to have a very retentive memory.'

'Objection, sir.' Counsel for the Crown was on his feet. 'Nobody has said Soldier B is a commissioned officer, nor has his unit been identified.'

'Come on,' Wedding – the reports all stated – laughed out loud. 'It might not be on record, but everyone in this room knows we're dealing with the Special Air Service.'

Soldier B spoke. 'I, for one, do not know that, sir.'

'Well, I *do* know, Soldier B, and I'm asking you to tell me if you have seen service in Northern Ireland.'

'Yes, I have, sir.'

'Then what's your score, Soldier B?'

'I don't follow the question, sir.'

'I said, what is your score? How many members of the Provisional Irish Republican Army have you done to death, and how many innocent Irish men, women and children have you destroyed?'

'I deeply resent that question, sir. It is offensive.'

'It is to the memories of those you have killed.'

'A soldier doesn't keep a tally, like a cricket match, sir. I still find the question offensive.'

Again, the Coroner interrupted. 'I rather go along with the witness, Sir Archibald. I believe this is an improper question.'

'I, sir, believe it to be very proper. This soldier *is* a member of a particularly ruthless unit of Her Majesty's armed forces. Their job, in Northern Ireland, is to *kill* members of the PIRA. That's the sole reason for their deployment in the province.'

Counsel for the Crown again objected, but it did not stop Sir Archie Wedding from pressing home the advantage already made. 'You mean – I am still addressing Soldier B – you mean you would deny that your orders are not to kill the enemy? Is it not true that, before a patrol goes out into the night, in Armagh, or Fermanagh, or Derry, or Belfast, you are told the object of the exercise is to kill the enemy? The enemy being members of the PIRA.'

'I have never been given that order, sir.' The journalists all agreed that Soldier B's voice had taken on an angry tone.

'Then why do you do it?'

'If you're talking about patrols, or operations in Northern Ireland, sir, we are under strict military discipline. We only return fire. We never institute it.'

'You wouldn't know that from some of the reports . . . but . . . ' Sir Archie let it go at that. Then, 'You were not returning fire that morning in Hong Kong, though, were you?'

'I have told you already, sir. We opened fire in self-defence . . . '

'Against thin air, Soldier B?'

'Against threatening movements, sir. *You* were not there. We were at the sharp end of a very dangerous and well co-ordinated operation. I had been ordered to shoot if I thought there was danger to anybody, and there *was* danger. I could smell the danger, sir. I saw it in their eyes. I . . . '

'You ordered the five men under your command to shoot the three men – O'Brien, Casey and Flynn – like dogs, to use a cliché. Just as your superiors had told you that you should do. Shoot . . . To . . . Kill, Soldier B. That's the policy isn't it? Shoot – To – Kill?' He had raised his voice, and the room shook to the sound of Sir Archibald Wedding's hand hitting the table twice at each of the words. Shoot – bam-bam – to – bam-bam – kill – bam-bam.

'This is monstrous,' Soldier B began to shout from his place, hidden behind the screen. 'You are suggesting what so many armchair tacticians like to believe, that there is a shoot-to-kill policy when it comes to dealing with the Provos. There's no such thing. They get shot – like our people get shot – through their stupidity, recklessness, and disregard for human life. They deserve everything that . . . ' He stopped, though the outburst had done exactly what Sir Archibald Wedding had wanted. Half his case was already proven.

Phillip Tarpin stretched, and thought of the seemingly insoluble problems in Northern Ireland. He glanced at his watch. It was not yet eleven and he wondered if he should call Liz Oliver – as she would have said, 'just for a cuddle'. A word of affection over the telephone line can be as much of a cuddle as physical contact.

He dialled her number and she answered immediately: bright

131

and happy.

'Liz, it's Phillip.'

'Oh,' the dazzle went from her voice. Phillip, I'm a little tied up at the moment. Is it important? I can call you back.'

'I think it's quite important, Liz. Could you call me back please? I'll be here.'

'Right.' She closed the connection, and the thought went through his head that she might well be one of those women who have to control relationships; who must always be the instigator; the first cause. That would account for the overt display of sexuality, and denial.

The telephone rang, almost before he had taken his hand away. The doorman told him that there was an important package from a Mr Palestino. 'It's marked urgent, Mr Tarpin, and the courier insists you sign for it, sir. Won't accept me.'

'Send him up.' He did not think twice, going through to the kitchen to put the coffee on. There was still a lot of reading ahead.

The bell rang.

Tarpin walked casually to the door and opened it.

Hell leaped into the room.

TWELVE

– 1 –

Elizabeth Oliver put down the telephone and smiled. It had worked. Perhaps, this time it would all really happen. She hoped so, for Phillip Tarpin was one of the nicest men she had met in a very long while. Beneath what she knew was a frosty exterior, Liz Oliver was still a young woman with a great gaping hole in her heart waiting to be filled by love, compassion and tenderness. She tried to control her short-fuse temper – which had been the downfall of a couple of budding romances – but Liz had to be careful. She had watched the nightmare created by her parents. She had lived a similar kind of horror created by herself – and she had no illusions about whose fault *that* marriage had been. She should have run from the altar. Once bitten, she thought.

All day she had wondered if Phillip would telephone her, and now he had done so. Well, she would give him half an hour, then call him back. This time she would control at least the early stages. It was like planning a siege, though she was realistic enough to know that, however careful she was, nothing might come of it. She had to be honest, she fancied Phillip Tarpin. The outcome might only be physical. There was no magic formula. Someone had once said to her that it is impossible to demand love, but you could kick-start it. Well, that was what she would do.

Half an hour later, right on the button, she called. The phone rang out, and to begin with she wondered if there was a fault on the line, so she called the operator who tested the number, and said she thought everything was fine.

By half past midnight she had become really worried. Constant calls were unanswered. He had said he would be there all night. At first she wondered if she should try calling the doorman. She knew there was one on duty, twenty-four hours. In the end she decided to go herself.

The chatty doorman opened up for her, and, when she spoke, Liz could hear a hint of desperation in her voice.

'Mr Tarpin?' she said. 'I've been calling him for the last hour and a half . . . '

'He's in. I know he's in. Took delivery of a package 'round eleven. Guy went up, and came down with his signature. I'll call him from here.'

There was still no reply. 'Maybe we should take a look-see.' The doorman frowned, and Liz saw he was concerned. 'Weird things happen these days. Had a guy – last year – Number forty. Fell in de bath. Konked out cold. Hadda get de cops to break de door down. Sumbitch had put in damned great security locks.'

He used his pass key. There were no security locks or chains on. The first thing Liz saw was the blood.

'Jesus!' The doorman just stood there, as though he could not think what to do.

'Call 911,' Liz shrieked at him. 'Ambulance and cops.' She followed the trail of blood that went from the living room, across the bedroom and into the bathroom, where Tarpin lay, face down, as if lapping his own blood from the tiled floor.

She grabbed a towel, turned him over, shrank back from the gaping wound in his face, cradled his head, and then snatched more towels, trying to stop the bleeding. The gash ran from the left corner of his mouth, opening up his cheek. He was breathing, and his head moved a lot, making it difficult for her to wrap a towel around the cheek. She had hardly got him comfortable – though she had remembered to get his feet up on the corner of the bath, higher than his head – by the time the ambulance arrived, and the two paramedics began to work on him. The bathroom floor was like an abattoir.

Then the cops came, and began to question the doorman and Liz. By this time she was almost incoherent. She telephoned Palestino, who sounded shaken, and asked to be kept informed.

'You wanna ride to da hospital with him, lady?' They were

bringing him out of the bathroom on a stretcher.

She looked at the cop who had been taking down the details. He nodded. 'You go with him if you wanna. We'll follow up.'

Another police cruiser had arrived, and when they got him downstairs Liz saw that, even at this time of night, a little knot of eyeballing people had collected on the sidewalk.

'Those people're fuckin' sick,' said the younger paramedic, and with quick efficiency they got Tarpin into the ambulance. They had a drip going, and asked Liz, about six times, if she knew his blood group. 'He's lost quite a lot.' They were radioing ahead, and the young paramedic kept telling her Tarpin would be okay. But he looked ghastly, lying strapped to the stretcher, the rent in the side of his face giving the impression that he was smiling lopsidedly, .hideously.

At the hospital they took him away, and the cops descended again. She told them all she knew, and they said the doorman had given them a good description of the courier who had brought the package. 'Big, tall, slim guy with funny eyes. We'll get a composite out by the morning. The fella at the building's coming down to the precinct.'

Then a woman doctor, who looked all of nineteen, with untidy hair and a stained white coat, came through and said they had put forty stitches in his face, and he had four broken ribs. 'He'd lost a lot of blood; he's in deep shock, but I think he'll be okay. Nothing more you can do for him tonight. Going to need some vanity surgery if he can afford it. Otherwise he'll be understudying for *Phantom*.'

She telephoned Palestino again, and by then he said that he would be in early, and would go straight to the hospital. The young doctor said she should go home and get some rest. The Emergency Room was like a butcher's shop. Tarpin was not the only one who had been cut that night. It seemed to be a spectator sport.

In the end, the cops gave her a ride home in their squad car. 'Your guy's lucky,' one of them said. 'We've had eight muggings, three shootings and half a dozen stabbings tonight. Five of the victims are dead already.'

Back in her own apartment, Liz Oliver sat down on the bed and wept.

He did not know where he was, and the only feeling, as he crept back to consciousness, was a splitting headache. Then he moved and felt the numbness in his cheek. He opened his eyes, and the whole thing came back, as though it had only just happened. By the time the memory had rerun itself in his head, Tarpin was shaking and gibbering like a frightened child.

Someone gave him a shot, and he retreated from the world again.

When next he woke, there was a policeman sitting by the bed. The cop called a nurse. He felt as though the whole of the left side of his face had been injected with massive shots of novocaine. The back of his head throbbed, his arms and legs trembled uncontrollably, and his stomach turned over with a switchback ride of anxiety. There were two drips in his right arm, and he could feel oxygen tubes in his nose.

'This one's for pain,' the nurse said, touching the drip secured to the lower part of his arm. 'Can you see the little plunger? If the pain gets bad, you're to press it. Each press gives you a morphia shot. There's no need to suffer agony.' She turned to the cop. 'You're not to get him upset.' She said it as though she meant it. If the cop disobeyed, Tarpin thought, she would probably not allow him a morphia drip if he was ever admitted to this hospital.

He was an elderly cop, near retirement, with a quiet slow voice, and spoke as a kindly father might talk to his child.

'You feel up to telling me about it?' he asked.

The abomination slewed into him again. The trembling got worse. Then stopped so that he could not move a limb. Somewhere in the far corner of his mind he realized that he was, literally, paralysed with the fear of it.

'Okay, son. Steady. It's not important. You'll tell us when you're ready.'

He must have called the nurse again, because she came back and the cop moved out. Tarpin gave himself a quick fix of morphine, then again drifted off into sleep. His last thought was that he had a funny lump in his mouth.

When next he woke, the raffish, neat Chilton was sitting by the bed.

'So, you're back with us, Mr Tarpin. Good. Some people seemed to think you'd be able to tell me what happened.'

'Mr . . . ?'

'Chilton. Call me Jackie, most people do.' He raised his hands to show he had a large loose-leaf ring binder, which he opened, rifling through it until he found what he was looking for. He lifted it, holding it in front of Tarpin's eyes. 'Recognize him?' he asked.

It was the man he had seen twice already. The one whose picture had been circulated in the UK. The man they were looking for after Sukie's murder.

He nodded. 'Saw him a couple of times.'

'Know who he is?'

His throat felt parched. He croaked, 'No.'

'Name's Paddy Flanagan. Was he the one who did this to you?'

His throat had become a desert. 'I don't know.' It was hard to get the words out, and in the back of his head, Tarpin wondered what *had* happened to him. All he could see was the ghoul coming through the door, wrapped in the long white robe. The words 'winding sheet' came to mind.

Chilton must have sent for the nurse who was now bending over him. 'You okay, Phillip?'

He pointed to his throat and mouthed, 'Dry.'

She brought a plastic beaker. 'Cranberry juice,' she said. 'Drink, it'll do you good. The doctor's coming up shortly. You'll probably be hungry. Drink the berry juice. Enjoy.'

Tarpin thought she had a great ass. His eyes followed its sway as she left the room. The morphia allowed him to retreat from reality. He wondered what kind of panties the nurse wore around those tight little buttocks, and was immediately shocked at the adolescent immaturity of the fantasy. Yet the shock did not stop him from becoming aroused, in a dream-like, far off way.

He gulped back the juice and motioned for more. When he had finished the second beaker he tried to smile, but his mouth did not seem to be working properly. 'My mouth,' he said, and the memory came flashing back. Jesus God! Oh, my God! Oh, Jesus! Judas Priest! He was not saying it aloud, but the memory came seeping into his brain. Out loud, he croaked to Chilton, 'Am I dying?'

'No, Phillip. You'll be fine. But you'll need some surgery. Not yet. Soon, but not yet.'

'Who was it?'

'Recognise this one?' Chilton held up another photograph. A thin-faced man, with terrible eyes. Cold, hard, the photograph of a killer or a victim. Like one of those pictures you got from an automatic machine.

He shook his head. 'I didn't see its *real* face. Then again, I might have done.'

'Well, he's the man who attacked you. The doorman at your building's identified him. Why didn't you see his face, Phillip?'

'Mask, I think. Opened the door and . . . ' He began to tremble again as the memory returned. He was so horrified he could not talk about it. 'I don't know. Don't know if it was a human or . . . '

Chilton disappeared when the doctor arrived. Doctor Maslek. A calm, precise, shortish man, with a friendly manner – full of Polish jokes – and the kind of optimism Tarpin needed after they had shown him his face in a mirror.

'A very precise wound,' he said. 'Almost the work of a surgeon.'

The rent ran from the left corner of his mouth, right up to the cheekbone. When it healed, Maslek told him, the mouth would be twisted, and the scar would bunch up the flesh. 'It'll take a year before we get you right. I figure three lots of surgery'll do it. When we've finished with you, the face'll be back to normal. Maybe you'll be more handsome than before.'

'What about work? I have so much work to . . . '

'Oh, you'll be back at work in a week. This is going to be a slow process. Just take it one day at a time.'

Eating was painful and difficult, for the inside of his mouth was swollen, and he was aware of another pain now, in his chest, making it difficult to move. He had night sweats, and things he thought of as 'the horrors' in which he relived those few minutes of absolute terror. They came at night. The days were not too bad. People visited regularly. Palestino was there every lunch time. Hilary Cartwright told him not to worry about Tim Clifford's book. He would still get first go. Every evening, Liz Oliver came and sat with him. She was sweet, kind, considerate, even loving. If he had but known, she was blaming herself. If she had not been so damned touchy, she might have been with him and whatever had happened could have been averted.

He looked at the wound while they were changing the dressings. An old Elton John song came back to him:

> Razor Face, amazing grace,
> protects you like a glove.
> And I'll never learn the reason why
> I love your Razor face.

He certainly could not bear to talk about it, and during the night horrors he wondered it he were going crazy. They talked about him leaving the hospital, and he went through a mild anxiety attack, concerned at what the apartment would unleash into his memory.

Chilton came three more times, and asked him a number of questions that did not make sense. Slowly Tarpin was coming to the realization that Sukie's death, and the attack on himself, were linked. Chilton was being very careful not to dig too deep – his words, and the questions, were chosen to head off the obvious. On the third visit, Mr Jackie Chilton, smart, smooth and impeccable, told Tarpin he would not be back.

'Why did you come in the first place?' he asked.

Chilton's eyebrows shot up, surprise written all over his face. 'Because you telephoned Gerald Rainbow, of course.'

'You could've talked to me over the telephone.'

'Yes, I could.' Chilton gave him a neat little smile. 'But then I wouldn't have had this jolly to the Big Apple, would I? Always wanted to see the Apple.' Then he left, as quietly as he had come.

That night, Liz Oliver offered to move in with him.

'I can manage, Liz. I'll be okay. Back to work next week.'

'The doctor – what's his name? – the one who's always telling Polish jokes . . . '

'Maslek?'

'Maslek. He doesn't think you should be living alone.'

Tarpin gave what passed for a smile, under the dressing. 'So, you're going to play Florence Nightingale, Liz?'

'No. I thought I just might be company for you.' Though she said it sharply enough, the acidity vanished in her smile, and she added, 'In any case, I'm rather anxious to sleep with you.'

It took him by surprise. All he could say was, 'Even with *my* face?'

'Especially with your face. Or, perhaps you don't fancy me. I got the impression you did.'

'I wouldn't be able to do it just for a cuddle, Liz. You're far too lovely for that.'

'Suits me.' She winked at him.

He knew that one of the doctors Maslek was bringing in was a psychiatrist. A Doctor Weiss. Young, bearded and overtly Freudian. The day before he was due to leave, Weiss came in during the afternoon, and seated himself next to Tarpin in the large sun lounge, full of greenery and potted plants, on top of the hospital roof. He said nothing. Just waited for Tarpin to speak.

'You think I'm nuts, Doc?'

'Do you think you're nuts?'

'No, but you'll drive me crazy if you just sit there looking at me much longer.'

'Why does that make you so uncomfortable, Phillip?'

'I feel you're just hanging around hoping your silence will break through my silence.'

'Ah, you admit to your silence?'

'Of course I bloody admit to it. I'm fully aware of what happened to me. It's unpleasant, and it's also so outrageous that I can't find the words to describe it yet.'

Weiss nodded. 'When you're ready, you'll *be* ready, Phillip. I just hoped you'd tell one of us before you left the hospital.'

'Maybe I'll write it down. If I do that it might not seem so crazy. If I merely told you . . . If I found the words to tell you, I think you'd have me committed to the funny farm.'

'Some of those farms ain't so funny, Phillip. Better you should work it out on your own. I'll leave my telephone number. Maybe one day I'll get lucky and you'll find the words.'

Late the next afternoon, Liz arrived to take him home. He would still have to go in every other day to have the dressing changed, but they said he could go back to work again on the Monday.

The second thing he did on arriving back in the apartment was to call Hilary and arrange to do the legal work on Clifford's book. She even said she would bring the lawyer to him.

The first thing he did was make love, for around three hours. It was worth the wait, for Liz proved to be inventive and liked games. At first she took all the initiative, stretching him out on his back, fondling him with hands and mouth, then riding him, like a jockey, towards a winning post of orgasms.

Later, she dressed, and said, 'Ravish me, darling. Ravish me hard with all my clothes on.' He was thankful that she looked straight into his face all the time, murmuring endearments. At one point she said, 'Darling, tell me you love me, even if it's a lie, just tell me.' In those first hours, Tarpin could not differentiate between truth and fiction.

– 3 –

Jackie Chilton had not left New York. He was living in an apartment owned by the British Embassy and used when the Ambassador made trips from Washington, or for visiting firemen. Chilton was very much a visiting fireman.

On the day after he had last seen Tarpin, he called Scarecrow in London.

'Well?' Scarecrow asked.

'He has no idea.'

'You're sure of that?'

'He hasn't a clue. I've gone through all the questions that would bring positive reactions from him. Nothing. Absolutely nothing. As they say here, zilch.'

'Let's try and keep it that way, then.'

'Oh, I intend to.'

'What about our American friends?'

'I think they believe me.'

'People usually do, Jackie. You're possibly the most plausible bastard I've ever known.'

'If I can help somebody, as I travel along the road, sir, then my living has not been in vain.'

There was a pause and some static on the line. 'You think they'll try again, Jack?'

'They always have before. It's the oral tradition. They have very long memories, and this is one they're not inclined to forget.'

'But will we try to stop it this time?'

'I'll do what I can. I want to stop it.'
'Keep an eye out, Jackie. Look after yourself, now.'
'I'll do that, sir.'

– 4 –

Peter Palestino came over on the Sunday night. He showed no surprise when Liz answered the door, then left him with Tarpin while she put the last touches to dinner.

Palestino lifted an eyebrow. 'Permanent?' he asked softly.

'Who can tell?' When he smiled, only the right side of his mouth moved, and he was now feeling the pain, in spite of the tablets they were giving him. 'She wanted it. I was not averse. We'll just have to see.'

'You've never said what actually happened.'

'No.'

'I mean, I've heard Liz's version. But . . . How?'

Tarpin looked away. Then: 'It's something I have to come to terms with.' He could not look anyone in the eyes when discussing this problem. 'Peter, I'm sorry. I haven't been able to talk about it with anyone . . . ?'

'The police . . . ?'

'Not the police, nor the guy they sent over from London. Not even the shrink they sicked on to me. He says when I'm ready . . . '

'You blocking it?'

Tarpin drew in a deep breath. 'I wish I was, Peter. No, I remember everything, up until the lights went out. I remember it all too clearly, and that's the reason I don't want to talk about it. I feel some of it would sound like the ravings of a lunatic.'

Palestino said he doubted that. 'You're far too down to earth, Phillip.' They chatted on.

During his visits to the hospital, Palestino had brought Tarpin up to date on the Hong King inquiry. In spite of many clashes between Sir Archie Wedding and the six Special Air Service men, the verdict had been returned as justifiable killing. There had followed a storm of protest in Northern Ireland. There had been six bombings, and three British soldiers had been shot dead while sitting in a public house in Aldershot – the great garrison town of Southern England.

'I signed the contract today for the *Sunday Times* book,' the CEO said. 'When we get the manuscript in, I'd like you to edit it, Phillip.'

'Delighted.' Then his mind made a strange connection, from the Hong Kong shootings to his real father. 'It's strange about the Provos.' He spoke almost to himself. 'For all the hypocrisy and evil, they did provide a good starting point.' He talked about the founding of SOE in Britain, the only truly free area of Europe, in 1940. Churchill had written in a memo that one method of bringing about the downfall of Germany was 'by stimulating the seeds of revolt within the conquered territories.' Later, one of his ministers suggested that they should, 'organize movements in enemy occupied territory comparable to the Sinn Fein in Ireland'. The Sinn Fein was the political arm of the IRA, and Churchill agreed to the use of its tactics in Europe.

Palestino nodded, and quoted from St Paul, 'Let us do evil, that good may come.'

Then, Tarpin glanced towards the kitchen door, dropping his voice. 'I've set up things with Hilary. The Tim Clifford book, remember?'

Palestino nodded.

'She's bringing his lawyer here tomorrow afternoon, with the manuscript.'

They had already agreed that Tarpin could work from home when he felt like it. He was going into the office in the morning for half a day. Palestino did not tell him that he had warned the entire staff not to be shocked by the editorial chief's condition. In fact, though Tarpin tried to act naturally, he was very aware that, even with the dressing in place, the left side of his face was grotesquely crooked. It would be worse when the dressings came off in a couple of weeks.

Liz had helped him accept the disfigurement. The fact that she would make love to him, looking him straight in the face, pouring endearments on to him, helped a great deal. But he dreaded the moment when he would have to walk into an editorial meeting without the protection of the bandages.

On the following afternoon, having spent a morning in the office catching up on paperwork, Tarpin let Hilary into the apartment.

She came with Professor Clifford's lawyer, a young and intense attorney called Robertson, who insisted on reading the legal commitment aloud, doing everything by the book.

The legal terms were exactly as Hilary had outlined. A solemn undertaking not to discuss the contents of the work with anyone until he had made a decision regarding purchase. Even then, the information contained in the book had to remain strictly confidential, shared only with people who had need-to-know until publication.

He signed, and the signature was witnessed. Then Hilary produced a thick, bound manuscript, tentatively titled *The White-chapel Victims*. There was also a small portfolio of photographs which Tarpin opened when the others had left.

There were the usual pictures – the five victims; sketches made of bodies before their removal to the mortuary; various press reports of the time, including artists' impressions of the main protagonists in Whitechapel, and drawings of the events during that autumn of terror – 1888.

He flicked over the final photograph and shrank back: violent images invading his mind. He was looking at a cartoon which had appeared in *Punch* – dated 29 September 1888. Under the title 'Nemesis of Neglect', there were six lines:

> There floats a phantom on the slum's foul air
>   Shaping, to eyes which have the gift of seeing,
> Into the spectre of that loathly lair.
>   Face it – For vain is fleeing!
> Red-handed, ruthless, furtive, unerect,
> 'Tis murderous crime – the nemesis of neglect.

The verse would hardly have won any prizes, but it was the drawing that had Tarpin shaking with fear. A tall figure stalked a derelict street, wrapped in a shroud with the word *Crime* on the headband. In its hand it carried a long, sharp knife, and its face was the pallid face of a ghoul, long, with staring eyes, the mouth open – a gaping, black, toothless hole.

The person who had come to his apartment had been dressed to re-create this very drawing, even down to the word *Crime* on its headband, and the death mask of a face.

This was no strange coincidence. Whoever had attacked him, or even ordered the attack, had gone out of their way to reproduce the figure from 'Nemesis of Neglect'.

In the sudden moment of reeling shock, Phillip Tarpin saw the whole thing again. He glanced uneasily at the door – the door he had opened that night – and the entire scene replayed itself in all its gory detail.

The bell had rung. He had opened the door . . .

THIRTEEN

– 1 –

The bell had rung. He had opened the door with a smile on his face, expecting to see a courier in uniform. Instead, he was confronted by this thing; this macabre fancy-dress thing, wrapped in a shroud, with *Crime* written on the headband, and a huge knife in the upheld right hand.

For a fraction of a second, a confusion of ideas bombarded his brain. It was somebody going to a costume party who had rung the wrong bell; it was an idiot joke; the dress was Mrs Bates, mother of Norman, from *Psycho*. It *had* to be a joke.

But in the same split second he knew it was no joke, for the thing let out a long, quivering sigh. He would never know if it was imagination, but he thought he could smell the fetid breath as it gave the half moan, half sigh again.

Tarpin now felt the fear. It streamed in on him, as though ice had invaded his body, and some violent poison had flushed into his bowels. Way off in the furthest dark lurking corner of his mind, he could hear the scrape of violins, high-pitched, jarring on the ear, like the constant squeak of chalk on a blackboard.

The Ghoul lifted its left hand and struck him, stiff-armed, palm outwards, in the middle of his chest. It did this with great force, like a jack-hammer.

Pain flared and Tarpin stumbled backwards, sprawling, then scrabbling, looking around wildly for some object with which to defend himself.

The Ghoul slammed the door behind him, moving robotically as Tarpin felt his legs and arms flailing. He must look like some electric toy, pushed over and going through its normal working walking movements, at speed, unable to perform properly until somebody picked it up.

His head hit the side of a small table near the couch. He grabbed, got to his feet, tipping a glass ashtray from the table, which he swung upwards, holding on with both hands, using it as a shield against the approaching horror.

The Ghoul swept one arm in front of itself as Tarpin pushed his shield towards it, then felt the table smashed from his hands. The thing advanced again, and, for the second time, flat-handed, stiff-armed him in the chest. This time the pain was worse and he felt something within him crack as he toppled over, his shoulder thudding against the floor.

He heard a whimpering, and, with revulsion, realized it was coming from him. He had always thought of himself as reasonably brave, but he now faced the appalling truth. He was not just afraid, but terrified. He was going to die, not standing up and fighting back, but in panic and gibbering dread.

Once more, he scrabbled backwards, making it to his feet in the middle of the room, before he was struck again. This time, as he fell, his eyes caught the glint of the knife, and he saw, as though eyes and brain were able to move into a huge close-up of the blade, that the instrument was razor sharp, honed, clean and glinting. As he hit the carpet once more, so the breath seemed to be knocked from his body and the pain in his chest became intense, exquisite, a raging fire surrounded by white-hot needles which made him cry out.

The attacker leaned forward and wrenched at Tarpin's shoulder, turning him around so that he was half sitting. He tried to wrest his shoulder from the vice that was the hand, and as he struggled, so he heard the long moan again, followed by a voice which was almost jolly, making it all the more chilling.

'I'm going to improve your smile,' it said, and he felt his hair being grasped, pulling his head back as he screamed, the high-pitched shriek reverberating through the echo chamber of his mind, and cut off, suddenly, as something stroked across his face. Just a sting, to begin with. A sting from the corner of his mouth advancing up his cheek.

The hand released his hair, and he saw the blood and, for the first time, felt the uncontrollable agony of the pain. His tongue probed to the side of his mouth, and the flesh gave way. He was drenched in blood, choking on it, spewing it out, splattering and stippling the white floating cloth of the shroud, while his would-be killer stepped back, quickly, as though revolted by the droplets of gore.

He crawled, listening to his heart pounding in his head, and watching as the blood dribbled from his cheek, feeling the side of his face cave in as he moved, like one of those truly awful child's dolls that crawl with a spastic rhythm.

He made it through the bedroom to the bathroom, leaving a damp crimson trail behind him – an exotic slug track. He was on his face, trying to push himself upwards with his hands, but the pain was too intense – in his chest and through his mouth and cheek.

Again the creature sighed. Then, as he said later, the lights went out. He remembered coughing, and looking incredulously at the blood dribbling on to the tiles as the back of his head seemed to explode.

Then he was in the hospital, not really knowing where it was. Someone gave him a shot and the retreat into oblivion was slower and more pleasant.

> Razor Face, amazing grace,
> protects you like a glove,
> And I'll never learn the reason why
> I love your Razor Face.

– 2 –

He could not stay in the apartment alone. Reliving the tiny fragment of time that was an intrusion into his life – changing it for ever – was too much. Before, he had allowed it to seep back into his head in flashes: small shards of the whole. The thing at the door; the first hit; scrabbling on the floor; the moan; the words, 'I'm going to improve your smile'; the wince of pain; his own gibbering; his scream; the blood draining from him. He knew it was part of a whole, but he only allowed the separate parts to come into his head, like pieces of a jigsaw puzzle.

All the reruns had been segments; now, for the first time, he had let the entire beast spread itself, chronologically, across his mind, like some slimy, red creature, full of pain and violence and terror.

One thing was certain. Having looked straight at the whole truth, Phillip Tarpin could never stay in the apartment alone ever again.

He almost ran for the elevator. In the lobby, the doorman smiled, 'How ya doin', Mr Tarpin? You okay now? Ya lookin' good.'

'Fine.' But he was not fine and he knew it.

Outside, it was a hot day. The kind of summer day New Yorkers hated. Where walking a block meant you had to change your shirt. Above the high-rises the sky was a dense blue, yet you felt the city had a lid on it. Fumes choked, people made quickly for the air-conditioned stores, and there was a daily tally of those who had fallen with heatstroke, dehydration, or worse, a sudden, final heart attack.

He crossed the street, having waited for the lights to change and, almost as a reflex, bending forward as though aping the little green walking symbol. They never gave you enough time: he was almost across when a car hooted him to jump out of the way. He glowered at the driver, and, for a second, caught his angry gaze and equated it with the cold, grey, bulging eyes of the attacker in the shroud.

The bookstore was nearest, and he went in, uncertain why he had come, but knowing only that he wanted to be out, among people, in the blazing heat of a midtown Manhattan afternoon.

The store was busy, the air-conditioning at full blast. People browsed, a few bought, and occasionally a man or woman would stride purposefully to the item they had come in to get, purchase it, then go out into the heat again.

He wandered, looking at titles, then with a sudden thought made his way to the music department where they sold tapes and CDs to the soft background Musak of Vivaldi. Why did they always play Vivaldi in these places? It was better than some dedicated music stores where only the latest cacophony for three electronic guitars, keyboard and a tempest-producing drum kit competed with a raucous, untrained voice. Usually the instruments won.

Tarpin wandered among the CDs, aimlessly, his eyes flicking along the racks, the speed of the way in which he searched increasing, becoming wild and losing any cogent pattern, until he realized he had reached a state of near panic. What was it he wanted? There was a reason for this erratic search. Quiet, Tarpin. Slow down. Think. What did you come here for?

But his eyes began to roam again, and he felt the anxiety rising, like a head of steam. Two men were scanning the Wagner section; a woman glanced over Puccini. He thought one of the men was staring at him. If the person in the shroud stalked him along the streets, or in a store, he would never know. Any tall, slim man could be the one who had come near to killing him. He could never be sure.

Then he saw the Bach. Got it. His brain began to slow down, and he knew he had been hyperventilating. He needed some soft, quiet music to calm him. Perhaps to make it possible to go back to the apartment. He was no great shakes at serious music, but knew what he thought of as the popular classics: the Rachmaninov concertos; Grieg; Beethoven; Tchaikovsky. Bach, he did not know, but somewhere – he thought it was from a book he had edited – he remembered something called the Goldberg Variations. It was a piece that could be relied upon to produce calm. He even remembered why. At the age of fifteen, J. S. Bach had written these harpsichord variations for a player named Johann Goldberg. Or was it Goldberg who was fifteen? He gave a silent laugh. Editors of non-fiction developed ragbag minds, filled with half-digested knowledge. You edited a book on the Queen of England, or the President, and immediately became an expert on royalty or the difficulties of the first family. Do a couple of volumes on computers and you were, to use the jargon, computer literate. Do the life of Bach and you remembered the Goldberg Variations and their calming influence.

Haltingly he asked a bored-looking male assistant if he could recommend a particular version of the Variations, and was surprised when the young man treated him to an erudite dissertation on various performances. He went away with Trevor Pinnock, captured on the little silver disc, playing on what the young man assured him was a Ruckers harpsichord dating from 1646. Tarpin would not have known a harpsichord from a Toshiba keyboard.

As he left the store he glanced at his watch and saw, to his confusion, that it was twenty minutes past five. He had left the apartment around three-thirty, maybe a quarter to four. Time had just slipped away.

Then, half a block from his building, he saw Liz, wild-eyed, concerned, near panic, slaloming through the late afternoon crowds towards him.

'Phillip! Oh God, where've you been? What happened?' She was on him with a rush, fear flashing behind her eyes.

'What's wrong, Liz? What's . . . ?'

Passers-by were turning to stare. Even a large black beggar, with a white cane and a tray of matches, stopped stock still in the middle of the sidewalk, listening to Liz' voice, high and near to hysteria.

'Did something happen? I've been frantic!' She held on to his arm, almost dragging on him.

'Nothing, I just had to get out for a while.'

She had called the apartment around four, and again ten minutes later. This time she had not waited. she dashed out of the building, grabbed a cab and rushed back, expecting to find chaos: death even. She was still panting, her face screwed into a frown of concern, when they got to the door of the apartment.

'Please, Phillip. Please, just for a while, if you're home by yourself, please call me. Call me if you go out.'

'Sure, but . . . ' He remembered her first question. 'You asked if something happened.'

'Yes.'

'Well, I suppose, in a way it did.' He sat her down and told her the whole story, everything, including his gibbering fear, all the things that had made him ashamed.

She sat, her face going grey when he described the assailant. He thought, as he finished, that she was going to be ill. But she swallowed hard, and said in a small voice, 'Phillip, could you tell that to somebody else now?'

'I think so. I've confronted it, in my head. I've acknowledged the fear. Why?'

She slid her tongue along her lips, and told him that, while he was in hospital, a detective from the local precinct had come to see her.

'His name's Bishop. Jimmy Bishop. He was waiting for me when I came out of your room one day. I took him back to my place and we talked: quite a long conversation. He said that you would probably block off some of the things that happened – close your mind to them. I told him, no. I said you could remember everything quite clearly: but just didn't want to talk about it.'

Detective Bishop had asked her to call if ever Tarpin changed his mind. 'He said that it might help them catch the guy who did this to you. Would you talk with him?'

'I don't see why not. It isn't the easiest thing in the world – telling people you're a coward. But, yes. Yes, I'll talk to him.'

What hit him now was the naked question mark. Why? Why Sukie, and then why him? Why the costume, the shroud, the copy of a *Punch* cartoon from 1888? Could there be some connection? But how? No, the only answer was that someone had seen the cartoon and realized its potency, for it was a powerful drawing: the kind of thing that stayed with you, possessed your mind.

Bishop arranged to come over within an hour.

There were things that had to be done. Tarpin realized that showing the copy of the *Punch* cartoon to the detective might lead to difficult questions about Clifford's manuscript, which he had locked in a drawer. So Liz accompanied him back to the bookstore, where he rummaged around among the social history and crime sections, until he came across a book on the Ripper murders, containing, among other photographs, a reproduction of the 'Nemesis of Neglect' cartoon. This he could show to the detective. Perhaps it was a clue that made sense. The thought came to him that, maybe, this was a serial killer, already active, whose modus operandi the police had kept out of the newspapers.

– 3 –

Detective Jimmy Bishop was a short, quiet man in his early fifties, who had spent all his working life with the NYPD, yet, on the surface at least, seemed to have been untouched by the daily catastrophes and quirks to which he must have been subjected.

'It's not easy,' Tarpin told him, explaining that, while in the hospital, he had recalled everything, yet not allowed the full memory to run, uncut, in his mind. 'It was rather like watching a badly edited movie,' he explained.

Bishop nodded, and said this was not unusual. 'Did you feel –
how can I put it? – violated?'

'Sort of.'

Victims often experienced a sense of revulsion towards themselves. 'A lot of rape victims get it into their heads that the rape
might have been their fault. Oddly, the same goes for people
who've been attacked – like yourself. The first reaction is anger,
then you get a period of soul searching. Victims sometimes find
facets of their character that they don't like . . . '

Tarpin said, yes. He had not been happy in discovering his
cowardice. 'I always thought I'd stand up to anyone who tried to
mug me. I found my own Achilles heel here, in this apartment.'

Bishop was a good listener, only intruding when he thought
something needed clarifying. By the time Tarpin had finished
talking he felt wiped out, as though he had spent hours on an
exercise machine.

'And you're certain the assailant was dressed like this?' Bishop
had a habit of looking people straight in the eyes, as though daring
you to break off contact.

'Right down to the word "crime". It was as though he was
sending me a message.'

'I think, perhaps he was. Would this have any special meaning
for you? Anything from the past?'

Tarpin said, no, it was quite crazy, and the detective followed up
with a volley of questions – Had he ever had dealings with anyone
who was a Jack the Ripper freak? Did he own any property? Had
he ever experienced really unpleasant difficulties with a landlord?
Had he ever been involved in litigation concerning disease, or an
accidental death? And so on and so on.

You did not have to be a psychiatrist to see where Bishop was
heading. One of the extraordinary results of those five murders in
London's Whitechapel had been attempted changes in housing
and living conditions for the impoverished.

'You know your Jack the Ripper then, Detective Bishop?' Tarpin
said with respect.

'Do you?'

'Not really. Not the full details. I edited an encyclopedia of crime
once. There was a lengthy article about the murders. I know the

basics.'

'Me, too.' Bishop gave one of his rare smiles. 'Tell you the truth, I read *that* book.' He touched the book which Tarpin had bought. 'Got it at home. Odd, isn't it, that five squalid murders, at the end of the nineteenth century, should have an enduring effect on people?'

Tarpin agreed, as he always did. Jack the Ripper had entered into international folk lore: a horror story, handed down from generation to generation.

'Maybe, the guy who tried to kill you is a Ripper freak.'

'I wondered. I even thought maybe you had someone on the books.'

Bishop shook his head. 'No. Afraid not. If we had, it would make life a little easier.' He seemed to be holding his breath, then: 'There is one thing, Mr Tarpin. I've read the hospital reports, and now I've heard the story from you. I've got to tell you this, and I think you have to hear it, and act on it.'

Tarpin experienced a butterfly roll in his stomach.

'I don't think this joker meant to kill you.' Bishop again locked eyes with him.

'What d'you mean. He nearly *did* kill me.'

'No. You were pretty well beat up, and badly cut. But, unless you'd had a dodgy heart, you were never in fear of losing your life. This guy had plenty of time. He went just so far, and no further. If he had wanted you dead, even if he was a crazy with blood lust on his mind and no other motivation, he could have killed you. No problem.'

'He might have been disturbed. My telephone might have rung. Anything . . . '

Bishop shook his head. 'No. This guy had enough time, and certainly the means to take you out and leave you on the floor, dead meat. He didn't want you dead, Mr Tarpin, which makes me think that either he did it for the kicks – just to hurt you real bad – or he's got more where this came from. Personally, I lean towards the theory that this is personal. Someone wanted to give you one hell of a fright. You say you can think of nobody who'd do a thing like this. I wonder? I want you to go on thinking. This character's dangerous, maybe a crazy. Now I hate to worry you, but you might not have heard the last of him.'

An edgy gloom fell over the apartment that evening, and Liz did her best to cheer him. Yet, no matter what they talked about, the conversation came back to the attack. It was as though some evil, life-threatening insect had crept into his mind and laid eggs there. The eggs were now hatching. With them, he thought, would come further nightmares.

About ten o'clock the telephone rang – Hilary with a load of fulsome apologies. 'I didn't hand over the most important photographs and documents,' she said. 'Sorry, Phillip, there's a whole folder of them. Where're you going to be this morning?'

He told her that he would be in the office, and she arranged to drop them off. 'Interesting stuff,' she told him. 'These are the documents that support Tim's main theory.'

'Maybe I shouldn't look at them until I've read the manuscript.'

'You sure?'

'Yes. There's no hurry. It's going to take a couple of days. Let me give you a call when I'm ready for them.' He put the telephone down and turned, to see Liz had changed into what she called her playsuit – a fantasy which could only have come from Frederick's of Hollywood: all tight silks and floating opaque lace. She was just pulling on the long black gloves which reached to her elbows.

The playsuit, and what was inside it, banished the nightmares for a while.

Across town, Hilary Cartwright opened the folder which should have been delivered with the manuscript of *The Whitechapel Victims*. There were two certificates of marriage, and several photographs. One of a man, photographed around 1889, looked oddly familiar: though for all the clichéd tea in China she could not think who it was.

– 4 –

Detective Jimmy Bishop was not a corrupt man. In his time with the NYPD he had seen many unscrupulous and venal policemen. It often amazed him that some had risen through the years, and eventually retired on full pension but with heavily swollen bank accounts. The fact that life was unfair had long made itself known to him, but he had also seen corrupt cops revealed for what they were, and thrown, in disgrace, from the department; or, as often as not, into jail.

Though he was not the kind of man motivated by a wink or a nod and a quick exchange of unmarked dollar bills, Jimmy Bishop had done deals. He found this morally acceptable. After all, lawyers, the DA and the courts, all of whom dispensed justice, cut deals the whole time.

His arrangement had been simple and not mercenary, except that the end result, should he keep his end of the bargain, would be a free jaunt to London, with special tours arranged so that he could see how London's finest operated. He argued to himself that it was the kind of arrangement made regularly in the world of business.

So it was, the following morning, that he drove out to an apartment building near the World Trade Center. He had telephoned ahead, simply saying that 'Robert's brother's going to be in town.'

'Good. Tell him to give me a call,' the voice on the distant end replied. Part of the agreement was that business should be conducted in person.

'I was called in to talk with Tarpin, last night,' he told the impeccable Mr Chilton after coffee had been served. They sat opposite one another. Outside the window there was a good view of the twin towers of the Trade Center and little else.

'So? Was it interesting?'

Jimmy Bishop told the whole story, just as Tarpin had told him. Jackie Chilton thanked him for it, saying he was sure the invitation would soon come. Detective Bishop would be visiting London this year. No doubt about it.

'Are you going to use this information yourself?' Chilton asked, as Bishop prepared to leave.

'I'll transcribe my notes. Maybe it'll be useful if something else happens.'

'Indeed, yes. The man's obviously some kind of obsessive.'

'To use the technical term, Mr Chilton, the guy's a loony tune.'

Chilton laughed, 'A fruitcake,' he said. 'But a very dangerous fruitcake.'

When Detective Bishop had left, Mr John Chilton dialled a London number.

The number in London rang at a little after five in the afternoon. Scarecrow answered in his usual quiet way.

'The lads are trying to give him a clue,' said Mr Chilton. Then he explained.

'Ah, d'you think you should fill in the blanks for him?'

'No. It's always been a case of the smaller the circle the better.'

'You'll keep an eye open for him though, Jackie?'

'Both eyes.'

– 5 –

At about the same time as Chilton was talking, via the long-distance line satellite, to Scarecrow, so Phillip Tarpin, having dealt with the morning's mail, and instructed Elaine that he was out to all callers, placed the large manuscript on his desk, looked at the title page – *The Whitechapel Victims*, by Professor Tim Clifford, © 1991 Clifford Enterprises – turned it and began to read.

Tarpin could not know that, by reading this manuscript, he was opening up his life to untold confusion.

Across town, Hilary Cartwright had slept in. She was tearing around her apartment, gathering things together, so that the day would not get too out of kilter.

She picked up the folder of Clifford's photographs and documents which would have to go into the office safe until Tarpin was ready for them.

The picture of the man she vaguely recognized had to be tucked back into the folder, and, even in her haste, she looked at it again, but could still not put a name to the so recognizable face. As she held it, she also glanced, for the umpteenth time, at the typewritten caption attached to its back. Photograph of Marc Jean Bartolemé, *c* 1889, she read. It made no bells ring for her.

FOURTEEN

– 1 –

I shall write in the first person, as though I am sitting with you, chatting in a garden on a summer's day, or by a fire on a cold winter evening,' Clifford began. Then, continuing, he wrote:

It will be easier to follow the facts of history – and the small answers I have managed to provide – if I tell this fascinating and bloody story in the manner of a confidential discussion. I am aware that you cannot ask questions; so, when I divine that there *are* questions which need answering, I will provide them, together with my replies.

One of the things I find strange about the Ripper murders is that, as I have travelled the world, conversations concerning crime and criminals, great social injustices, or even plain tales of horror, always seem to lead back to Jack the Ripper: the great universal Bugaboo, the horned Bogeyman. It is as though the Ripper has become the outward sign of terror and evil, in a way which sometimes even surpasses the appalling truth about the Nazi Holocaust, and other barbarous acts of attempted genocide. He is the monster who lurks in the closet; the devil made man who stalks a nightmare land in people's anxiety dreams. The Ripper, above all other mass or serial murderers, takes pride of place. Maybe because he was never brought to judgement.

In India, Thailand, Hong Kong, the United States, Canada, France, Germany, Spain – take your pick – I have listened as arguments, or plain after-dinner talk concerning murder, have inexorably turned to Jolly Jack. Once you touch on Jack, you immediately encompass the events of the autumn of 1888, in that area, hard by the City of London, known as Whitechapel.

The thing which has surprised me, and other Ripperologists, is how little is really known by the otherwise intelligent man or woman. In spite of the many popular books and studies, the vast majority of those who show a sudden, conversational, interest, imagine that the crimes of Jack the Ripper went on for a considerable period of time, and that his victims ran into the hundreds. Part of this myth can be firmly laid at the door of the movie makers who, over the years, have done irreparable harm to social historians and criminologists. In the main they have made two errors:

First, they have fudged the issues by giving life to already demolished theories regarding the identity of the Whitechapel killer. Second, they have presented the inner district of Whitechapel in 1888 as a fairly reasonable, if slightly soiled place, where the whores were young, and even quite attractive.

A case in point is the last Ripper movie I watched. A piece which presented us with an old, and well debased, theory involving Sir William Gull, the royal physician, who – with a manic coachman – growls into Whitechapel, performing his hideous work. There is a novel based also on the Gull theory. Neither takes into account that by the autumn of 1888, the good Dr Gull could hardly walk: a victim of a stroke over twelve months before the Ripper murders began. There are further demonstrable proofs which nullify this fanciful piece of fiction.

Having said this, I should reveal now – at the start of our journey – that, in my studies and my work as a historical detective, I have never set out to beard the criminal. This book does contain some startling proofs about what is considered to be the Ripper's last victim, but do not look for any strong leads towards naming the killer, for this is an impossible task, best left alone.

To those who already know all the facts: who have studied the extant information regarding the Ripper and his victims, I would suggest that you skim this work until you reach the two chapters on victim number five – Mary Jane Kelly, or, as she sometimes liked to be called, Marie Jeanette Kelly. For well-read Ripper-ologists, the rest is silence.

So, let us begin, remembering that the Ripper's certain victims have been reduced to five (though I will remove one from that list); and his jig through the mean streets of Whitechapel lasted a mere ten weeks.

Come, I am beckoning you now to follow me into the early hours of Friday 31 August 1888. See, we are in a place named Buck's Row. Smell the early morning here – unpleasant, sooty, with an overlay of human stink: and it is dark. Not a pleasant time or place to be out alone . . .

Tarpin smiled, for, having read Tim Clifford's book on Richard III and the young princes, he was aware of the man's technique. This almost folksy opening would haul readers in and then close, snap, sharp as a steel trap, thrusting them headlong into the revolting facts: hanging on to them so that the book became impossible to cast aside.

Clifford, being a scholarly historian, left nothing to chance, yet he purposely set aside the more obvious approach of beginning the work on the most famous sexual serial killer of all time, with a lengthy dissertation on the social conditions prevailing in White-chapel of 1888. Instead, he told the story of the murders, as they occurred, and into the warp and weft of the telling he planted what appeared to be asides, yet were, in fact, carefully concealed windows into the appalling state of the poor and homeless of that area of London.

Starting with the first victim, Mary Ann (Polly) Nichols, he was able to lead the reader into the pungent stew that was the daily, and nightly, state surrounding the lives of the hundreds of impover-ished, shifting unfortunates who found themselves existing in that small part of London towards the end of the nineteenth century.

With not a little drama, he began by describing, in almost clinical terms, the discovery of Polly Nichols' body by a market porter, George Cross, who thought he had come upon a rape victim, still unconscious. In the flickering light of a single gas lamp at the end of the street he could not, as yet, see the terrible mutilations or the blood which had soaked mainly into her clothes.

In fast, dramatic paragraphs, Clifford laid out the whole scene and the events which followed – the summoning of a fellow worker, John Paul, and the arrival of the police in the person of Constable 97J, John Neil; the sending for Dr Llewellyn, and the fact that the corpse's arms and legs were still warm, indicating that she had been dead for less than half an hour, though nobody in the immediate area had heard a sound, nor even a cry for help, let alone a struggle.

He wrote of the removal of the body to the workhouse yard – the nearest mortuary – where it remained until a pair of paupers – one of them an epileptic – had completed their meagre breakfast and were ready to strip the body.

All these events allowed Clifford to draw in details of the daily lives of the poor, and those institutions which gave them scant assistance. Later, he was able to give a picture of the common lodging houses of the area, and the crushed, stilted lives of the wretched women who sold their bodies for the price of a loaf of bread, or for a night indoors and the use of a blanket.

He was also careful to describe the wounds inflicted on poor Polly Nichols who, slightly drunk, had boasted, 'I've had my lodging money three times today and have spent it. It won't be long before I'll be back. See what a jolly bonnet I've got now,' as she went unsteadily into that dark night to sell her favours and meet her nemesis.

Her windpipe and gullet were slashed through to the spinal cord, her throat cut from ear to ear. A jagged, deep wound opened up the abdomen from ribs to pelvis. Other downward cuts ran across the stomach and there were two stab wounds in the vagina. The jolly bonnet lay beside her.

In recounting the details of Polly Nichols' drab life, Clifford added much in the way of social comment, for the first victim was almost a perfect case study in degradation. Married to a printer at the age of twelve, she had borne five children and soon became a drunkard, leaving her husband and family in the early 1880s for a life on the streets, in the workhouses and common lodging houses – her days and nights numbed by hard liquor, her body a means of supporting her in this dreary habitual existence. There were many like Polly in the East End of London.

The fact that Polly Nichols' brutal murder began to spark fear among the sad women who roamed Whitechapel's streets, Clifford pointed out, was due to the earlier murders of two prostitutes, almost certainly not victims of the Ripper. This pair, Emma Smith and Martha Tabram, had both died, badly mutilated, during April and August respectively. Horrible though these crimes were, they had no place in Jack's throat-slitting, mutilating spree. Smith survived for twenty-four hours and claimed she had been set upon by a gang. Tabram, though killed by multiple stab wounds, almost certainly died by the hand of a soldier who was one of her clients.

It was Polly Nichols' violent end which began that period of terror in the streets of Whitechapel, and a second murder quickly stoked the fires of alarm.

'So we come to Saturday 8 September 1888,' Clifford's chapter on the second victim began. As though to put some kind of perspective on the chronology and the distance in time, he added: 'Far away, across the Atlantic Ocean, in Boston two days earlier, a child was born into an Irish immigrant family. His name was Joseph Patrick Kennedy, and he would live to see his son, John F. Kennedy, become President of the United States.'

He returned quickly to the matter in hand: the body found at six in the morning at the back of a lodging house: 29 Hanbury Street. A woman, her throat cut in two places, and her body mutilated. As the police report stated – 'Lying on her back, dead, left arm resting on left breast, legs drawn up, abducted, small intestines and flap of the abdomen lying on right side above right shoulder attached by a cord with the rest of the intestines inside the body; two flaps of skin from the lower part of the abdomen lying in a large quantity of blood above the left shoulder; throat cut deeply from left and back in jagged manner right around the throat.' In fact, it seemed to Doctor Bagster Phillips, who conducted the post mortem, that the killer had tried to sever the head from the body.

She had been seen alive but half an hour earlier by a park keeper's wife. Then Annie Chapman, as she was later identified, was haggling with a man who, as the park keeper's wife reported, asked, 'Will you?' Annie Chapman replied, 'Yes,' and went to her death at the age of forty-eight years, to be carried to the mortuary in the same coffin shell that had been used for Polly Nichols the previous week.

When Dark Annie's body was discovered, a piece of muslin, a comb and a paper case were lying close to the body and a few pennies, together with two new farthings, had been laid at her feet. Near her head, the killer had placed part of an envelope and two pills in a piece of paper.

Again, the victim had been seen thirty minutes before her body was found, and nobody in the lodging house had heard a sound. The killer had come and gone, leaving no real clues.

At the inquest there was a startling revelation, though members of the public were withdrawn from the court and the full details published only in *The Lancet*. It appeared that, 'From the pelvis, the uterus and its appendages with the upper portion of the vagina and the posterior two thirds of the bladder had been entirely removed and carried away.'

In the opinion of Doctor Phillips, the murderer *had* to have anatomical knowledge. Doctor Llewellyn, who had carried out the post mortem on Polly Nichols, had made the same observation with regard to her killer.

Tarpin remained glued to the pages, for Clifford was far more readable than most popular novelists. He talked of the larger portion of those who inhabited Whitechapel as being 'People of truth and virtue, men, women and children who lived hard, but fruitful, lives, God-fearing, and man-fearing also, for these folk would rarely venture into the quarter-mile square area into which evil was packed so densely that you were obliged almost to shoulder your way in'.

'Murder,' he wrote, 'was nothing new to these inner conclaves of crime and amorality. To be honest, murder was a regular occurrence, but those murders were, in nature, either domestic, or what can be termed murder for gain. The rivers of blood which flowed from Polly Nichols and Dark Annie Chapman seemed to bring out a primeval instinct among the inhabitants of Whitechapel who lived perpetually on the dark side of the moon.

For those who scraped a living from the streets, venturing outside their locale only to commit other crimes, returning with the proceeds which would allow them to exist for a few more weeks, the Ripper seemed to pose a greater threat than their natural enemies – the law, the landlords and the lodging house keepers. These were people motivated simply by survival. The grit of the city had burrowed into their pores, soaked its way into their clothes, while drink and the Devil did for the rest. They lived in this twilight world and some, possible many, occasionally glimpsed the better times of their past as though looking at an almost forgotten dream. Annie Chapman had certainly seen better days; Polly Nichols was the child of an artisan – a blacksmith – and wife to another, a printer. She was enfolded into the impossible drudgery of childbearing and managing a family, as a child herself, and paid the price extracted from so many.

Of the Ripper, he said:

We can only guess at the hobgoblins which drove the murderer to acts of unspeakable violence. We know, without doubt, that his crimes were sexual in nature, and, possibly because of this, they were half-recognized by the Victorian collective consciousness as something different, a new development in man's most hideous excesses.

Certainly there have been worse, and more terrible, crimes since the autumn of 1888. Think of Albert Fish; Son of Sam; the Hillside Stranglers; John Reginald Halliday Christie, who murdered at least seven women and one child in his minute London house of 10 Rillington Place; or Brady and Hindley, the Lancashire Moors murderers, who tortured and killed children for the sake of it, for kicks. Jack's crimes pale, almost into the proverbial insignificance, next to these monsters. Yet it is Jack who, in the imaginations of so many, continues to live.

Tarpin was engrossed. As the title of the book indicated, Clifford was writing more of the victims than their killer. His descriptions were stark, bare and brutal. While he included all the known evidence, the transcripts of the coroner's inquests, and the many stories of the police investigation, the book led the reader from murder to murder, victim to victim, hardly letting up, so that the horror and tension became almost the motive for turning the pages.

'Now,' the author wrote, 'it is the early hours of Sunday 30 September 1888: the night of the double killing, the "Double Event" as it has been called. The anxiety, not simply in the Whitechapel area but throughout London, has not relaxed, though two weeks have passed since Dark Annie died with her small possessions placed around her, as though in some bizarre ritual.'

The first body was discovered at one in the morning in a small courtyard off Berner Street, which ran from Commercial Street down to the London, Tilbury and Southend railway. The court was pitch dark, though lights blazed from the first-storey windows of the International Working Men's Educational Club. Indeed, though it was past midnight, people living in the vicinity were kept awake by the singing and noise coming from the club. Earlier, there had been a debate, and this was followed by music and dancing.

The club's steward, Louis Diemschutz, was not on the premises during these festivities, for he traded in cheap costume jewellery, leaving the running of the club to his wife. At one in the morning, Diemschutz led his pony and barrow into the yard. He was returning from the market near Crystal Palace. Suddenly the pony shied away from something lying in the dark. It was the body of the Ripper's third victim, later identified as Elizabeth Stride, originally Elizabeth Gustafsdotter, a Swedish prostitute, known locally as Long Liz.

The doctor – Frederick Blackwell – arrived at one-sixteen. Her throat had been cut, and she was still warm.

The police had started to take elaborate precautions by this time and, knowing the murderer could not have gone far, began an exhaustive search. Already they had instructions to question all couples seen in the street after midnight. Stride and her murderer had somehow slipped the net. Now the police questioned and searched numerous people – including members of the club, who took great exception to having their hands examined.

The search went on, redoubled at the news of yet another victim. This time, the police must have missed the killer by minutes, while the victim, Catherine Eddowes, was doubly unlucky. She had been in custody at Bishopsgate police station since eight-thirty the previous evening, having been discovered dead drunk in Aldgate. The City Police had kept her until she had sobered up. They released her at one in the morning. Three quarters of an hour later she was found dead, four hundred yards away in Mitre Square.

As Clifford wrote:

This was Jack's most audacious crime yet, for Mitre Square had three entrances; it was also close by a warehouse which employed a night watchman. If this was not sufficient, the local beat policeman's patrol took him through Mitre Square every fifteen minutes or so.

Constable 881 Watkins entered the square at one-thirty. At the inquest he stated that he 'had [my] lantern on – fixed to my belt. I looked into the different passages and corners. There was no one about.' Fourteen minutes later he returned. In that time, Jack had cut Catherine Eddowes' throat and ripped open her stomach. The uterus and left kidney were missing.

Clifford described the lives of these two unfortunates – Stride and Eddowes – in some detail, and ended the chapter –

'So, Jack had disposed of four prostitutes. From two of them he had removed organs. On every occasion he seemed to have come and gone like a wraith. There was worse to come with the fifth victim, and here I part company with practically all students of these crimes. Not only do I believe that the fifth victim was not killed by the Ripper, but also I can prove it.'

Tarpin had learned nothing new about these abhorrent crimes, but Professor Clifford had done something that no other writer on the subject had really managed: the period, time and place came alive on the page. You could almost smell the sooty streets, and feel the fear. The reader would, if nothing else, go away with possibly the most accurate description of London's East End during those troubled days.

He was about to begin the next chapter, when a steady tapping at his door made him jump. It was a tribute to Professor Clifford's skill that a sudden, normal noise like this could cause him to start, almost with fear.

Liz Oliver peeped around the door. 'Your sweet Elaine has been very good,' she said. 'She has things to ask you, but you said you were not to be disturbed.'

He looked at his watch. It was almost six-thirty. He had spent the entire day engrossed in Clifford's book, as it gripped, bubbled and flowed, transporting him to another time and place as very few boks on that subject could have done. He had even missed lunch. That night, Liz could have tried all her natural feminine charms, and they would not have worked. They dined out, yet Tarpin remained distracted, his mind back in the late nineteenth century, with the many puzzles surrounding the Ripper, both fact and legend, circling in his mind.

It was the first time that Liz felt Phillip Tarpin had ducked from under her shadow, escaping the potent magic she tried to create: her personal love potion.

They left the restaurant at nine-thirty and were back in the apartment by ten.

– 2 –

In London it was three in the morning. Professor Tim Clifford spent most of his time either at the Cambridge college of which he was a Fellow, or in a small, convenient basement flat, which doubled as an office, in Wells Street, off Oxford Street.

On this particular night he was in Cambridge, and the fact was known to the two men who, in these small hours, approached the outer door of the building: once a terraced house, now a series of small flats.

They let themselves in and they wore gloves. They also carried two large briefcases. One contained a portable photocopier, the other held paper. Once through the main door they went straight to Clifford's flat, entering with a key, deactivating the sophisticated alarm system with an ease born of their professionalism.

The master copy of the manuscript was locked away in a floor safe, set in cement within a walk-in broom cupboard. One of the men flicked the combination to the desired numbers which, in fact, consisted of the year in which Tim Clifford had been born.

Remaining in the comparative darkness of the cupboard, using the light from a small pocket torch, they set up the photocopier, plugging a long lead into one of the kitchen sockets.

It took them an hour to copy the eight hundred pages, which they returned to the safe. They let themselves out in the manner in which they had come in. Nobody, they considered, would be any the wiser.

Skilled at surreptitious entry, they had made one small error. During the copying, one of the men had almost subliminally noticed that two pages, near the beginning of chapter seven, had been reversed. They thought nothing of returning the pages in the correct order.

When Tim Clifford returned to London on the following evening, and retrieved the manuscript which he was taking with him to New York, the first thing he did – as always – was to check the two reversed pages of chapter seven. Believing the price of freedom was a little paranoia, he knew immediately that the master copy had been tampered with. Accordingly he called Hilary Cartwright in New York, and his local police station which was West End Central. A couple of officers who worked out of West End Central already knew the manuscript had been copied. But, then, they would not say a word. They had not done the copying.

– 3 –

The horrors of Whitechapel remained with Tarpin through the night, hanging in his brain like an old-fashioned Victorian fog, through which the voices of the damned women drifted, calling of their sins. He woke from this troubled sleep, remembering the words of one quoted by Clifford from a newspaper description given by the benevolent Dr Barnardo. 'We're all up to no good,' the woman said. 'No one cares what becomes of us. Perhaps some of us will be killed next. If anybody had helped the likes of us long ago, we would never have come to this!'

On the following morning, Tarpin went to the hospital to have the dressing changed on his cheek. They were pleased with the way the wound was healing. 'In another couple of weeks we'll have the stitches out,' Doctor Maslek told him.

He had lunch with Peter Palestino, and could not talk of anything but the Clifford book. 'With luck, I'll finish it today,' he said. 'We'd be fools not to get it. It has huge best seller written all over it.'

Once more in his office, he gave instructions to be left alone. Then he turned to the chapters on the last Ripper victim – Mary Jane Kelly, whose murder had interrupted the Lord Mayor's Show in 1888. Or had it?

FIFTEEN

– 1 –

'So now we come to Jack's last stand,' Clifford wrote.

Jack's *pièce de résistance*; Jack's last waltz; Jack's night of the long knives; Jack's trial by fire; Jack be nimble, Jack be quick. At least that is what all the experts have said – until now.

I trust you are not squeamish, because if you do not know the story of how Jolly Jack the Ripper upstaged the Lord Mayor of London on 8/9 November 1888, it might make you a little, well . . . As one of the witnesses at the inquest said, of finding the body 'I have not broken my fast since then. The sight made me sick and it will be a good many years before I forget it.'

Let me tell you of this murder in a clinical fashion. No atmosphere, no drama. Just the plain, unvarnished facts: though, as you will see, I believe the facts to have been liberally varnished, and are far from plain.

It all starts late on the night of Thursday 8 November, continuing until the morning of Friday 9 November 1888. The place? Miller's Court, Dorset Street, about a quarter of a mile from Hanbury Street, where Dark Annie met her death. The area around Dorset Street was about as unsavoury as you could get. A place of warehouses, squalid streets, and a very large number of registered lodging houses.

The entrance to Miller's Court was from Dorset Street, next to No. 26, through an arched passage not more than three feet wide. Dorset Street itself was quite well lit, but the passage to

Miller's Court was unlit. The following description is from *The Daily Chronicle*, 10 November 1888:

'. . . from this passage open two doors leading into houses on either side. The house on the left hand is kept as a chandler's shop by a respectable man, named John M'Carthy, to whom also belongs [the house on the right-hand side].

'The court is a very small one, about thirty feet long by ten broad. On both sides are three or four small houses, cleanly whitewashed up to the first-floor windows. The ground floor of the house to the right of the court is used as a store, with a gate entrance; and the upper floors are let off in tenements, as is the case also with M'Carthy's house.

'Opposite the court is a very large lodging house of a somewhat superior character. This house is well lit and people hang about it nearly all night. There is another well frequented lodging house next door to M'Carthy's, and within a yard or two of the entrance to the court is a wall-lamp, the light of which is thrown nearly on the passage.

'But, perhaps the most curious item in the entire surroundings is a large placard pasted on the wall of the next house but one from the right-hand side, offering, in the name of an illustrated weekly paper, a reward of £100 for the discovery of the man who murdered the woman in Hanbury Street.'

Well, that is what the papers say on the day after the shocking discovery in Miller's Court, the houses and tenements being occupied for the most part, one suspects, by prostitutes. Not a pleasant place: dirty, dangerous. The kind of place where it is best to take no notice of a cry in the dark; or a banshee wail in the desperate wee small hours.

Room 13, as it was called, is in the house on the right hand of the passage. Originally it was part of the back parlour of 26 Dorset Street. The back parlour was divided, with a fairly flimsy partition, making Room 13 – unlucky for some – accessible from the door on the right of the passage.

In the spring of that same year, Room 13 was let to an attractive young girl by name of Mary Jane (or Ann) Kelly, or Marie Jeanette Kelly, as she liked to style herself. She did not mix well, and many considered she thought herself to be a cut above the other tenants. Be that as it may, she rented the room, together with a friend – often referred to as her common-law husband: Joseph Barnett. The rent was four shillings a week.

Barnett was later to tell the coroner's court that Mary Kelly was born in Limerick, and her parents moved to Wales when she was a child. She was married when she was sixteen, to a miner who was killed in an explosion. After the death of her husband she moved to Cardiff with her cousin. From there she went to France, but only stayed for a short time. Next she lived in a fashionable house in the West End (presumably as a servant), before coming into the East End, very down on her luck.

All appeared well until 30 October, when Kelly and Barnett had a fight – during which a window was broken – over the fact that Kelly had invited another prostitute – Maria Harvey – to sleep in the room. This Maria Harvey was still in Room 13 on the afternoon of Thursday 8th, for Barnett saw her there when he looked in to see that Mary Kelly was all right.

Kelly was *not* all right. In spite of Barnett's claims that he looked in on her every day, and gave her money if he had any, Mary Kelly was very short of cash. Barnett is on record that he considered Kelly to be 'a superior person' when judged against the other drabs who walked the streets in that part of London. Streets with names like Flower & Dean, or Thrawl. She was more experienced in life, even though she was younger than most. She had seen a little more of the world, and had even glimpsed life among the wealthy upper classes – albeit as a servant. Now she was drinking more than usual, and was also some three months overdue with her rent.

It is claimed by some that she was also three months overdue in another sense, meaning that she was three months pregnant, though there is no supporting evidence, except a conversation which has been – maybe deliberately – misunderstood: just as the three months overdue was misunderstood.

On the night of Thursday 8 November she was certainly out to get money. She was seen, very drunk, entering her room at around 11.45 pm, by Mary Cox, of 13 Miller's Court. There was a short, stout, shabbily dressed man with her. He carried a pot of ale, and wore a long dark coat and a round billycock hat.

Mary Cox called 'Goodnight, Mary' and Kelly, about to close her door, said, 'Goodnight. I'm going to have a song.' She then began singing 'I plucked a violet from my Mother's Grave, as a Boy'.

According to Catherine Picket, a flower seller, she was still singing this sentimental ballad at twelve-thirty.

Mary Cox, who had said goodnight to Kelly, went back to her room for only a quarter of an hour. She then left again – presumably to solicit. When she returned at one o'clock in the morning – with a client? Maybe – Kelly was singing. Then she went out again. Mary Kelly was still singing. She returned, for the last time, around three in the morning, and by then the light in Room 13 was out. There was no noise. Miller's Court was in nightmareland.

Elizabeth Prater, another prostitute, lived directly above Room 13, and it is important to note the salient points of her evidence, given at the inquest, First, she maintained that the floor between her room and Kelly's was so thin that she could hear Kelly if she simply moved around in Room 13.

Prater was away from her room from five o'clock on the Thursday afternoon until one in the morning. In fact she stood on the corner until twenty past one. Nobody spoke to her, and there was no sign of life from Kelly's room. Prater went to her own lodging - from which she claimed to be able to hear Kelly if she even walked in the room below. Not a sound was heard. Not a funeral note. She barricaded her door, and went straight to sleep. At between half past three, or a quarter to four, Prater was woken by her pet kitten. As she was turning over she heard a faint cry of 'Murder!' She claimed that it appeared to come from the court. Certainly if it had been from Kelly's room she would have known. In any case, she took no notice, went back to sleep and was awake in time to be in the Ten Bells public house by a quarter to six in the morning.

The cry of 'Murder!' was also heard by a laundress, Sara Lewis, who was visiting a friend's house in Miller's Court. She described the cry as faint, and could not say where it came from.

One other fact emerges at this point. Mary Cox, who had bid Kelly 'Goodnight' at 11.45 the previous night, woke at six in the morning and distinctly heard a man's footsteps leaving the court. She is on record as saying she thought it was the beat policeman; and so begin a number of strange anomalies.

During the night of 8/9 November, there is no record of a beat policeman going into Miller's Court. There may well be a good reason for this. Friday 9th was the day of the Lord Mayor's Show. It was also the Prince of Wales' Birthday. The police might well have been preserving manpower. The fact remains, there was no policeman on duty covering Miller's Court, and you might find this interesting when I present my new evidence.

The dawn came. A new day had begun. At around 10.45 am, M'Carthy sent his assistant, John Bowyer, to Kelly's room to see '. . . if she is going to give me any money'.

Bowyer knocked, looked through the keyhole, then went to the window that had been broken during the quarrel between Kelly and Barnett. Kelly had stuffed an old coat into the window, behind which was a muslin curtain.

John Bowyer pushed the coat to one side, then reached through and pulled back the curtain. The twelve-foot-square room was almost bare: two tables, a chair and a bed. On the bed lay a naked, bloody mass, that had once been a human being.

Bowyer had been a soldier for twenty years, and had seen active service, but nothing had prepared him for this. As he said, 'She was mutilated out of all recognition.'

Some time was lost with police haggling – instructions came, via various officers, that the door was not to be forced until the bloodhounds were brought, so that an attempt could be made to follow the murderer's scent.

In the end, the door *was* forced at around one-thirty in the afternoon. What had been a woman, now lay on the bed, entirely naked. Her throat had been cut from ear to ear, right down to the spinal column. The ears and nose had been cut off. The breasts had also been removed and placed on a table at the side of the bed.

The stomach and abdomen were ripped open; the face slashed so that the features were beyond recognition. The kidneys and heart had also been removed and placed, beside the breasts, on the table. The liver had been removed and placed on the right thigh. No portion of the body had been taken away. The thighs had been cut. It took five doctors six hours to put the pieces together and produce the semblance of a human being.

The victim's clothes were lying in an orderly manner by the side of the bed, and there had been a fire in the grate – so hot that a kettle spout had melted. Some clothes left by Maria Harvey had been burned, but nobody could account for the extraordinary heat given off by the fire.

The inquest was held on the Monday morning, though it was a hasty affair. Anyone with a suspicious mind might say that it was hurried through. The fact was commented on by the press. The jury very quickly returned a verdict of wilful murder against some person, or persons, unknown, after having been shown the remains, Kelly's room in Miller's Court, and hearing a very small amount of evidence.

The evidence did not include a couple of interesting points. First, an out-of-work labourer, George Hutchinson, maintained that he saw Kelly in Thrawl Street, at around two in the morning, and Kelly had asked him for the loan of sixpence, which he could not give her.

She then said, according to Hutchinson, 'Good morning. I must go and find some money.'

As she walked away, he saw a well-dressed man tap her on the shoulder and whisper something, at which they both laughed. As Hutchinson described it, the man was carrying a parcel, with a strap around it. He heard Kelly say, 'All right.'

The man replied, 'You'll be all right for what I've told you.'

Hutchinson followed the couple, and watched them as they talked, in Dorset Street, near the entrance to Miller's Court. He heard Kelly say, 'All right, my dear. Come along, you will be comfortable.' Then the man kissed her.

As they went towards the court, she said she had lost her handkerchief, and the man immediately pulled out his handkerchief which he gave to her. It was red.

Hutchinson, according to a statement given after the inquest, said he hung around for a while, and Sara Lewis, the laundress, reported seeing a man outside Room 13 at two-thirty in the morning which could have been him.

None of this – including a detailed description of the man with Kelly – was given in evidence during the inquest. Neither were two other witnesses heard. One, a tailor, claimed to have seen Mary Kelly at eight in the morning; another saw her at ten. This is strange as the doctors put the time of death at between three and three-thirty.

However, one dissenting voice *was* heard at the inquest, though the evidence from her seems to have been completely disregarded. She was a Mrs Carrie Maxwell, wife of a Dorset Street lodging house keeper, and, knowing what she was about to say, the coroner, Doctor McDonald, a former police surgeon, carefully warned her before she gave evidence. Here is the direct transcript:

Coroner: You must be very careful about your evidence because it is different to other people's. You say you saw her standing at the corner of the entry to the court?

Maxwell: Yes, On Friday morning, from eight to half past eight. I fix the time by my husband finishing work. When I came out of the lodging house, she was opposite.

Coroner: Did you speak to her?

Maxwell: Yes. It was an unusual thing to see her up. She was a young woman who never associated with anyone. I spoke to her across the street. I said 'What brings you up so early, Mary?' She said: 'Oh, Carrie, I do feel so bad.'

Coroner: And yet you say you had only spoken to her twice previously? But you knew her name, and she knew yours?

Maxwell: Oh, yes – by being about in the lodging house.

Coroner: What did she say?

Maxwell: She said: 'I've had a glass of beer and brought it up again.' And it was in the road. I imagined she had been in the Britannia beer shop at the corner of the street. I left her, saying I could pity her feelings. I went to Bishopsgate to get my husband's breakfast. On the way back I saw her outside the Britannia talking to a man.

Coroner: This would be at what time?

Maxwell: Between eight and nine o'clock. I was away about half an hour. It was about a quarter to nine.

Coroner: What description can you give of this man?

Maxwell: I couldn't give any. They were some distance. But I am sure it was the dead woman. I'm willing to swear to it.

Coroner: You are sworn now. Was he a tall man?

Maxwell: No. He was a little taller than me – and stout.

Coroner: What clothes was he wearing?

Maxwell: Dark clothes. He seemed to have a plaid coat on. I could not say what sort of hat he had.

Coroner: What sort of skirt had the deceased?

Maxwell: A dark skirt, a velvet bodice, a maroon shawl, and no hat.

After reading that evidence, and the reports of the two other persons who claimed to see Mary Jane Kelly walking and talking after she was supposed to be dead, the coroner, students, authorities and assorted Ripperologists have all simply shrugged their shoulders. Mrs Maxwell must have been mistaken, they say. Or, this proves that witnesses are notoriously unreliable.

Not so. There is plenty of evidence that Mary Kelly was a better-educated person than the other Ripper victims. She was certainly the youngest and most attractive. Yet, when I first encountered the description of the body in Room 13, and then began to look at the three sightings which could only have taken place after death, I became concerned. Soon I began to wonder if the body, discovered in that drab room in Miller's Court, just conceivably, might *not* be that of Mary Jane Kelly.

It is now some twenty years ago that I entered this ghostly, bleeding tunnel of discovery. Since then, I have worked at the problem, and worried at it also. I felt that I should not look for motives, but for the bare truth, and that, I felt, lay in the state of the body in Room 13, Miller's Court.

In the November of 1888, and since, the butchery which took place on that night has been explained as the last mad, deranged frenzy of the Ripper. True, we know now, from criminological studies of sociopathic sex murderers, that, as they progress with the killing, so the acts perpetrated become more violent and more random.

They did not know this in 1888, but, looking at the descriptions of the body, I became almost certain there was a reason for this killing. The ears and nose were cut off. The breasts had been removed, and the face slashed so that the features were *beyond recognition*. Those last two words made sense only if we are dealing with a crime which was meant to look like something it was not. The whole feeling about the body was that it was mutilated so it could *not* be recognized: and the only way this makes sense is if someone wanted the authorities to believe the body was that of Mary Jane Kelly, when it was not.

Once you have made that step forward, the evidence that she was alive, after three in the morning on 9 November 1888, begins to make sense. Do not try to fathom the reasons for it. Do not, yet, look for motive. Three people claimed to have seen a dead person walk and talk; while those who saw the body accepted it was that of Mary Jane Kelly. Now, I know it was not.

Where would Kelly go, if she also wanted to play dead? There was only one place I could think of – France. So, initially, I began to make quiet forays into the French Channel ports, and those along the Normandy coastline. Mary Jane Kelly, who liked to call herself Marie Jeanette Kelly, might just have crossed the Channel into France, and – while I thought it unlikely there would be any evidence – I went to the *Marie* (the French equivalent of our Town Hall) in many towns in Northern Europe. It became almost a hobby. I spent some three weeks of each year in France, and, wherever I went, I searched for traces of Kelly.

Then, two years ago, I picked up the scent, in the ancient city of Poitiers. I recall that I could hardly believe it when I first saw the name in the list of marriges for 1889. But it is there – and I publish a copy here for proof. On 25 August 1889 Marie Jeanette Kelly was married to Marc Jean Bartolemé. There is even an address, as you will see, and, later, I was able to talk with at least one of M. Bartolemé's descendants, from whom I received more proofs – and more mysteries.

Before explaining these things in detail, let me give you a brief peep into Mary Kelly's later family tree – knowing that I am about to bring before you proofs of what happened. As yet, I cannot explain why these things occurred, though I can make a number of intelligent guesses.

Marie Jeanette Kelly married Marc Jean Bartolemé in August

1889. M. Bartolemé was a baker with his own shop where he sold his bread and high-quality pâtisserie. He was well thought of in that part of Poitiers where he had followed his father into the trade. Two years after the wedding, Mary Kelly gave birth to their first child, a little boy, baptized Paul. A year after that there was a second boy, Jean Marc.

I cannot yet explain the reasons for what follows. It is as though the curse of the Ripper, and the scourge of Miller's Court, fell upon the Bartolemés.

In the summer of 1900, the children, who were aged nine and eight, respectively, were sent to an aunt – the wife of a farmer – who lived near Crécy. It was a kind of summer holiday for them. A change. While they were away enjoying the country life, fate struck, as though Mary Jane Kelly had been missed once, maybe by the Ripper, yet was never to be free of him.

On the morning of 28 August 1900, Marie Jeanette and Marc Jean Bartolemé were found, slashed to death in the bakehouse behind Marc's shop. The killer was never caught, though the weapon was still at the scene – a large carving knife, taken from the Bartolemé's kitchen.

Alas, this was not the end. The children remained with their aunt, Hilde Bartolemé, in Crécy, and she became a mother to them. The war came, in 1914, when both boys were in their early twenties. Miraculously, they survived the carnage, both of them serving France with courage.

In 1918, Paul, now twenty-seven years of age, returned to Poitiers and took over his father's bakery, while twenty-six year old Jean Marc went to England, where he married a girl called Margaret Fenton, but the curse had not finished with the Bartolemé family.

In 1922, Paul Bartolemé was shot dead in what seems to have been a tragic hunting accident. Jean Marc, who had his own bakery business in England, sold up and brought his wife, and their small son, Paul, back to Poitiers.

In 1931, Jean Marc Bartolemé was, himself, murdered by a thief whom he disturbed in the shop. His widow almost immediately returned to England, where she changed her name, not back to Fenton, but to a kind of Anglicized version of

Bartolemé – Bartholemew . . .

Tarpin stopped reading. He could hear his heart thudding in his ears. His hands trembled like a man with Parkinsonia. Paul, son of Jean Marc Bartolemé and a direct link to Mary Jane Kelly, supposed final victim of Jack the Ripper, was his father. For a few moments the world spun around him, and it took a while for him to separate the ringing in his head from the ringing of his telephone.

'I'm sorry, Mr Tarpin, I know you asked not to be disturbed.' It was Elaine, his PA. 'Miss Cartwright insists on speaking with you. She says it's urgent.'

'Put her through.'

'You okay, Phillip?' Hilary Cartwright's voice seemed distorted on the line.

'Sure. Yes. Of course . . . ' Only he was not okay, and his entire life had changed. 'Yes, Hilary,' pulling himself together. 'What can I do for you?'

'A couple of things. I don't want to pressurize you . . . '

'Oh, you're not. We'll be making an offer. I'm sure of that . . . '

'Good, because Tim Clifford's coming into New York tomorrow. He wants to add – or enlarge – a chapter or two. Come up with more dirt, I think. It'd be nice if you could meet.'

'I want to see him as soon as he gets here.' He knew the words were tumbling out in desperation.

'You sound serious, Phillip. You sure nothing's wrong?'

'Nothing that your Professor Clifford can't put right.' It seemed unbearably hot in his office. In his head he saw a bleak, bloody room with a fire roaring out of control in a small grate.

'Well, he's coming on Concorde, in the morning.'

'Can we lunch?' Tarpin asked, hearing his own voice rasp in his throat, and the drumbeat of his heart, like a death march, in his head.

SIXTEEN

– 1 –

Tarpin speed-read the rest of the manuscript, taking in the salient points as the author presented them. Clifford had simply gathered together all the information concerning the violent deaths within the Bartolemé family: extracts from local newspapers; a couple of French police reports; a statement from an old friend of Paul Bartolemé, who had been in the hunting party when he was killed; and a small amount of uncorroborated information on Margaret's flight to England following Jean Marc's death. Clifford pointed particularly to the odd spelling of the assumed Anglicized name, Bartholemew which is usually spelled Bartholomew. He had been unable to trace the last male child, the second Paul, son of Jean Marc and Margaret (neé Fenton).

Clifford summed up.

He was of an age to have fought in World War Two. Many records appear to have gone astray, and all that is left is the fact that this last remaining male, direct descendant of Mary Jane Kelly, lived for some time in Bedford where his mother – Margaret Fenton – had family. An exhaustive search of the records has produced little, though I did speak with one old lady who claimed to be Margaret Fenton's sister, and almost certainly the last member of the family. She was already very old, with her mind wandering, when I saw her in St Catherine's Home for the elderly near Bedford.

I tried to ask simple questions, the kind of thing that might jog her memory, but I got nothing back until I was leaving. Quite suddenly she looked at me – squinted at me really – and asked if I was Jack.

I told her no, and inquired why. Quite clearly – and I have the witnessed transcript of that conversation – she said, 'Poor Margaret. She was always worried about Jack. She said Jack had taken all her husband's family. She was afraid for Paul. She said he must be careful or Jack would get him, like he got his grandmother.

So, the trail dies out. How, then, do we make any sense of this? Can any deductions be drawn regarding the identity of the Ripper, or why Mary Jane Kelly's family – the males certainly, if not all the females – died violent deaths? Is this simply one of those stranger-than-fiction coincidences? Or is there a reason? Did Mary Jane Kelly lend out Room 13 in Miller's Court – as she seems to have done with Maria Harvey? Once having allowed someone else to use the place, had that someone got unlucky? I think so. Whoever killed in Miller's Court that night, wanted the authorities to believe two things: that the victim was Mary Kelly, and that the murder had been committed by Jack the Ripper.

Tarpin was in no mood to go on. He flicked through the last pages, to find that Clifford had not really attempted to find a solution to the puzzle within the mystery. He went through all the old theories of who the Ripper might be, but it was obvious that his heart was not in it. His energies were being channelled into the further conundrum – the flight of Mary Jane Kelly, her marriage, and the dark shadow which seemed to follow her descendants down the years.

There was no doubt that this book would cause a stir, for the author had genuinely produced something startlingly new out of the facts and legends of the Ripper. Countless students, historians and authors had claimed there had been some cover-up concerning the Whitechapel murders of 1888. Some had claimed a royal connection, which had swept the truth under the carpet of Victorian morality. If there was any kind of whitewash, then the publication of *The Whitechapel Victims* might flush more facts from the buried woodwork of history.

Now Phillip Tarpin had accepted the truth about his own lineage, he understood that, whoever wanted to see his real family name blotted out, were already on to him. The death of Sukie Cartwright; the terrifying spectre of the 'Nemesis of Neglect' cartoon; the knife rip in his cheek – all these things began to make sense. He was not a random victim, and Sukie had probably died for him.

He looked at his watch. A quarter to six. Slowly he dialled Hilary Cartwright's number.

– 2 –

Earlier in the day, Mr John Chilton, known to his friends as Jackie, took a call from the man he knew as Scarecrow.

'Had an interesting day,' Scarecrow said, his voice plummy and affected. Chilton thought he sounded like a very English actor, though he could never remember the man's name.

'Oh, yes?' Chilton remained reserved.

'Read the professor's manuscript.'

'How the hell . . . ?' Chilton began.

'Ask no questions, and you'll be told no lies, Jackie.'

'Right. What's the verdict?'

'Quite surprising. He's got most of it right, but he doesn't even have a stab at the reason.'

'Well, that's all right.'

'Hardly.'

'Why?'

'Because, my dear Jackie, he'll put the cat among the pigeons. They'll be over the records and files like a swarm of tom cats after a tasty pussy.'

'We do anything?'

'Doubt it. Nothing legal anyway.'

'And when did that stop us, sir? With respect, of course.'

'Rarely. But we can give no reason for this. Doesn't jeopardize national security.'

'Mmmm.'

'Just thought you should know, Jackie. If only because the clever professor's on his way to your side of the pond.'

'Ah, but we can't really do anything.' There was a subtext in the way he spoke. It was something that Scarecrow quickly jumped on and squashed.

'No, Jackie. I mean it. We do *absolutely* nothing. How are the lads on your side of the pond?'

'Quietly active. I think they'll have another go, and this time they could be successful. The shoot-to-kill policy still hitting the headlines, is it?'

'Since Hong Kong, and then the other business in June, yes. Never stops. Accusations flying around. Statements being made. Her Majesty's government denies any such goings on in the North.'

'Quite right,' said Chilton.

'Pity our friend isn't on this side of the water.' Scarecrow was musing, dropping the word in the hope that Chilton might be able to do something with it.

'You want me to arrange that?'

'Could you?'

'Maybe. Maybe not. I can but try.'

'We could protect him here, Jackie. I can't let the boys from Hereford loose in New York.'

'Hardly, sir.' The boys from Hereford, as Mr Chilton knew, meant the Special Air Service, the élite unit constantly blamed for a shoot-to-kill policy against the Provisional Irish Republican Army.

– 3 –

'So, you think we should make him a high offer.' Peter Palestino looked concerned. He always did when it came to paying authors large sums of money.

They sat in the CEO's office: Tarpin, Liz Oliver and Palestino.

He had caught Hilary just before she left her office. 'I want your authorization, on Clifford's behalf, to talk about the book to my CEO and one other senior editor,' Tarpin had said.

'You *are* going to make an offer, then?'

'That will be my recommendation, yes.'

'You got a figure in mind?'

'That's the other thing I need to talk about with you.'

'Go on. Say a sum.'

'Come on, Hilary, we both know how the game's played. What did you get in London? The truth, now.'

'One hundred thousand sterling.'

'Just for *The Whitechapel Victims?* No hidden clauses? No two- or three-book deal?'

'They have first refusal on Tim's next book. It's the usual, standard, thing.'

'No outline for the next?'

'No, just the clause about first refusal of the next work. With a time limit, of course.'

'Okay. You looking for us to match this?'

'I would expect a little more.'

'Hilary, wait a moment. This is the American publication, remember. This is a particularly English crime.'

'And you come on as well, Phillip. As you've already said, we both know how the games's played. The Ripper is international. You'll clean up.'

'Possibly. If we do, then Clifford'll make his money. Give me a ballpark, Hilary.'

'Okay. How about three-quarters of a million?'

'You're joking?'

'I'd get it from Pallisers.'

'Think again.'

'No, Phillip, my dear. *You* think again. You have my okay to talk with your people, but I'd like an offer before we meet for lunch tomorrow.'

'I might have something more than an offer.'

She laughed, uncertain. 'Something more? What?'

'Wait and see. I'll call you in the morning. Early, before you go out to meet the professor.'

'I'll be at my home number until nine-thirty.'

'Right.'

'Right.'

Now, Palestino was quizzing him about the book and the expected price.

'She's talking seven-fifty.'

'Dollars?' Palestino hoped.

'Naturally. She'll take five, maybe even lower, once I've talked with Clifford.'

'Phew,' from Liz.

'Phew, nothing, honey. Other authors did deals in the millions earlier this year, and they're fiction.'

'Funny money,' Palestino laughed. 'Crazy money. How can you tempt Professor Clifford, Phillip?'

'Let me tell you a story.' Under the dressing his wounded cheek began to throb, as he went through his own connection with what Clifford had uncovered.

'You mean someone's still after you?' Palestino looked dismayed.

'This isn't plastic surgery!' He touched his cheek. 'Whoever came after me was dressed like a bloody Ripper cartoon, Peter. I guess that was only a warning . . . '

'Hadn't we better get you some protection?'

'I suspect I have some protection.' He was thinking of the omnipresent Mr Chilton. 'Though I could be wrong. But, that's all one, as the Bard would say. For the time being, I'll take my chances. What's your first offer, Peter? Let me have something to start the bidding.'

Liz was looking shocked, staring at Tarpin in horror, for the truth was only now starting to seep into her mind.

Palestino shifted in his chair, looked away, then said softly, 'Two-fifty.'

'Okay. I'll call it a quarter of a mill. Sounds more. They can have my story for nothing.'

'Surely . . . ?' Palestino began.

'Is that really wise, Phillip?' Liz still looked horrified. 'I mean, if someone is out to . . . '

'Kill me? Yes, it's the wisest thing I know. Come out in the open, and let it be known before publication. In fact, let it be known as soon as possible. Truth might just blow the bogeyman off course.'

On their way out, in the elevator, she held him very close. He could feel her breasts through the thin material of her blouse and his shirt. 'Can we have fun and games tonight?' She tried a smile, though it did not blot out the clouds still furrowing her brow.

'Sure, why not?' He gave her a squeeze.

That night, he laid Sukie's ghost and taught Liz how to play trains. They chugged their way half around the United States until two in the morning, after which Liz fell into a deep, satisfied sleep, with a smile on her face.

Tarpin found sleep a little more difficult. In that twilight time, drifting between the day and unconsciousness, he heard footsteps in his head, and then the faint cry of 'Murder!' He knew where he was, and, when his eyes snapped open, it was a relief to realize that he slept next to Liz, above Fifth Avenue, a long way from Miller's Court which had ceased to exist, trampled under by a multi-storey car park.

– 4 –

Timothy Clifford was younger than Tarpin had imagined. Younger and very shrewd. They met at The Four Seasons – in the Pool Room even though Hilary had turned down the quarter of a million out of hand.

'Wait, Hilary,' he had said to her. 'Let me talk with your author. I'm sure we can do better.'

She sounded reluctant on the telephone – 'You are not to discuss money in front of Tim' – but, when they all met, she described the situation as ' . . . being in negotiation'.

Clifford was in his early forties. Boyish, with an unruly mop of black hair, and the manner of one who could probably get you interested in the most prosaic side of history. Enthusiastic was the word Tarpin would have used. Everything came in superlatives. The trip over had been ' . . . Splendid. Never done Concorde before. You ever . . . ?'

He suspected Hilary had kicked the young professor under the table, edging him away from anything that might remind Tarpin of Sukie's death.

Then: 'It's wonderful to be in New York. Frightens some of my colleagues, but I adore it.'

'You don't have to live here,' Hilary said with a smile.

Then he did a big hype for his British publishers, and Tarpin said it was a pity Hosier & Whitehead had not bought the book.

'Their offer was almost insulting,' Hilary said.

'You should've asked me first.' Tarpin was actually a little put out. 'I oversee everything after they've bought it. I might have done something for you.'

Clifford just went on telling them the plans in the UK for a huge publicity campaign, until Hilary stopped him again. 'I think Phillip wants to talk about the book. He has some questions, haven't you, Phillip?'

Tarpin nodded. 'Questions and answers.' He told Clifford that, should they successfully buy the book, he would be editing. 'Hilary said you wanted to add some things?'

Clifford raked his thick hair with open fingers. 'Well, the people in London say they want some more. A tad more detail about Mary Kelly.'

'Have you more detail?'

'Not much after she went to France – that's the big news in this book. All I'm doing is adding a lot of quite old stuff from the London records. About Kelly I mean – in Miller's Court.'

'The sightings after death. And the inquest, that kind of thing?'

'Lord, yes. I'm putting everything in but the kitchen sink now. I was a shade selective, I suppose. Wanted to get to the big news that she had married in France.'

'What other evidence, then?'

'Oh, Carrie Maxwell first. It was suggested, at the time, that poor old Caroline Maxwell – wife of Henry, who owned and ran that damned great lodging house in Dorset Street – had muddled the days. Not so. They knew by the end of the week, after she had given evidence, that she was sure of the day.'

'How?'

'Because a London newspaper followed it up. You might recall she said she spoke with Kelly, then saw her again, later.'

'After she'd been to Bishopsgate to get her husband's breakfast, yes.'

'Well, what she was doing was getting *milk* for his breakfast. She *always* got fresh milk on a Friday. The dairy bore out her story. They also checked the other two people. Man called Lewis – I don't mention his name in the version you have – saw her in the Britannia beer shop. Oh, and there's a lot more.'

'Such as?'

'Such as the identification by the boy friend. Barnett identified her by the eyes, but he'd have identified a horse as being her by the time he saw what was left. It really was identification by association. The body had been found in her room, therefore it had to be her, poor cow.'

'Anything else?'

'Kelly herself.' He paused to thank the waiter for his smoked salmon. 'She really *was* out of the ordinary. Somehow she didn't belong. Old Inspector Abeline, for instance, who did a lot of the investigation and is often, wrongly, invested with being the police officer in charge. Well, Abeline had known her since she moved into the area, a year or so before she went into Miller's Court. She really *was* a cut above the others. She was also one hell of an actress. She was there, I'm certain, for a purpose.'

'I think I might be able to provide you with a whole new chapter.' Tarpin dropped his voice, but he could feel the static coming off Tim Clifford. The professor had a kind of electric aura. He gave off the passion and drive of a creative person.

He waited, and Tarpin let him hang on for a good twenty seconds. 'Mary Kelly was my great-grandmother.'

Clifford's mouth dropped open, and Phillip Tarpin had him. The entire room seemed to go silent, but for the sound of the water. Clifford hardly ate a mouthful while Tarpin told of his mother's affair. Of the letters; of Paul Bartholemew's work in SOE; his death in Belfast; and lastly, his own brush with death in New York. By now he had made the full and obvious connection.

'Jesus!' said the professor. Then, again, 'Jesus!'

'I'm going to offer you all my mother's papers, and my own story for inclusion in the book. The rest'll have to be between Hilary and my boss – Peter Palestino. I just hope you can come to some agreement, because I for one would like this whole damned thing solved as soon as possible.'

'So would I.' Clifford gave a little smile, as though glad to have a surprise of his own. 'The manuscript in my safe has been tampered with. I had a feeling, an intuition. I thought my London flat was under surveillance. So, I set a small trap. They got a peep at a very early first draft.'

'Who're they?' Tarpin asked, leaning forward, tense.

'No idea, but they might well be what we call "the authorities". Now, with your story, it looks as though someone *still* doesn't want the truth to get out. After all these years.'

'Over a century.' Hilary stated the obvious, and then looked a little sheepish.

– 5 –

That night, after Hilary had another lengthy session with Palestino, Liz and Tarpin learned that the deal had been done for three hundred thousand, with bonuses. Tarpin spoke with Tim Clifford on the telephone. They arranged to meet the following afternoon. Liz had already weeded out all of what she called The Millstone References from Paul Bartholemew's letters to Vera Tarpin.

'It'll take about half an hour for me to put them in order,' she said when they got back to the apartment building.

The doorman seemed to be waiting for them. 'There's a registered packet for you. Mr Tarpin. I'll get it for you. All the way from England.'

It was a padded bag, registered and addressed to Phillip Tarpin Esq., which must have puzzled the doorman who knew Tarpin was not a lawyer. The sticker on the front showed that it had come from Cox, Russ & Pembeton.

Inside was a heavily sealed envelope and a letter from old Mr Pembeton:

Dear Mr Tarpin,
I am sorry this was apparently overlooked when we were settling up your mother's estate.

She left it in our keeping some years ago. I remember well that she told me it was to go to you, and she asked us to keep it secure. It has been in one of the firm's strongboxes ever since.

Your mother was a little mysterious about this, though she told me she had never read the contents, and never would.

My apologies for not letting you have it sooner. You will see that the seal on the inner envelope has not been broken.
With my good wishes,
Yours sincerely.

Tarpin opened the second large envelope. Inside was a letter and another envelope. This one was of a strong thick brown paper. It had also been sealed with wax.

With Liz peering over his shoulder, Tarpin read the letter, which was dated May 1944.

'Darling Muffin', it began.

Liz laughed, 'Your father had some odd names for your mother.'

Darling Muffin,

As you know, I shall be away again for a while. This time I feel you should take charge of the only proofs there are regarding what we both refer to as Millstone.

These papers belonged to my grandmother. She apparently told my father's brother that they should not be opened except in a dire family disaster. I think my father, in fact, read the contents after his brother died in the so-called hunting accident. He sealed them again, according to my mother. All I will tell you is that they provide the truth about Millstone.

If, for some reason, I do not come back – perish the thought – you should read what is inside. Maybe you will then want to take some legal advice. Maybe not, it depends on how you feel.

As ever with all my deepest love –

His hands trembled as he broke the seal. Inside the thick envelope was another packet which had been opened but was now bound with a tight red ribbon. The stamps showed the head of Queen Victoria and the packet was addressed to Madame M. J. Bartolemé at an address in Poitiers, France.

Inside was a small oilskin packet and another letter, this time yellow and old, the page written in a firm, clear copperplate hand. There was no address at the heading, but it was dated 20 June 1893. It began:

Dear Marie Jeanette,

I am done for now. The doctors say that I will not see next Christmas, but I am to go into hospital where they say I will be more comfortable. I shall miss the occasional letters we exchanged. But now to business.

You will remember me as a cautious man. I am also a man with a conscience, though you may find that hard to believe. I still have the occasional nightmare about what we did on 9 November 1888 in Miller's Court, and I have often wondered if the powers that be might one day come after us and alter the facts – or try to alter them.

Against that day, I will now tell you that I kept a diary of all the events of that year, from the time you went into the East End, so bravely, to pose as a little whore, right up to the final act. I do not know if I ever told you I followed your career, even though we only met on that last terrible night.

You were a brave girl, and did what was to be done as a true patriot. If England was to know the truth, we would both have been given medals, and our families would have been proud of us. As it is, my name has remained a mystery, though the Micks still have yours, so, presumably they know the truth – or at least suspect it.

I leave you my little diary. Who knows, one day it could be of use to you. If you are in need of help, I think a copy might give the people in Whitehall, and particularly what we used to call the Irish Branch, the Special Branch, at the Yard, second thoughts. It could see you quite comfortable – like you promised me on that dark night when we met, and did what had to be done.

God bless you, Mary Jane. And God help me.

Your friend,

It was signed, 'Detective Superintendent Daniel Drover, (Retired)'.

'Who the hell . . . ?' Liz began, but all Tarpin could think of were the words in Clifford's manuscript. The description given after the inquest, by the man Hutchinson:

'Hutchinson followed the couple, and watched them as they talked, in Dorset Street, near the entrance to Miller's Court. He heard Kelly say, "All right, my dear. Come along, you will be comfortable." Then the man kissed her.'

He put his hand on the oilskin packet, and looked Liz in the eyes. 'It's a hundred and one sticks of dynamite,' he said. Then he swallowed. 'This is the diary of the man who killed Mary Jane Kelly in Miller's Court in November 1888.'

He began to unwind the oilskin and remove the small bound book which lay inside.

In his head he heard that faint night cry of 'Murder!'

SEVENTEEN

– 1 –

They sat close together on chairs pulled up to the dining table, the book open between them. It was bound in grey and black marbled board, with a strong spine, about three-quarters of an inch thick. On the first page, in the same firm copperplate hand as the letter, were the words: Daniel Arthur Drover. Inspector. Department I, Formerly of the Special Office, Scotland Yard. Notes and observations. 1888.

The first entry was dated *Monday, 2nd April 1888:*

I have decided to renew my old practice of keeping an occasional journal, together with notes and observations. My reasons are that I have been moved to a most secret department, and am no longer with the Branch, but simply a group known as Department I. None of us have names, it would seem, and we refer to the Super in charge as the Chief. I know his name, of course, but we are to be answerable to nobody. This is mainly on account of the Fenians, and there is to be no communication with our old friends in the Branch.

Interesting that I came to this resolution over the weekend because, no sooner do we seem to have put away the two Irish Republicans (Callan and Harkins, who were sentenced to fifteen years apiece on 3rd February last), than others have sprung up. We still have the informant Beach, who penetrated the Fenian Brotherhood some time ago, and from him the Chief has learned of at least three new cells – of four men each – which have now established themselves in the East End, we believe.

Unhappily, Beach is not able to give us the names, or any full details, but says he got the intelligence from a source near James McCarthy – a known Fenian who has been responsible for infiltrating groups into the capital before. McCarthy is a slippery customer, and, though we know what he is doing – preparing lodgings or houses that will be safe for the cells; supplying them with dynamite and weapons etc. – we have never been able to lay hands on him. Today, the Chief said, 'Damn it, we can't even arrest him under the Explosive Substances Act!' It was through this Act that the Branch nailed Callan and Harkins.

Someone else, I think Willis, said, 'I know what I'd do with those Fenian bastards. I'd just have them shot out of hand. They plan assassination and the laying of bombs, like the Jubilee Plot, and serve hard labour when we get them. They wouldn't think twice of blowing innocent people to tarnation, the buggers. It would be cheaper and more merciful, to our pockets and our time, if we just did away with them.'

The Chief told him to watch his language, then laughed and suggested that we should put some of them away on the quiet if we got a chance. I would certainly go along with that, and I said so. I do believe that the Chief means it.

Tuesday, 10th April 1888
It has been a busy time, and at last McCarthy has been brought to book. The method is irregular. We all know it, just as we know the Chief, and others, are turning a blind eye. It was Saturday last at about five in the evening. Evans and Church were on duty, keeping a watch on McCarthy. At dinner time, in the Four Bells, Cheapside, they saw another man, now identified as Joseph Boland, pass him a small haversack containing a pistol.

Both Evans and Church were armed and they followed him back to his lodgings in the next street. Their story is that, when they forced an entry, McCarthy drew his pistol and fired at them. They returned fire and killed him stone dead with the second shot.

I spoke with Evans later and got the truth. When they forced McCarthy's door he said, 'Right, you have me fair and square now. But long live the Brotherhood,' or some such. Evans told me that Church went to the haversack and pulled out a Webley revolver and ammunition. As he walked back towards Evans, so he turned and fired two bullets from his own weapon into McCarthy, and then shot at the wall with the Webley which he threw down next to the body.

'It saves a lot of time and work,' Church apparently said to Evans. I agree, and I suspect Evans did also, though he was a little shaken.

Met Church in our local later this evening, and said to him that it was good shooting. He winked, and I said I would do the same. After all, we are only attached to the department. Nothing is permanent any more. In fact, this morning I saw Mr Quinn, who was once the Queen's bodyguard, and is now high in the Branch. He passed by me, in the corridor, without even acknowledging my presence. So, we know how the land lies. We shall be responsible for our own actions. Answerable to none.

Monday, 18th June 1888
It seems the Chief is a cunning one. Today at the weekly meeting he revealed that, not only are we running the informant Beach, but he has also put a young girl into the East End. She is Irish, from Limerick, but very loyal to the Queen and the government. It seems she has been working for us since long before we became this ghost department (Department I), and lives in a certain amount of squalor, even taking a man as her lover. I would not like to be her, for she lives among the dregs of mankind. I know that area well, and it's thick with Family people, whores, and every conceivable vice. However, we were told today that she has made contact with one of the Fenian cells, and we should be getting good intelligence from her. The Chief himself maintains contact with her.

Tarpin looked at Liz, and knew there was fear in his face. She winced when she looked at him. The whole thing was bizarre, and there could now be only one conclusion. He talked to her in quick, short sentences, laying out the story of Jack the Ripper's Whitechapel victims, just as Clifford had written of them.

'That's what all this is about?' she asked.

'Mainly.' He did not look her in the eyes.

194

They continued to read. In July 1888, Drover wrote –

I have not had a chance to make notes recently, for we have all been busy trying to deal with the cell that the Chief's informant (the girl from Limerick) has opened up to us. None of us has any doubt now where our duty lies. I suppose there would be many who, should they know, would say we are nothing but paid asassins. This is not the bone of contention. The problem of Ireland can only get worse as the years go by. These people wish to press their cause, which is not just, by violent and terrible action. They will do anything to foment disquiet. What we do now might help in future years.

The great problem facing the Empire lies in the long and desperate memories these people gather together. Through these recollections, which are often warped, they will bring about rebellion. That is a word which chills all of us to the bone, for, if Ireland rebels, and carries its mutiny into the very homes and hearths of people here in the mother country, where will it end?

As the Chief has said, 'If they succeed in their evil ways, there is nothing to stop the huge brush fire spreading through the Empire, and then this glorious country of ours will descend into a dark chaos. For certain the Empire will go with it.'

As for this particular cell, there are four men: Judge, Cavey, Fearon and Smart: and this is what they all are – smart. We know the houses they use, and we have an idea that they are preparing some terrible deed. They have spent much time, in pairs, or individually, looking around the Crystal Palace, and the pleasure gardens surrounding. If they were able to secretly amass a huge amount of dynamite for a bomb, it could cause untold damage. Hundreds of innocent men, women and children might die. It is for the children I fear most, for they are the future for Queen and Empire.

Monday, 4th August 1888
Over the past weeks, things have gradually come to a head. Through the girl (her name is Kelly) we have discovered that the man Fearon has been planning to purchase a horse-drawn van, and we believe they will fill the van with explosives and drive it, possibly on a weekend, into the Crystal Palace area and so

explode it.

Kelly has made a good contact, and it certainly seems as though this is the Fenian plan. We cannot stand by and just see this happen, yet we have no way of arresting them. They have done nothing as yet, and we believe they expect explosives any time now. On Friday last, it was discovered they have moved to lodgings in Limehouse, close by the docks. Perhaps we have waited long enough. Tonight I believe we shall take action.

Tuesday, 5th August 1888
They are gone. Finished. Late this forenoon we heard from the girl, Kelly, that the other cells are in disarray. None of the Fenians in London know what to do.

Last night, I went with Church, Dobbs, and the others, to carry out our plan. We were in the Three Bells public house in Limehouse, and there saw the man Fearon, who had been talking with Smart and Cavey. Eventually Smart left, and Church went after him.

Shortly after, Dobbs and I began to engage Fearon and Cavey in conversation. They are quiet, somewhat hard men, and did not seem to enjoy our company until Dobbs asked Cavey what trade he was in. Cavey did not answer directly, but Fearon said they were in the business of buying arms for a dealer in Dublin.

I asked what kind of arms, and he said mainly for hunting purposes, for the gentry paid good money for shotguns and the like. He also talked of antique pistols, and said he had a market for all types of weapon.

We bought them more drink. After a while, I took Fearon to one side and told him I knew of a warehouse where there were two hundred rifles stored, together with explosives. He said, 'What's that to me?' So I replied I knew the night watchman, and he might be able to get some of the rifles without payment. He made a gesture as if to say that he could be interested, so I offered to take him there and introduce him to the night watchman. I said he was my cousin.

He became more interested, and suggested that we should all four go. I told him, no, that would not be safe, but I would take him alone. We had been plying both of them with drink, and they were now quite drunk and full of bravado.

In the end he told Cavey to stay in the public house. 'I'm going with this feller,' he said. 'We will not be long. He's a good man.'

The streets were very dark, and I led him to an agreed point, behind the old Tate warehouse which is to be pulled down. One blow felled him, and I finished him off with a knife, then bound the feet together with a cord I had with me. This I attached to six heavy bricks – part of the crumbling warehouse. He went into the water with hardly a sound. I doubt they will ever find him.

This morning we compared notes. All four have gone into the river. Now we wait for some reaction from the other cells.

'My God, talk about shoot-to-kill,' Liz muttered.

Tarpin just nodded, and read on.

Thursday, 30th August 1888

They seem to have scattered, and lost contact with one another. These remaining Fenian cells are in complete disarray, and we now have a bonus. Today the chief told us that his girl – Kelly – has befriended a young woman from Dublin. Her name is Maureen Casey, and Kelly says she thinks Casey is the go-between for the Fenian groups. We expect to hear more soon.

There were no more entries until *Friday, 6th October*. Now, they came to the first mention of a connection between Drover and Kelly. Tarpin saw the whole picture, and could hardly believe it. Drover wrote:

There have been a number of murders by the man everyone is calling either Leather Apron, or Jack The Ripper. The Force is at sixes and sevens, for they fear demonstrations from the East End.

Tonight, the Chief asked me to present myself at his house. He had a cab waiting and we drove quite deep into the East End. It is as foul as I remember it. The smell is soot, beer and human excreta. Along the streets there are men and women drunk, or offering themselves for hire. Both sexes. It is disgusting to see.

We drove down the Flowery Dean – as the locals call Flower & Dean Street – and the Chief told me to sit well back, in the shadows. Then, at the corner of Thrawl Street, he pointed out a young woman. She was tall, and handsome, parading herself as all the women do in that place.

'That's our girl, Kelly,' he told me. 'Look at her and remember her face, Dan. We might have need of making contact, and you are my choice.'

Poor wretched girl. She must indeed be very loyal and courageous. I would not like to work in disguise in this part of London.

On the way back, the Chief told me of a friend of his who came across children of nine and ten trying to copulate in the road, near Dorset Street, 'They copy their elders,' he said. 'It is truly appalling.'

There was a long gap in time now, and Drover resumed with an entry made on:

Tuesday, 6th November 1888
There is good news about the murders, though, for various reasons, neither the City, nor Metropolitan Forces are yet releasing it. One explanation is that the Chief, who obviously has friends in very high places, has asked for it to be kept quiet.

We now know the Fenians are in complete confusion. The girl Casey is, apparently, the only person who can make contact between the separate cells, and she waits for orders from Dublin, which are long in coming. If it was not for Casey, they would be in complete rout. Meanwhile it seems she pretends to be a working girl on the streets, though Kelly says this is only a dodge. She is very friendly with Casey, and the Fenian trusts her – Kelly, that is.

Late in the afternoon, the Chief called me to his office and said we should take a ride around the park, which we did. During the ride he spoke very frankly to me. 'If the girl Maureen Casey disappears, then the cells will wither until they have a chance to rebuild them,' he said as we drove in a cab. I agreed. 'My girl, Kelly, can trap her,' he continued. 'She can arrange to have her come to the place where she lodges. It's no bigger than a broom cupboard. In Miller's Court, off Dorset Street. You know it, Dan?'

I told him I knew it well. Then he said he had been looking at my file, and had seen that I started life as a butcher's apprentice. I laughed and said that was why the others spoke of me as 'Butcher Drover'. 'Ah', he said softly. 'I thought that was for another reason. Are you up to doing some butchery for your country, Dan?' I asked what he meant, and he put the idea to me. It will have to be done before the week is out. He says he can arrange it with the girl Kelly. Probably the early hours of Friday.

I asked him what would become of Kelly, for the Fenians must know she and Casey are thick together. Kelly would be taken care of. 'She would be taken out of the country as fast as can be arranged,' is what he said. Then, 'You'd have to make it look real.' He stared at me, hard. 'People would have to think it was Kelly that was killed. That'll make it a bloody business.'

I repeated that the Fenians would eventually know who it was, and he nodded. Mary Jane will have to look out for herself in the coming years. When the Fenians work it out, her life will not be worth a brass farthing. In the end, I told him I would do it on one condition: that I go back into the Branch and my name is taken off any paper connected to Department I. He says there is nothing in writing about the Department, and I tend to believe him.

Wednesday, 7th November 1888
It is to be tomorrow night. At least, early on Friday morning. I have to meet the girl in Thrawl Street, around two. There are passwords to be exchanged, and she has promised the Chief that she will have Maureen Casey already at her lodging.

This afternoon, I went down to take a look in daylight. It should all be easy enough, though I trust the girl Kelly has the stomach for what has to be done. It will be butchery, there's no doubt about that.

Tarpin had to steel himself for the final entry:

Friday, 9th November 1888
It is over and done with. I trust that I will never have to look upon the like again. All I can say is that the young girl, Mary Jane Kelly, was the bravest I have ever seen a woman. My hope is that the Chief kept all his promises. He has told me that she got off to France this afternoon. We took a ride in the park again and

talked everything over. It appears that he had hoped the body would not be discovered until late tonight, or even tomorrow, so that Miss Kelly could make good her escape. I deduce that he is concerned, for she was out in the streets not long before the body was discovered, and he is afraid for her.

I waited in Thrawl Street, as arranged, and she arrived on the dot of two in the morning. There was another man loitering nearby, and she spoke to him briefly before proceeding towards me.

As arranged, I whispered in her ear, catching hold of her as she passed. The first password was to be 'A little of what you fancy does you good'. She was to laugh and talk some nonsense. I was amazed, for she appeared quite calm and collected, though she had fortified herself with drink. The Chief had already told me that she has been feigning drunkenness and poverty for several weeks.

I was a little concerned, for the fellow she had spoken with appeared to be following us, but she said to take no notice. When we got to the little archway that leads from Dorset Street into Miller's Court, she gave the second signal, saying she had no handkerchief. I did as I was told and handed her the one provided by the Chief.

I next asked her if the woman was in her room, and she nodded, so I warned her it would be a horrifying business. Again she nodded, though I saw that she bit her lip.

When we got to her room, she went in first and said to Casey, 'This is the man I told you about.' Casey had been sitting on the bed, but she rose and said, 'I'm so glad you have come. The Brotherhood needs instructions. We are all to pieces. None of the men dare show themselves in the streets.'

Then I did it very quickly, knocking her unconscious so that she fell to the floor beside the bed. I stepped back and unrolled the surgical apron and gloves that I carried. It only took half a minute to put them on, and a few seconds to cut her throat with the knife the Chief had provided – double-edged, and sharp as a razor. She did not make a sound, though there was a great spurt of blood, and Kelly gave a small cry, then said, very quietly and in control, 'My God, you're Jack the . . . '

I turned to her and shook my head, telling her that we took Jack earlier in the week. 'You will not hear of it,' I said, giving her the truth. 'He was a strange little man. Hanged himself in his cell, so there will be no report. He admitted to Nichols, Chapman and Eddowes, but to none of the others.' This is what I was told on Tuesday.

Kelly helped me lift the corpse on to the bed, and I told her she need not stay to watch. That it would be a terrible sight for her young, pretty eyes, and would take a long time. She had locked the door, and now she said she would stay as long as was necessary.

There was only one candle, so she helped by making a fire out of old clothes that were in the room. We also burned all of Casey's clothes, leaving a set belonging to Mary Kelly neatly beside the bed. The fire did not give much light so I handed her the magnesium they had given to me in case I could not disfigure the face. It had been suggested that I might disfigure her by fire: burn off the skin and her hair, using the magnesium powder. The hair was not a problem. She was the same colouring as Mary. Same eye colour as well. Kelly threw the magnesium on the fire, and it blazed so ferociously that I thought the whole place might go up. The sudden heat was enough to melt the spout of an old tin kettle.

The work was not too bad, though I would not do it again. When I had cut the face, and begun on the breasts, Kelly said she felt sick. I asked her when she had to make contact with the man who would get her out of England, and she said not until between nine or half past in the morning. So I told her to get out into the air. She gave me the key and I even kissed her on the cheek, telling her she was very brave. When I locked the door behind her, I felt her weight leaning back on it, and heard her sigh, 'Oh, murder!' in a low, ghost of a voice. I wonder how she will fare? The Chief has said he will provide me with an address so that I can write, though I have promised not to mention what passed between us.

I finished at a little before six. It had been an unpleasant and rainy night and I had a mind to burn the apron in the fire, then thought better of it.

The cab was there, exactly where the Chief promised. I expect this will go down as Jack's last crime. I will not do more, and I cannot get the horrible smell of hot blood out of my nostrils. It seems to have oozed into every pore. I bathed twice today, but can still smell it on myself. I shall use carbolic soap, later. The smell of that will be better than the stench of raw death.

Tarpin took a great breath, and realized he was shaking. Down the years they had remembered, and hated, and taken their mindless revenge. The Fenians; Sinn Fein; the IRA, who had eventually won their fight and made a republic of the South; then the Provos. All of them blamed Kelly for the disruption of some long-lost campaign in London during the late 1880s.

Mary Kelly, and all her male offspring, had died. He, Phillip Tarpin, was the last of the line. He too was marked for death, and he knew also that, even over a century ago, there had been a crude shoot-to-kill policy. Not condoned by any government, but known of and carried out nevertheless.

He could see that sooty, dark satanic place that was Miller's Court, with its smudged brickwork, and the pathetic reward poster soaked with rain on that dank November night. He could smell the blood and sweat. It was as though he had travelled in time. He looked at Liz Oliver as though he did not understand who she was.

Then, the telephone began to ring.

– 2 –

'He claims it's for your health, Phillip, and I believe him.' Peter Palestino sat at his desk. He heard Tarpin give a small sigh at the distant end of the connection.

'What's his name, Peter?' Tarpin's voice was very low; quiet, like someone who has just witnessed a terrible tragedy.

'He doesn't say, but I believe he only has your safety in mind.'

'So, what am I to do?'

'I'm coming, personally. I'll bring the ticket and pick you up at seven.'

'In the morning?'

'Yes, you're getting a ride to London on Concorde. It leaves at nine-thirty. Please be ready. Don't open up to anybody but me, and then only if I say, 'What is the stars? What is the stars?'

'I know the quotation. I used to like Sean O'Casey. Now, I wonder. They killed Sukie, Peter. They want to kill me, and they'll probably go after Liz here as well. I shouldn't be surprised if they have a go at Tim Clifford once his book's published.'

'You'll be ready, though?'

'Yes. Okay. Peter, tell the man who's with you that I know about Butcher Drover.'

'That all?'

'It's enough. I'll be waiting.'

The man had come into Peter Palestino's office just as he was about to leave. Palestino was often the last man out of the building, and his visitor obviously had ways of getting past the security.

He had settled himself opposite Palestino and talked for nearly half an hour. When he finished, Palestino telephoned British Airways and booked the ticket on Concorde. They said a courier would come to his office.

'I'd best wait to make certain,' Mr John Chilton — Jackie to his friends — said. 'Now, will you ring Tarpin? Truly, sir, I'm trying to save his life, and I can't do it here in New York.'

Palestino had nodded and dialled Tarpin's number.

When the conversation ended, he told Chilton what Tarpin had said. 'He knows about Butcher Drover.'

'Does he now?' Chilton appeared distracted for a second. 'I fear Tarpin knows more than is good for him.'

On Fifth Avenue, at about the same time, two men met, seemingly by accident. They stood on the sidewalk, not a block from Tarpin's building.

'You're to see to it tonight,' Connor Murphy told Flanagan.

'He has the woman with him.'

'You're good at women, Paddy. Remember his other woman, in London?'

'That was reflex. I don't like doing women. She's an innocent.'

'Do it! Just get it over with! Now!'

'I'll give it a try.'

'Get the fecking man. Tonight. Okay?'

'I will, so.'

Flanagan crossed the road, and walked a couple of blocks until he found a coffee shop open in a hotel. He drank several cups of coffee before going out again into the night.

It was after four in the morning when he stopped outside Tarpin's building.

EIGHTEEN

– 1 –

He told her everything as he understood it, and at the end she held him close and asked, 'What've we been doing in all this, Phillip?'

'I suppose we've been comforting, healing, playing house as well.'

Even a week ago, she thought, if he had said this she would have exploded with rage. Playing house? Was that all? 'Let's play house again, now, my dear.' She led him towards the bedroom and took charge of what would happen between them. She could feel his fear, hidden just below the surface. 'I *do* understand, Phillip.' She held him close again. 'I understand. All I ask is that, when all this is over, you just give us a try. The two of us. See if we can stop playing and come out into the light. Do something real.'

'You know I will.' As he said it, Tarpin had an awful premonition. It was as though he knew this would be the last time with her. The final hours of his life. It bore down on him like some freak storm: rattling the windows of his mind; whirling black thunderheads in his brain; dashing lightning against his eyes.

They played honeymooners. She showered, then came to him in pure white silk and lace underwear, and pleaded that he be gentle with her.

She cried out the second time: a wild, high shriek that lanced his mind and brought back the foreboding.

Eventually they fell asleep, and he dreamed of ruined buildings; of a man's shadow sprawling against dirty brickwork, thrown menacingly against it by flickering gaslight. In his dream, Tarpin turned to face the man, and the cry split the night, so that he woke to the violent howl of the telephone.

The digital clock by the bed showed that it was just after four in the morning.

– 2 –

Flanagan pressed the night bell, reaching into his pocket and finding an old envelope which he transferred to his left hand. His right gripped the automatic pistol, snug against his back, jammed into the waistband of his uniform trousers. Just a simple pair of khaki trousers, and a jacket to match made him look official; and the cap, of course. That helped a lot.

He pressed the bell again, waiting, his face hard against the glass of the door.

The night-shift doorman shuffled out from his room behind the reception desk. He was putting on his coat, grumbling to himself. Flanagan, proud of his literary skills, thought of the porter in Shakespeare's Scottish Play. Once he had known actors at the Abbey Theatre, Dublin, so he knew the play was unlucky, and that you should not voice its true name aloud. He thought the doorman's lips were mouthing the words, 'Knock, knock, knock!'

The doorman spoke into the security mike on the other side of the door: 'Whaddya want, dis time in da morning?'

'I've a special delivery letter for Ms Townsend.'

'Candit wait till da morning?' Mike, the night doorman, should have remembered the trouble they had the last time someone had come in with a special delivery, but sleep had caught him off guard. Anyway, who would want to hurt old Ms Townsend? Mutton dressed up like lamb, that one.

'It can, but *I* can't. Just wanna leave it with you.'

'Okay.' The doorman pulled the locks and opened the door.

'I've gotta check the apartment number's right.' Flanagan reached behind him for the pistol, as the doorman stretched out his hand through the narrow gap.

'Apartment Four-twenty. Fourth floor. Gimme the letter.'

Flanagan shot him once in the chest, and slipped inside the door as the man was punched backwards by the blast, his head thrown high, arms suddenly splayed out, heels dragging on the marble floor. For a second, poised like something in mid-flight, Flanagan

206

thought he looked like the figure of Christ crucified. The image was so strong that he crossed himself.

He took the man under his armpits, dragging him back behind the small curved reception desk. The doorman was still breathing, so maybe he would live. Flanagan hoped so, for he had no argument with the doorman. He saw that the duplicate keys to Three-fourteen were hanging by the pigeonhole. He reached up with a gloved hand, unhooked them and stepped back over the doorman's body.

For a moment he stood listening, fearing someone else might be on the ground level. There was no sound but his own breathing, and a low moan from the doorman.

Holding the pistol in his right hand and the keys in his left, Flanagan walked quietly across the entrance lobby to the elevators. Both were up: one at the fourth floor, the other at the sixth.

He pressed the call button and stepped into the elevator as it arrived, the doors hissing open with a long sigh. It seemed a very loud noise in the silence of the building.

Gently, Flanagan pressed the button for the third floor, and the cage began to rise.

Below him, in the lobby, the doorman stirred. He had fought, and been wounded, in Vietnam. For a second as consciousness and the pain hit him, he thought he was lying out there, on the sodden ground. He even imagined he could hear the medevac chopper getting closer. Then he realized it was the sound of the elevator doors closing, and the cage rising.

He took a deep breath and pulled himself towards the desk. This was bad, he realized, as he saw his own hand, wet with blood. Godda get help. Jesus, Joseph and Mary, the guy did not want old Ms Townsend. This was like before. Gotta warn Mr Tarpin. He pulled at the telephone cord and the instrument clattered down beside him.

For another second he wondered if he had broken the damned thing. Then he heard the dialling tone in his ear. He pressed three – one – four, and it seemed to ring for an hour before the voice answered, gravelled with sleep.

'It's Mike, the doorman. A guy shot me. On his way to you.' His own voice sounded strange: distant, and he could not wait for

Tarpin's response. He pressed the *Flash* key and the button they had marked for 911. 'Ambulance and police,' he grunted when the emergency operator answered like a robot. He gave the address, then his name, then the one word 'Shot'. As a kind of afterthought he added, 'Intruder. Armed. Apartment Three-fourteen.' Then he passed out again.

– 3 –

Tarpin came awake in the time it took for his brain to register the full impact of the doorman's words. He pushed Liz, hard, rolling her out of bed, so that she gave a series of cries and started to ask, 'What the . . . ?' But by then he had his hand over her mouth.

'Sssshhhh! Danger, honey! Stay down. Here, behind the bed.'

Naked, he slung his robe around him, struggling for a second as his right hand missed the sleeve. Then he walked rapidly, pulling tight at the tie around his waist. He went to the kitchen, feeling his way towards the work surface, reaching for the wooden angled block with slots in it for the cooking knives. He tried to remember if they were all there, or if some had been left in the dishwasher. Then his hand touched the block and he pulled out the large carving knife. Whenever they used it, Liz told him to be careful.

'It's so damned sharp,' she would say. 'It's like a razor.'

He held it away from him, hoping he could make the door before the nameless thug who had shot the doorman managed to get in. As he reached the living room, he heard the key click into the lock.

Slowly, trying to remain silent, Tarpin negotiated the furniture and made it, to the right of the door, just as the handle turned and the wood strained against the safety chain. He flattened himself against the wall, as though trying to push himself through the plaster, the knife close to his body, hand raised as high as his chest, heart thumping in his ears. As though answering his fear, a jab of pain slid up the scar on his cheek.

He saw the dark shape of bolt-cutters clamp against the safety chain, and almost jumped at the sound of them snapping through the metal. Then the door swung open, and the intruder stepped past him into the room, his right arm half outstretched, and the shape of the pistol visible.

He was a pace away, his back towards Tarpin, who took a deep breath and aimed for the man's right shoulder, pushing himself from the wall and putting all his weight behind the stroke. The knife seemed to flash for a second, then he felt it hit, and heard the cry as the dark shape tried to turn away.

The pistol fell, skittering over the carpet, and the handle of the knife was wrenched from Tarpin's hand as the figure spun away from him, giving little terrified yelps of pain. He snapped the light on and recognized the face. The face that had haunted the wanted posters; the face of the man who had murdered Sukie; the face which leered from the Photofit; the face he had seen in the crowd outside J. B. Pudney, Sons' building on Madison; and the face he had glimpsed outside the restaurant.

Tarpin did not recognize his own voice as the stream of abuse exploded from his mouth and he launched himself at the man, fists flailing, muscles suddenly bursting with a strength he had never known existed.

Then the police were suddenly in the room, pulling him gently from the figure who lay, bloody and prostrate on the carpet. He saw Liz, draped in a robe, standing at the bedroom door, her hands to her face, hair rumpled, and horror shouting from the wide open eyes.

'You stopped him, buddy,' one of the cops said quietly. 'He bring that gun in here?'

Tarpin only nodded.

They told him the doorman, Mike, would be okay, and he heard one of the plain-clothes police mutter something to the uniformed sergeant as they dragged the half-conscious man from the apartment. He was sure the plain-clothes cop said, 'He's the guy the Brits're after. Flanagan. Fucking IRA.'

It took an hour for them to hear his statement.

'You might have to give evidence in court,' the plain-clothes man told him.

'I'm off to London tomorrow.'

'For good?'

'A week. Two weeks. As long as it takes.'

'As long as what takes?'

'Work.' He explained his job, and the cop said it was okay. 'We can check it out at your office. Don' worry about it, Mr Tarpin.'

Outside, as the sun began to rise, Connor Murphy passed by, walking. He saw the ambulance and the police cars. He joined the knot of rubbernecks and media people, happy at first, angry and jolted when he saw them bring Flanagan down strapped to a stretcher.

Casually, he asked one of the cops what had happened, and through him knew that Tarpin lived. He hung around, watching, taking in any half heard conversation.

He was still there when the tall figure of Palestino unfolded itself from the limo, and when he returned with Tarpin who carried a small suitcase. He even heard Palestino tell the driver, 'Kennedy. We've got plenty of time.'

Only then did Murphy leave, returning to his hideaway. He called Belfast just after eight o'clock New York time.

— 4 —

Before leaving the apartment, he gave the oilskin package containing Daniel Drover's book to Liz. 'See Hilary gets it,' he said. 'Tell her to hand it on to Clifford. Say it's the final link. Then you'd better tell him that I'm the final link as well.'

She clung to him, like someone saying goodbye in wartime, and he thought that was apt because he was going off into the killing fields where the Provo guerrillas fought with remote-controlled bombs, and bullets that came from nowhere.

On Concorde he was given a window seat, and he did not even see Chilton come down the narrow aisle. The first thing he took in was the well-cut grey suit. Then Chilton turned his face towards him as he lowered himself into the next seat.

'Good morning, Mr Tarpin. Chilton.' He extended a hand. 'John Chilton, though my friends . . . '

'Call you Jackie. I know.'

'You remember me. How nice.'

'How could I forget, Jackie? You're my Alpha and my Omega, I believe.'

'Nice of you to put it like that.'

Tarpin turned his face away and watched as they taxied out, only half listening to the drone of safety instructions he always thought of as the dance of death.

It was not until they had been shot from the runway, and the Mach numbers were beginning to climb, that he turned to Chilton:

'Why?' he asked.

'Why what? Why the Irish? Or why us?'

'Both.'

Chilton sighed, and the steward brought their drinks, taking the meal orders. When he had gone, Chilton looked Tarpin straight in the eyes. 'I understand you've seen Butcher Drover's book.'

'Seen and read.'

'We've been after that for a long time.'

'I should imagine they've been wanting to take a look as well.'

'Oh, I think they've seen it. You see, Mr Cox – old Mr Cox, of your mum's solicitors, Cox, Russ & Pembeton – was of Belfast stock. I think they've had a good look. But, of course, they knew it already. They knew it was Maureen Casey who was done in Miller's Court; and they knew why. It's obvious they soon found out where Kelly had gone, whom she'd married. They swore they'd wipe out the male children. I only bring up Cox, because we think it was through his family that they got to you. The Irish have long memories. It's really mindless revenge, down the years.'

'Over a century?'

Chilton nodded. 'Yes. First the Fenians, Sinn Fein and the old IRA. Now it's the Provos. They call it the oral tradition. Maureen Casey's death put the cause back for a long time. You know how the Irish are. For good or ill, they're like elephants. They do not forget. Not ever.'

'And still they come after sons of Bartolemé.'

'The fathers and the children, yes. They've hunted you all across the years.'

'But what are you . . . ?'

Chilton held up a hand. 'Phillip, don't ask *what* I am. I'll tell you that I began work for the government more years ago than I like to remember. I am, let's say, something to do with old files, and a guardian of secrets. Does Butcher Drover mention for whom he worked?'

'Some secret part of Scotland Yard. He was in the old Irish

Branch, then the Special Office . . . '

'Special Branch, yes.'

'He wrote about a Department I.'

'I for Irish, yes. Us Brits've sometimes been blackguards. In our colonies, and across the old Empire. You'll know that there are very few records left concerning jolly Jack the Ripper?'

'Police records lost. Other records that tell nothing.'

'Correct. They tell nothing because they've been filleted. That's one of my jobs. We made a lot of mistakes in the days of Empire. The problem is that once you've stripped a file, people read it and come to wrong conclusions. The Ripper files have been filleted: freed of any possible contamination with the old Department I. Look what happened. People invented all kinds of reasons. They mainly said that Jack's identity was withheld because there was a royal connection.' He gave a beaming smile. 'No way. There was very little on paper about that strange Department I. What we did have was enough, so it got stripped out. Who'd ever want anyone to even think there was a tacit murder squad within the police?'

'And was it? Was it what Drover claimed?'

'I really don't know. But I doubt it. I think maybe some top brass turned a blind eye to things which should not have been done. Department I was disbanded, by the by, in 1892, yet there was a legacy. You don't have to be brilliant to know what the legacy is.'

'A shoot-to-kill policy against the Provos.'

'Quite. One of my jobs is to keep snoopers away from anything that might be misconstrued as a shoot-to-kill policy in the North.'

'Which *does* exist.'

Chilton paused, waiting as they served the first course. 'Hardly,' he said very quietly. 'Oh, yes, sometimes there have been surgical strikes. That's obvious, but I'd deny saying it to you, or anyone else. If any hint of the old Department I ever got out, we'd all have explaining to do. It's proof of shoot-to-kill by inference. Let me ask you, Phillip, if you were threatened by, say, a Provo hit squad, wouldn't you feel safer if you were guarded by men who could kill without asking for written instructions in triplicate?'

'I can't answer that. I abhor *all* violence. I think war, in every guise, is wrong. It is the final basic resort, and it is evil.'

'Even when terrorists get blown away?'

Tarpin remembered what he had long held to be the truth. 'One man's terrorist is another's freedom fighter.'

'Well, we shall see.' Chilton attacked his meal.

About fifteen minutes out of London he said, 'I want you to remember something.'

'Yes?'

'You're a marked man – you know that. The lads will not rest until they've got you, though they might just give pause if certain stories got out. Stories that show the sins of the past have been forgiven. That people have atoned. But, until that day, they'll be watching and waiting.

'I just want you to know that the whole time you're in London, and going about your business, we'll also be watching you. Every minute of every day, we'll be guarding you.'

'Comforting,' Tarpin said, turning away to look down on the late summer evening patchwork quilt that was England.

'One more thing.' Chilton had stopped smiling. 'The government'll move heaven and earth to see Clifford's book is never published.'

'I look forward to the fight.' Tarpin turned away.

They landed on time. At ten past six in the evening.

– 5 –

At the same time, four men drove fast from a secret retreat in the Republic of Ireland, to Rosslare, from where the night ferry would take them to Fishguard. All four men were old trained hands. Members of the Provisional Irish Republican Army. They were men without records.

Two of them carried British passports, and two were equipped with American papers. These men, trained a long time ago in the desert camps of Syria, knew how to kill. They were, in effect, a death squad. They went where they were told, and killed who they were ordered to kill.

By the early hours they would be in the United Kingdom. By tomorrow all four would be in London.

What they had to do was to be accomplished quickly, and their target was a publisher called Phillip Tarpin who would be staying in a flat he owned behind Kensington High Street. They had even been told that one of the things he would be doing in London was putting that flat on the market.

A telephone call, earlier in the day, from Belfast to a man called Connor Murphy, had indicated that Mr Tarpin was as good as dead.

NINETEEN

– 1 –

When the taxi stopped and he climbed out to pay off the driver, Phillip Tarpin found himself crushed hard against reality. The sound of a London cab ticking over outside a building was unique and, for him, almost unbearable. He looked around like a man in a daze or a dream, knowing that, for the past three months, he had, quite consciously, blotted Iverna Court from his mind.

Slowly he walked from the road, across the narrow pavement of the cul-de-sac which fronted the building. Inside, and at the front door of the flat, his courage almost failed him as the sounds returned, and a million memories were unleashed.

Within the flat it was worse. Sukie's ghost roamed the rooms where they had shared so much happiness. He went to the bedroom, and thought he heard her voice as it had been on their last night together: the night she had cooked dinner, while he made his romantic proposal and gave her the ring which had been buried with her. He moved slowly, wondering if he could, after all, stay here. Too much of his past was invested in these rooms.

Putting down his case, Tarpin returned to the living room and noticed the light was blinking on the answerphone. He rewound the tape and listened, with horror, as an unfamiliar female voice said, 'Hi, Sukie, I'm back in London. It's me, Chris. I'm at my father's place. Give me a call when you've got a minute. Three years is the hell of a long time. See you.'

It was the only message, and he snapped off the machine, rewound the tape and set it to answer, leaving the flat and the building, as though all hell's demons were chasing him. He fled up into the High Street, walking the mile to the Royal Garden Hotel.

Before they landed, Chilton had said, 'I've no doubt they'll come for you. Don't be afraid. Just wait it out. Behave normally, as though you haven't a care in the world. Do what has to be done, but remain alert. If you think someone's following you, take no notice. Don't try to work out if it's them or us. It'll probably be them. You should never be aware of our people.'

He ate in the Garden Room, aware that he had awakened in New York, to horrors, then bridged the time gap. He still wore the clothes in which he had travelled, and he felt sweaty and unkempt, though that did not seem to bother the waiters.

Back in the flat, he called Liz in New York: a stilted conversation which ended with her saying, 'Phillip, I love you. I want you to know that.' He could not respond. For one thing, he did not love her, and Sukie was there, invisible, at his elbow. He even thought he could smell her scent.

When they had lived in the flat, high in Iverna Court, they had revelled in the silence. No cars could pass directly below them, and the traffic noise of Kensington High Street was blotted out, the sound baffled by the buildings which stood between their windows and the constant clamour of that famous street.

Now, in the night, he loathed the quiet and could not sleep for it. Her presence was so strong that he expected her to appear, even as an apparition, in the doorway. At three in the morning he gave up all thoughts of sleep, brewed some strong coffee and sat up in the wide bed, propped with pillows, as he tried to concentrate on a manuscript about the American Civil War.

Chilton had given him a number to call if he needed to make contact. The smooth voice answered with a plain, 'Hallo?'

'I don't think I can stay in this place.'

'I understand that, but it's necessary. Please try.'

Tarpin gave a long sigh, and noticed his hand was trembling. 'Is it absolutely imperative?'

'I would think so. Give it another couple of nights.'

He nodded, as though Chilton could see him. 'I'll try.'

'And for God's sake don't get drunk,' Chilton commanded.

On Concorde he had said, 'You're the last of the line. I believe that if we show strength they'll reconsider. If it works, they should leave

216

you alone.'

Tarpin had not seen the logic in it. He could not understand why the Provos would give up on what they called the oral tradition, if one of their hit teams got a bloody nose. After all, Mary Jane Kelly had left a legacy. All those long years ago she had given the Fenians succour, and then turned, not only informer, but the finger who had led their go-between, Maureen Casey, to her violent and horrible end. He could not see them stopping now.

Still, he would give it a try. He wished, for a moment, that Liz had come with him after all. Then, with sudden clarity, he realized the absurdity of that. He saw Liz as he had left her. Heard her voice appealing to him and, in this moment, Tarpin knew their brief, uncertain relationship was over. He could never marry her, for she carried too much emotional baggage, and any union would be cursed.

He showered, shaved – stubble covered the area around the scar – and dressed, then took a cab to the Hoiser & Whitehead offices where he was greeted like an old friend who had moved on to better things. People seemed to want just to touch him, as though he would pass on his luck. They had been warned of his arrival, and everything was laid on. The day passed very quickly, with meetings, arguments, even pleas for one project or another to be kept alive, or prodded on.

At five-thirty, one of the secretaries came through – he was talking to the senior editor, Richard Lucas, and the publicity director, Tony Bridge – to tell him there was a call for him. He thought it was probably Palestino, but when he heard the voice his heart gave a leap, and he felt his stomach roll over.

'I came on the red-eye,' Hilary Cartwright said, cheerful and relaxed. 'Slept all day, and I'm now ready for the fray.'

'How long're you here for?'

'A week or so.'

'You got the book? I told Liz to give you the book.'

'Tim's doing handstands. Came all the way out to Kennedy with me. Didn't stop talking once.'

'Great. Is he going to take long – the rewrites and extra information, I mean?'

'Peter's given him three months, but I bet he'll do it in two.' She paused, and before he could speak, she blurted. 'I called in case you felt like taking a lonely girl out to dinner.'

They arranged for him to pick her up at seven, and he dashed back to the flat, shaved again and changed. He redressed the wound on his cheek, thinking how terribly it twisted his face. The scar was sore and red, throbbing slightly. If it got worse, he would go over to St Mary Abbot's Hospital nearby.

At about the same time as he was putting a new dressing on his wound, Connor Murphy entered England, undetected, via Gatwick airport. He came into London by train, then took a taxi to a hotel near Marble Arch. The four men detailed as the active-service death unit were already there.

Murphy was irritated by them, for they had been drinking a lot, and two of them had sampled the whores who use that area of London. He told them what they should already know: London whores would be the first to identify them should it come to that. 'The police have the girls by the short hairs,' he said. Then he talked of the way they would dispose of Phillip Tarpin, the final link in the oral tradition.

– 2 –

Hilary Cartwright's London flat was in South Audley Street, an impressive and very expensive part of Mayfair. 'I've been lucky with it,' she told Tarpin when he picked her up. 'It belonged to my godfather. I hardly knew the lovely man, but he left it to me in his will. Sukie was furious, I remember . . . ' She pulled up short. 'Oh, I'm sorry, Phillip.'

'Don't worry. I don't think I'll ever be rid of her from my mind, but life goes on.'

'I noticed.' He detected a tinge of acid in her tone, and wondered what all that was about. She was wearing a neat blue Chanel suit, with a skirt which ended just above her knees, and she walked like Sukie, long-legged strides, confident and firm. She held her body in the same way, with a secret pride. As she walked to the cab, he saw her thighs and hips move under the thin material of her skirt.

They took the cab to the Tiberio – 'They have a band there. We can dance if you like.' She sounded even more like Sukie now she was back in London, and her hair had the same smell, the summer hayfield scent that he had so loved.

Halfway through dinner she asked, 'What's between you and Liz Oliver?'

'Why?'

'I'd like to know. You were very keen to take me to dinner in New York, then you went cold on me. Next thing I knew was you and Liz were an item.'

'Not any more.'

'That's not what she says, Phillip.'

'That doesn't surprise me.' He knew he was looking embarrassed. 'We had a little thing, yes. Now it's over.'

'So you won't mind me being blunt?'

'Blunt away, Hilary.'

'Liz Oliver's a splendid editor, but she eats men up, then spits them out – or at least *they* spit *her* out. She's an obsessive. Take her out to dinner and she thinks you're proposing marriage. I only know because a friend of mine went through a very hairy rollercoaster ride with her. She threatened suicide and God knows what. The guy had to put an attorney on to her.'

'Thanks for letting me know.'

'You said I could be blunt.'

'And I appreciate it. Really, she's history now, and I think she knows it.'

'Good.' Very pert. Satisfied.

They ate, danced to the little band, and talked exactly the kind of shop he used to talk about with Sukie. Hilary seemed very comfortable. 'How's the face?' she asked towards the end of the evening.

'Throbbing a bit. I think I'll pop into Mary Abbot's and let them take a look.'

'Drop me off first, okay?'

He got out of the cab and saw her to the door of her apartment where she put out her arms, pulled him to her and kissed him hard, her tongue leaping into his mouth, so deep that he gasped.

'Same time tomorrow?' she asked, smiling. The little brackets of laugh lines creased at the corners of her mouth, in just the same way as Sukie's.

He moved to kiss her again, but she held him off. 'Phillip, don't mistake me for my sister. I've told you that before.'

'I wasn't . . . '

'I was hell's jealous of Sukie. Thought you should know that.' She disappeared and the door closed quietly behind her. He took a deep breath, inhaling through his nose, filling himself with the scent of her, as though taking some kind of fix that would have to last twenty-four hours.

He told the cab to take him to Emergency at St Mary Abbot's, where they tutted and clucked. A young doctor finally told him there was a slight infection, gave him an injection, and he came away with a container full of antibiotics.

The telephone was ringing when he walked into the flat.

'You went to the hospital, what did they say?'

'That was good timing, Hilary.'

'No, I've been calling for the past half hour. What did they say?'

He told her.

'Hope it's nothing serious.'

'What about you?' he asked.

'What about me, what?' She all but giggled.

'You said you were jealous of Sukie.'

'I said I was hell's jealous of her.'

'Good.'

'Phillip, don't confuse us. I mean that. I know I could take Sukie's place, but I have to be certain that you don't get bewitched and think I'm her.'

'I understand, but you have to know something as well.'

'What?'

'That it might be difficult for me. You're very like her, in many ways.'

'I know. Hope the face gets better, Phillip.'

By the morning the swelling and redness was down, and the throbbing had stopped. He went first to an estate agent, as a prelude to putting the flat on the market. He owned it leasehold for another fifty years. 'There's still a lot of life in it,' the severe woman at the estate agent's said. 'You'll get a good price.'

She went back with him straight away, and they did all the measuring and note-taking. 'I'd like someone to come over and do some photographs,' the woman said. 'Perhaps tomorrow morning.'

'It'll have to be early. Eightish.'

'That's all right. He's my husband. I'll kick him out of bed. Eight on the dot.'

There was a lot to do at the office and it was not until late afternoon that he realized that last night in the flat had been easier. Had Hilary suddenly laid her sister's ghost? As he thought about it, there was a small pang of guilt about Liz Oliver. He banished it with the thought that she had tried to push, running before they even walked.

'I understand,' Liz had said. 'All I ask is that, when this is over, you just give us a try. The two of us. See if we can stop playing and come out into the light. Do something real,' she had said, and the light in her stare was not to do with affection, but with winning: trapping, ensnaring a man.

'You know I will,' he had replied. Now he felt inadequate.

He dialled Liz Oliver's New York number.

She gushed for the first couple of minutes, filling his ear with questions, telling him she missed him, asking when he would be back. Then, almost as though she could see his face, she said, 'You're not coming back, are you?'

'I'm coming back, Liz. Of course I'm coming back.'

'You're not coming back to me, though. Right?'

'Let's see.'

She gave a hard laugh at the distant end. 'I know what "let's see" means, Phillip. I asked you to give us a chance.'

'You did, yes.' He was being weak, and he consoled himself with the idea that this really could not be done over a long-distance telephone line.

'But you're not going to. Don't worry, Phillip. I understand. I told you that as well. Goodbye, Phillip.' The line went dead, and he knew this was not the last he would hear from Liz Oliver. He had tried, though there really was no going back. He had seen that lust in her eyes, and it had nothing to do with love or physical desire. Or was he being an absolute grade A shit? They had not talked permanence, he thought. He had never talked eternal love. He had not even spoken of love. Yet it made him uneasy. What had taken place in New York did not make him feel very good about himself.

That evening he took Hilary to an Italian restaurant he knew well, at the junction of Fleet Street and Chancery Lane. It was always full of journalists at lunch time, but moderately quiet in the evening.

'Mr Tarpin, nice to see you.' The owner embraced him. 'What you do with your face, hu?'

'He cut himself shaving,' said Hilary, all bright and bubbly.

'Looks like you bit him, I think.' The *padrone* grinned.

'Chance would be a fine thing.' Then she mumbled to Tarpin, 'That was a *terrible* line. Obvious. You deserve better conversation and backchat than that.'

They ate as though they were making love, and he knew she was teasing him as she inhaled spaghetti into her mouth as though fondling it with her lips.

Back at her flat, Hilary asked him in –'Just coffee.' Then, wagging her finger. 'Nothing else. No nookie. Understand?'

'Of course.'

He left at one in the morning, with lips sore from the kissing, and went to bed thinking of Hilary and how they had been together. He could smell her hair and her body in his pores. Her scent was close to him in the wide bed where he had spent so much time with her sister.

The man turned up to take the photographs on the dot of eight. He was small with wary eyes and ratty hair. It was easy to see how the woman from the real estate office controlled him. Uninvited, a truth slid in and out of his head. Liz Oliver wanted dominance. If he had been foolish enough to let things follow a natural course, that could be him, being kicked out to take photographs. Liz would have run his life to her timetable, and all freedom would have gone. It would not have been a question of mutual love, but of her iron will trying to change him. She would have dictated my every move, he thought.

It was well after nine before the photographer left. 'My wife says she'll be in touch,' he said, almost making a little bow as he mentioned his wife.

Tarpin was ready to leave when the telephone rang. For a moment he wondered if it was Hilary.

Instead, he just recognized the voice. 'Mr Tarpin? Oh, I'm so glad to have found you. I rang your New York office yesterday and they said you were in England. I found this number late last night, and hoped you'd be there.'

'What can I do for you, Mr Pembeton?' Tarpin thought the man sounded older, more frail.

'It's what I can do for you, actually. You did get the package I sent on to New York?'

'Yes.'

'Well, I hate to bother you, but there's another set of papers. I must be getting old. I'm so sorry. My secretary came across them yesterday morning.'

'Can you put them in the post?'

'I'm afraid not. I'm really rather thankful you're here. In England. I don't have to come over to New York. You see there's a legally binding document with these. They are very important, and essential to the will. One of the partners has to hand them over. I could be at your flat in twenty minutes if you like.'

'Can't I come to you?'

'When would that be?'

'Oh, tomorrow some time, or the day after. I am rather busy.'

'I'd much rather deal with it all today. If I could drop them round . . . '

Tarpin looked at his watch. 'If you really mean twenty minutes,' he said.

'Oh, yes. Twenty minutes at the latest. Probably fifteen if I get a cab straight away.'

He agreed, and went into the kitchen to pour another cup of coffee. Then he called the office, where they rearranged his schedule with great efficiency.

When the buzzer went, he walked straight to the door, then paused, the memory of that other doorbell, ringing in New York, darting into his mind.

Bending forward, he squinted through the security wide-angle door viewer he had asked to be put in, with the new locks, before he went to New York.

The solicitor stood in front of the door, looking greyer, older than he had at Vera Tarpin's funeral. Tarpin even saw the briefcase.

He opened the door, putting on a happy face.

'Mr Pembeton. Do come in . . . '

Someone stepped from Pembeton's right, smashing a hand into the elderly man's shoulder, throwing him to one side. 'Make yourself scarce, old man. You've done well.' The accent was unmistakable, as was the automatic pistol in his hand as he stepped into the doorway.

'Now don't you be making more trouble for yourself, Mr Tarpin. We're going on a little jaunt. I've a taxi waiting. Best move quickly because I, for one, don't want to do it here, in your flat, in broad daylight.'

TWENTY

– 1 –

He found that he was strangely unafraid, and it was to do with him, not Chilton's assurance that he would be guarded every minute of every day. As they walked towards the lift, he remembered the premonition in New York: the knowledge that he was not coming back. Well, at least Liz Oliver would know. She would not go on living with the idea that he had died yearning for her. On the other hand, Hilary . . . Oh, to hell with it, he thought. Let them do it and get it over with.

The man jabbed his pistol into Tarpin's side. 'When we go out the front,' he said quietly, 'you'll find there's a taxi drawn up to the left, by the pavement. This isn't the easiest place in the world, what with one walk-through on the right, and no drive through at all.'

'I always found it convenient.' He was quite surprised that his voice did not shake. 'Don't hurt the old man. That's all I ask.'

'The old man, is it? His partner's a very good friend to the cause, so Pembeton does what he's told. Very useful to have a sensible middle-class solicitor at our beck and call.'

The lift stopped, and the doors slid open.

'Now, remember what I said, Mr Tarpin. Nice and gentle. Just walk ahead of me. I'll be three paces behind you, and I'm sure you've got into taxis at that spot many times before. Now, my finger's itchy.'

The sunlight seemed very familiar, an old friend, slicing up from the High Street, flooding the front of the building, a solitary tree making a dappled pattern across the steps.

The taxi had its engine running. The driver looked towards them as they walked slowly towards the vehicle. Another man stood by the open door, and he could see a fourth figure sitting in the back. So, they were taking no chances. Four of them just for him. He wondered what his great-grandmother would have thought. From Miller's Court to Iverna Court. Rags to riches. Murder to murder.

The man walking behind him muttered something about moving nice and easy.

He was almost at the cab when he saw them appear from the High Street end. Two of them in drab denim trousers and olive green jerseys, with reinforced leather shoulder and elbow pads, their faces hidden under woollen ski masks, their hands forward, clutching weapons.

Then everything happened quickly. There were shouts from behind him, and the whole narrow cul-de-sac exploded with sound. If he had been asked about the entire sequence, he would never have been able to say which came first, the shouts or the rapid thwack-thwack of the pistols.

He saw the three men in front of him collapse as one. The driver seemed to spin in his cab; the one standing by the door arched his back slowly, then lifted two or three inches from the ground before he was thrown down on to the pavement; while the one who had been sitting in the back simply appeared to disintegrate: a red film hovering where his head had been.

Behind him someone yelled, 'Tarpin! Get down! Hit the deck!' But he did none of those things. He turned, to see another two hooded figures walking steadily towards the bleeding body of the man who had been urging him towards the cab.

He was conscious of Pembeton being led from the house by a further hooded figure, and behind it all came the sudden wail of sirens. The hee-hawing of police and the cacophony of ambulances.

Someone took him by the arm, hard, spinning him around and firmly leading him away from the High Street end of the little walk-through court.

At the far end an official-looking black Rover sat, with a man at the wheel, and someone else in the back. He looked up to see that the man propelling him towards the Rover was dressed like the others: olive green drab, a ski mask and a Heckler & Koch pistol in his right hand. He smelled of oil and cordite – or, at least, what

Tarpin took to be cordite.

Then he was in the car, and Jackie Chilton patted his arm as the Rover drew away, picking up speed.

'We're going to try and keep your name out of it, old boy,' he smiled.

Phillip Tarpin felt slightly sick. 'Did they have to kill . . . ?' he began.

'It was you or them. Aren't you happy it was them?'

'Did they *have* to shoot to kill?' he asked again.

'I saw no other way for them. Our people shouted warnings. The man behind you almost got a shot into the back of your head, Phillip. I, for one, am glad he didn't. The SAS are very well trained, you know. They even practise with live ammunition in a room with three dummies and two of their colleagues. Usually it's the dummies who collect the bullets.'

'There must be another way.'

'I very much doubt it.'

– 2 –

They were married less than a year later, by an Episcopalian priest in a small church in upstate New York. Phillip Andrew Tarpin and Hilary Mary Cartwright plighted their troths and took their vows. They wanted to live happily ever after, and eleven months, almost to the day, Christopher David Tarpin made his entrance, via Hilary and a private maternity hospital in New York.

They took him home, and Hilary vowed to give up work until he was old enough for pre-school.

Two days after they brought their baby from the hospital, a tall, quiet man, with a smile that made girls go weak at the knees, gave his AT&T card number to an operator from a telephone booth at Grand Central Station. It was the morning rush to work.

In Belfast a telephone rang four times before it was picked up.

'Brian?' the man with the smile asked.

'You're speaking to him.'

'For what it's worth, if the oral tradition's still alive, another man child has come from the Miller's Court informer.'

'Give me the name, and I'll pass it on. We've still got the little fella's father to deal with, I think.'

'You're right there, Brian. The baby's name is Christopher David. You know the surname.'

'Christopher David, is it?' Brian said. 'Well, I'll bet he's a lovely little fella. We'll see what's to be done. There's been talk about seeing to the father. I'll pass it along.'

The tall, quiet man put the telephone down, smiled his wonderful smile, and disappeared into the commuting crowds at Grand Central. Outside it was a lovely day, and the girls would be out in their summer dresses.